BREAK US

JENNIFER BROWN

BREAK
US

A SHADE ME NOVEL

KATHERINE TEGEN BOOKS
An Imprint of HarperCollins Publishers

Katherine Tegen Books is an imprint of HarperCollins Publishers.

Break Us
Copyright © 2018 by HarperCollins Publishers
All rights reserved. Printed in the United States of America.
No part of this book may be used or reproduced in any manner whatsoever without
written permission except in the case of brief quotations embodied in critical
articles and reviews. For information address HarperCollins Children's Books, a
division of HarperCollins Publishers, 195 Broadway, New York, NY 10007.
www.epicreads.com

Library of Congress Control Number: 2017938883
ISBN 978-0-06-232449-8

Typography by Carla Weiss
18 19 20 21 22   PC/LSCH   10 9 8 7 6 5 4 3 2 1
❖
First Edition

FOR SCOTT
YOU ARE THE SUNLIGHT THAT
MAKES THE RAINBOW POSSIBLE.

PROLOGUE

THE DOOR SEEMED flimsy. She probably could have kicked it in if she wanted to. And, at the moment, she really, really wanted to. She wanted to kick in everything in sight. She wanted to kick in the world. She had lost, and if there was one thing she could not stand, it was losing. If she kicked in the world, she could let everyone know—she had lost for now, but she would win in the end. Make no mistake about it.

She followed him through the flimsy door and dropped her bag on the carpet just inside, then peered around. Tacky, tacky, cheap, tacky, common, tasteless.

"I'm already bored," she said.

"Don't be like that. Give it a chance." He hurried across

the room and threw open the curtains, revealing a window almost the length of the whole wall. Sunlight flooded into her, causing her to squint, a small stab of pain lighting up in her temples. She cursed, but he ignored her. "What do you think?"

She followed him to the window, pressed her hand against it. It was warm. Her heels sank into the carpet, so she kicked them off and curled her toes into its fiber. At least the carpet was plush. Still tacky, but plush. A gull swooped past the window and winged into the distance, until it was a tiny, squawking dot. She turned, pressing her back against the toasty window, and faced him. "I'm not doing this forever."

"Of course not," he said. "There's no intention of that."

She paced through the living room, testing the cushion of the sofa with her palm. Plush, just like the carpet.

Okay, so maybe not quite as cheap as she'd originally thought.

"Let me show you the rest," he said. He'd somehow gotten back over by the door—this place was way too small—and grabbed her bag.

She sank onto the sofa, propped her bare feet up on the coffee table, and closed her eyes. "I don't feel like it."

"At least let me show you your room. You can freshen up. I'll make us some sandwiches."

Her lip curled in disgust. Sandwiches? She didn't eat sandwiches. Sandwiches made people fat. Sandwiches made people ordinary. She didn't know why she kept having to prove it over and over again, but she was not ordinary. She was special. She was meant for better than this. She was meant for better than anything she'd ever been given in her life. How was it fair that she'd been gifted with so many talents and not one person—not one!—who could truly appreciate them?

"Well? You hungry?"

"I don't think so."

"We can talk."

She opened one eye. "And what exactly is it you think I want to talk about?"

"You know exactly what," he said, his face grave. He gestured toward the hallway with her bag again.

She sighed and pulled herself off the sofa. Already she felt herself getting cankles and dull hair and ragged cuticles. No, she could not do this forever. He stood aside and let her go down the hall first, even though she didn't know where she was going. But damn straight she would lead. Because leading was what she was meant to do.

"Are we going to talk about getting rid of Nikki Kill?" she asked. So casual, even though the name Nikki Kill made her insides boil.

"No," he said. "We're going to talk about getting rid of you."

She stopped, causing him to nearly bump into her, and

turned her deadest eyes on him. Her lips pulled back in a snarl. "I told you I'm not doing this forever."

"I told you, I have no intention of you doing this forever." He grinned. One tooth stood just the tiniest bit out of line with the others. His lips looked dry. "Trust me," he said. "I have something much better in mind."

1

THE MINUTE I stepped out of my car, I knew I should have rolled down my window before lighting up. I stank. That's what he would say, anyway. If he remembered how much he hated my smoking.

He might or he might not. The doctors said it would be that way. He'd remember some things and not others. He would forget again things he'd remembered just the day before. He would suddenly recall something silly and unimportant, or maybe something serious and very important, but there was no way to tell what would trigger him and no way to force him to recall everything we wanted him to recall. Basically, they said, the brain was as mysterious in injury as it was in health, and we just had to learn to live with it.

I was not great at *learning to live with* things.

We also had to learn to live with it if he got frustrated and headachy and short-tempered and tired. He'd been through a hell of a trauma, and it would take a while to put all the pieces of Chris Martinez back together again, even if he looked whole on the outside.

Those conversations happened in the early days—the ones right after he woke up, opening bloodshot eyes in swollen, purple sockets, darting glances around the room warily, as if he had come back from the other side and wasn't sure where, or who, he'd come back to.

Maybe I was being dramatic. Maybe Chris Martinez was behind those eyes, present and accounted for, so serve-and-protect upstanding yellow you could get a sunburn off him, and I was too distracted by the blissful release from my crimson prison to see it.

I was so sick of crimson. Death, death, death. It followed my life like a grim shadow, rolling in and out on tides of deep, burnt red.

Mom, Peyton, Dru.

Vanessa.

And almost Chris.

Almost.

It had been three months since I'd last seen him. Right after he'd woken up and it had been clear that everything between us had changed. How could it stay the same when he didn't remember anything more than my name? It hurt too much to be forgotten. And it annoyed me too much to be hurt.

Besides, his gaggle of cop buddies hung around, watching me like I was a suspect, like I had done this to him just by virtue of being in his life.

And they might not have been altogether wrong. If I hadn't been in Chris's life, he might have never been following Rigo Basile. Peyton's murder would have remained an unsolved case, but he wouldn't have had any reason to be at Tesori Antico, trading bullets with Bill Hollis. He wouldn't have been walking across the street, distracted by the blood seeping through his shirt. He wouldn't have been there at all when that black Monte Carlo rounded the corner.

But that Monte Carlo had nothing to do with the Hollises. At least not that I could tell. That black Monte Carlo was about something else. Something Chris wouldn't let me in on. Something that had him driving around with bullet holes in the front panel of his car and had him checking sidewalks and doorways like he expected someone to jump out at him.

He'd been right to expect that, apparently. They'd caught him in that one rare instant that he wasn't watching for them.

Whoever *they* were I had a name—Heriberto. Someone he'd been searching for. But the last name was escaping me because it was associated in my mind with a color I didn't expect and I usually relied on my synesthesia to help me remember things like words, numbers, and names. Heriberto's last name wasn't red, and it wasn't exactly purple. . . .

Basically, I had nothing for the cops who caught me in the hallways, the waiting rooms, the cafeteria, peppering me with questions. *You're . . . close. What do you know? What did he tell you? Who did this?* My answer was always the same: *I don't know. I don't know. I don't know. We weren't that close.*

We weren't that close.

We were that close. But I was the only one who knew it. Even Chris didn't know it anymore.

So I stayed away. It killed me, but I didn't belong by his bedside. Not like the others. I paid attention to his progress from afar.

One thing I had learned while working with Chris was that it was so easy to fool people into giving you information you shouldn't have. And once I found out he was discharged, it wasn't hard to follow him from his apartment to physical therapy.

You don't just go charging into someone's workout session when it's been three months since you last saw him. Instead, I found his car in the parking lot and sat on the hood, holding a manila envelope in my lap, my feet crossed at the ankles and rhythmically thumping against the bumper.

He'd parked under a cottonwood tree, and I enjoyed the shade, along with an intermittent breeze that blew the smoke out of my clothes. Summer was on its way out. My peers had long since packed and headed off to freshman orientation at whatever schools they'd chosen. They were stuffing their valuables into plastic tubs and vying for bathroom space in their dorm rooms and doing icebreaker exercises on campus quads.

And I was wasting time, waiting for my recently attacked unofficial-as-hell partner in justice to hobble out of the hospital and talk me down off the ledge . . . again.

After what seemed like forever, I finally saw his form making its way to me. He was walking with a cane now—how ironic, I thought, given that this whole ordeal had started with a cane—his limp pronounced, but his gait quick. He paused when he saw me, raised his hand to shade his eyes, then continued his journey.

"Hey," I said, when he got close enough to hear. Like it was nothing to run into each other here after all this time.

"You're sitting on my car."

I glanced down. "You're right. I'm so sorry. I'd hate to do something to take away the aesthetics of your bullet holes there."

He stared at me, his face giving away nothing. I hated this. Normally, he would have a smart-ass comment to throw right back at me. This new and unimproved Martinez was so serious.

"Fine," I said, sliding off the car. I took a few steps toward him, holding out the manila envelope. "I just wanted to let you know that I can't do it. I thought I could, but I was wrong. I can't. Sorry. I know you'll be disappointed, but I've gotta look out for numero uno, you know? And numero uno is not interested after all."

At first he just stared at the envelope, looking from it to me and back again. Then he reached out slowly and pulled it out of my hand. "What is this?"

"The application," I said. "Police academy? Ringing any bells?" I was hoping it would, for more than one reason. I wanted him to remember pushing me about becoming a cop, because that would mean he remembered something about our time together after Dru's death. I wanted him to remember, and be ready to help me get to the bottom of everything once and for all, even though the doctors had said that pushing him to remember things was likely to do the opposite.

He leaned the cane against his leg and opened the envelope, sliding out its contents. "Of course I know what the police academy is," he said. "I've lost a couple months, not my whole life."

"But you don't remember forcing me into it."

He gave me a look that couldn't even be called incredulous. It was more like *you have got to be fucking kidding me.* The same look Dad had given me when I mentioned that I might be looking into pursuing a career in law enforcement. The same look I'd given Chris when he'd first suggested the idea to me. Guess Nikki Kill playing the role of Upstanding Administrator of Justice wasn't believable to any of us.

At the time that I picked up the paperwork, Chris was lying in a hospital bed, unconscious. He had just saved my ass in every conceivable way. And I'd saved his. We'd become a team on a level I'd never imagined we could. I'd thought he was dying. I'd thought of making a promise to go into the academy as some kind of tribute. Or maybe a bargaining chip with God—*make Chris pull through and I'll become a decent person after all.* I honestly didn't know why I was doing it. I only knew that I'd told myself, sleeping Chris, and my dad of all people that I was going to do this.

And there was no way in hell I could do this.

"It doesn't matter now," I said. "I'm not going. I can't."

He glanced at the application, which was blank, pushed it back into the envelope, and held it out for me to take. "Okay. Why not?"

"Because. I can't be a cop. I mean, who would want to be one, right?" I gestured the length of his broken body.

"I did. I still do."

"Yeah, but you're not normal. You've got all that crazy annoying yellow, and . . ." I trailed off, realizing too late that I'd casually been talking about my synesthesia. Of course, I'd told him all about it at his bedside, but he apparently didn't know that, and now that he was alive, awake, looking right at me, it felt weird to talk about it. Why was I able to do so many things when he was sleeping that I was unable to hold to when he was awake? Why was I such a chickenshit? It was disgusting.

"Yellow?"

I shook my head. "Never mind. I just mean . . . you were meant to be a cop. I wasn't."

He thrust the envelope toward me again; I still didn't take it. "Listen, Nikki. I can't remember what happened that made me give you this, but if I thought you could be a cop, then I probably had a good reason."

"The reason was charity. Or, I don't know, recruitment quotas? Do you have those? I told you then that I couldn't do it, and I'm still telling you that."

"Okay." He dropped the envelope on the ground between us. He started to make his way past me and to his car.

"Okay?"

He turned. "Okay."

"That's all you have to say? I'm telling you that I'm giving up on the cop thing, and it's just okay?"

He shrugged. "What's it supposed to be? No, please, think about it some more? Don't give up? You can do it? It's natural to be afraid? Will any of those things help?"

I gritted my teeth. "No."

He shrugged again. "Then okay. You already told me you

didn't want to do it, and I don't remember any of this anyway. So do it or don't do it. Nothing I can change about it. All I know is I'm exhausted and my leg hurts and I want to sit down and drink a beer and get this day over with." He started toward his car again, his limp more pronounced now that he'd been standing for a while.

"This is the first time you've seen me since you were mowed down right in front of me and you want to go home and drink a beer? Nice."

He turned back to me. "Mowed down. You were there?" he asked. Or maybe he said it: "You were there." I couldn't tell. Maybe he couldn't tell, either.

I nodded. He shuffled toward me.

"Why?" He licked his lips. "Why did I do it? What had me so distracted?"

"What do you mean?" I asked. "Why did you do what?"

"Walk out in front of the car," he said. "Was I going somewhere?"

Jagged-edged mint built a bridge between us. His confusion was obvious. He was searching for answers. He had only pieces of what happened—the ones told to him. Somehow he'd gotten the impression this was a true accident, maybe even his fault. Of course he had. Nobody else had been there but Arrigo Basile's mother and me. I could tell them it looked like a purposeful hit all day long, but I had nothing to prove it, other than the fact that the driver hadn't stopped.

God knows what Arrigo's mom would have told police. She had been half-crazed with fear, and had an entire family of criminal thugs to protect—including Arrigo himself.

And, damn it, I had been too busy rushing to Chris's crumpled body to think about looking for a license plate. All I knew was it was a black Monte Carlo. Not like there weren't a few zillion of those out there or anything.

"You didn't walk in front of it," I said. "They came out of nowhere. They hit you on purpose. And then they ran."

He frowned, as he tried to take it all in. "Who?"

I deflated. "I was hoping you could tell me," I said. "You were being really secretive about something. You wouldn't let me in."

Suspicion stretched between us in mints and ferns and lime sherbets. I worried that I'd sounded bitter about him not letting me in. How rich, given that I'd made it my life's mission to let nobody—especially him—in. "Why were you there?" he asked. "Why were we together?"

"Oh God," I breathed. "You really don't remember anything."

He shook his head, slowly at first, and then with more conviction. His forehead creased. "I'm trying. I remember being at your graduation. And then . . . pieces. You were in jail, right?"

"That's what you remember, out of all this time? That I

was in jail? Yeah. I was in jail. For a night. You got me out. We were looking for Rigo Basile, and we found him. You sh—" I stopped myself short. *You shot Bill Hollis*, I was about to say. But was that something you sprang on someone—that they'd killed somebody? Would he understand why without me retelling everything that had happened? It didn't seem like it. And where did I start, anyway? With my arrest at the graduation party? With the day we busted into the Hollis warehouse? With my mom dying right next to me when I was eight? It all seemed to go together, to get scrambled into one long event. And I wasn't sure how he would take it, or even if he could take it. "You should go home and get that beer," I said instead. "You'll remember more tomorrow, probably."

He grunted, frustrated, as if he wanted to say something else, but then he thought better of it and started limping away from me again.

"And for your information, I'm not afraid," I said to his back. He stopped, turned. I kicked at the manila envelope. "It's the written test. I can't pass that. You know how my grades were." What he didn't know was that it was the distraction of my synesthesia that made my grades suck. And what neither of us knew was whether or not I could use it to my advantage now that I'd learned how to rely on it in the right ways. But what I didn't want to know was if I sucked just as bad in the real world as I did in school. You suck at school, you get an F; you suck at the real world, you get a shitty life; you suck as a cop, you get dead.

"Sounds like you're afraid," he said. "Afraid of taking a test. I don't know what to tell you. I, personally, think you could pass it without a problem. But I'm not the one who has to go in and take it. Already did that. And, yes, I do remember taking it. You want, maybe I can help you study for it. Or not. Entirely your call."

I felt irritation well up inside me—piping-hot ink with steam—and I clenched my fists. The *rah-rah-you-can-do-it* Chris was annoying, but this Chris was . . . well, he was just an ass.

"No, I don't need your help with anything," I said. "I'm not taking it." I bent and picked up the envelope. "And I can study on my own."

He smirked. I realized what I'd just said, how it made no sense that I could study alone for a test I wasn't taking, and the fact that he'd reduced me to idiocy only served to enrage me further.

Still, it was kind of good to see the old Chris come through a little, even if just with that maddening smirk.

"Got it," he said. "It's good to see you, Nikki. I missed you. You shouldn't have stayed away so long. I could have used a friendly face in that therapy room."

I frowned, cocked my hip to one side. "Does this look

like a friendly face to you?"

"No, not exactly," he said. "But when you're around, something inside me remembers that it can be." He opened his car door and tossed his cane across to the passenger seat. "Don't be such a stranger," he said, then got in, started up, and pulled away.

I stood in the shade of the cottonwood tree, listening to the warning cries of a mother bird above me, and held the manila envelope, which felt heavy and impossible in my hand. I watched him go.

At least he remembered something.

TELLING DAD THAT I was thinking of becoming a cop may have been the least of the problems we had between us, but it was a problem nonetheless. He wasn't happy about it. He didn't like the police any more than I did. Maybe even less. They'd never solved my mother's murder, and in his eyes, that was just as bad as being the murderer. It wasn't logical, but I could understand where he was coming from. The crimson memories of my mother were the worst memories I had, and every time I thought about her murderer, walking around in the world, totally free, while she rotted beneath the ground, the crimson fused with indigo betrayal that blanketed me with such hopelessness, it was like I was the dead one. At least on the inside.

But how much of Dad's outrage over Mom's death was genuine, and how much was a front? This was a question that had been nagging me for months now, ever since I'd discovered Mom's ties to Vanessa Hollis's escort service, and Dad's complete and total lie about not knowing anything about the Hollises at all. Something fishy was going on, and I hated that the one man in this world that I thought I could trust was the source of my unease.

I hated it, but I accepted it. Because I didn't have a choice.

Every time Dad left the house for any amount of time—and with his job as a photographer, he was constantly on location—I busied myself with trying to figure out what exactly he was hiding from me, and how. The problem was, when you've been hiding something from someone you live with for over ten years, you get pretty good at hiding. I had searched the entire house, top to bottom, twice, and had found nothing. Only a dusty, locked metal box beneath his desk, and even that I had run across by accident. And I couldn't crack the combination to save my life. Or to avenge Mom's. Or whatever it was I was trying to do.

I came home from the physical therapy parking lot and plopped the manila envelope on the kitchen counter, grabbed a glass from the cabinet and turned to the refrigerator to fill it. I was so irritated by my run-in with Chris, I almost didn't see Dad sitting at the kitchen table, poring over some paperwork of his own. He looked up when I dropped the envelope.

"Bad day at the station, Officer?" He said it like he was teasing, but he still had a bitter edge to his voice whenever he brought up my future plans. And to think, just a few months ago at my graduation, he was desperate for me to have future plans.

I took a long drink of water. "For your information, I'm not even applying. I decided today."

He blinked, pulled off his glasses, and laid them on the paperwork. "Oh, really? You okay with that decision?"

"Would I make it if I wasn't okay with it?"

"Maybe."

"Well, how about, yes, I'm totally okay with my decision."

"Doesn't really seem like it."

I took another drink. "Don't pretend like you're not thrilled about it."

He rubbed his eyes with forefinger and thumb. "Well, no, if you're not happy, I'm not happy. You know how this goes. I'm your dad. I love you."

I ground my teeth together to keep myself from asking why a dad who loved me so much was keeping things about my own mother from me. How a dad with such love for his daughter could lie to her for her entire life.

"I'm happy," I said instead.

"Nikki," he said, in that voice I'd grown so sick of ever

since that night at Tesori Antico. I'd been a mess when I came home from the hospital that night. Filthy, bloody, emotionally wrecked. There was no hiding anything from Dad at that point. Luna had gotten away again, and Chris was at death's door, and every time I closed my eyes, I saw Vanessa hitting the ground, blood blooming around her, the same crimson that bloomed around my mom. How was it possible that they bled the same?

After, there had been investigations and statements and questions and questions and questions. All the while, Dad tiptoeing around me, using that voice, as if he was half-afraid that talking too loud would make me break. And, honestly, it might have. "You don't have to keep up the act with me. I know you're scared. They'll find her. They will. In the meantime, let me help."

I rolled my eyes. *Here we go again.* Was I scared? Hell, yes. I was scared shitless. I would be a moron not to be scared. Luna had attacked me too many times for me not to be scared. And she obviously could literally get away with murder. She was still out there, and someone was helping her. And I'd killed her mom. With Chris out of commission, she and I were the only two who knew, and I intended to keep it that way. She could hardly turn me in to the police, so she had to want me dead more than ever. Every time I thought about her, my whole world filled with asphalt gray and black. I was so scared I could hardly walk upright.

But I was tired of being scared. I was tired of looking over my shoulder. I was tired of Dad's goddamn annoying Soothe Scared Nikki voice. And at the same time, I wished like hell that I could just let him soothe me. That he could make things better. I wished I could open up to him, tell him about everything that had gone on, cling to him for help and support. I hated myself for being so stubborn, but I'd done it for so long, I didn't know any other way.

"I know they'll find her," I said. "But I'm not going to be out there looking for her. And before you ask, no, I don't have another life plan. But I will come up with one. Maybe I'll . . ." I paused, at a loss. My life had been all about the Hollises for so long, I didn't even know how to think about anything else.

"You'll . . . what?"

"I don't know . . . paint swimming pools or fix roofs or sell refrigerators. Does it really matter?" I heard the defensiveness in my voice and tried to force myself to tone it back a bit.

"Yes. It does. It matters a lot. It's your life we're talking about. You're an adult now. It's time to start acting like one." He replaced his glasses and checked his watch. He took a deep breath and began gathering together his papers. "And we'll have to talk about it later, because I have a meeting to get to. I'm sorry."

Thank God.

"It's okay. I've got some thinking to do, anyway." Translation: *I have to go through your shit while you're gone so I can figure out what you're hiding from me, and why. One plan at a time, Daddy. One plan at a time.*

He stacked the papers in the middle of the table and stood. He came over to me and kissed me on the top of the head. "You okay?" he asked. I nodded. "I'll set the alarm, just to be safe."

"Fine."

"You know where the panic button is."

"Yes."

"Let Hue in."

"Dad, I've got it. Go."

He looked at me a second too long, as if he was debating whether or not to leave, then nodded once and headed out. "You know how to get ahold of me. I won't be long. I can be right here if there's an emergency."

"Okay, okay, okay," I mumbled, going to the back door to let in Dad's latest safeguard—a lumbering boxer with too-big feet and more slobber than you could stuff into twenty dogs' mouths. Dad thought his name was Hugh, and I was fine with that. But really it was Hue—a nod to Peyton's rainbow. I liked being the only one who knew that. I opened the door and Hue bounded in, stomping across both of my feet on the way by. "Ouch. Good to see you, too, buddy. Guess you're on duty." I reached down to scratch his ears, but he was circling me too fast to catch. I laughed, despite myself.

I hadn't been lobbying for a dog, and part of me thought this was more overkill in the Kill Family Homestead Arsenal of Self-Defense, but if I were being totally honest, I slept a hell of a lot better when Hue was beside me than when he wasn't.

I sat on the floor and let Hue leap and bump and cover me with kisses, trying to catch an ear here or a neck there for a good scratch, then finally stretched out on my back, giving in to the crazy dog frenzy until I heard Dad set the alarm, and then the click of the front door closing behind him.

"Okay, okay, dinner," I said, pulling myself up off the floor and filling Hue's bowl with kibble. He dove in eagerly, making disgusting crunching and slurping sounds, just like always. *"Bon appétit,"* I said. "I've got work to do."

I went upstairs, detouring to paw through Dad's dresser for the thousandth time. Nothing but socks and underwear and T-shirts and an old pair of swim trunks that I had literally never seen him wear. But nothing that answered a single question, or raised a single doubt. To any casual observer, Dad was just a normal, kind-of-boring dad.

Which I knew was a fucking lie. Normal, kind-of-boring dads didn't hide potentially deadly secrets under their desks in a little locked box.

In my desk drawer, under the black notebook where I'd stashed the letter Peyton had left for me, was a pocket-sized spiral notebook. I opened it and was immediately showered with colors. Purple, sea green, black, orange, red, cornflower blue. Row after row of numbers. Every possible combination I could think of that might have meaning to Dad.

Sea green, bronze, mauve, melon, silver. Mom's birthday. *Neon pink, purple, mauve, melon, pink.* His birthday. *Pink, black-and-white checkered, mauve, bronze, cornflower blue.* Mine.

I went downstairs to his office, crawled under his desk, where the box was, and stretched out on my belly. For a while, I had been taking the box to my room to work on, but I was jumpy as hell when I did that, and convinced that Dad would notice that the dust had been wiped off in the move. Every tiny noise made my heart leap into my throat, and once Hue came into the room and startled me so much that I had to curl up around him and sit quietly for half an hour to calm myself.

I spun the dial a few times to clear it, took a deep breath, and started trying combinations.

Our house number.

Our phone number.

Mom and Dad's anniversary.

Model numbers of all his cameras.

My license plate.

His license pl—

I froze, my fingers still clutching the dial. License plate.

I was blasted with a memory, an image that sucker punched me. Luna, sprinting through the parking lot behind Tesori Antico, her blond hair flying out behind her like a cape. The smoky chemical smell of fired gunpowder enwreathing me, my ears muffled and ringing from the gunfight inside. My chest hitching with quick breaths from fear and exertion as I chased after her. My eyes burning. My throat dry.

My stomach sinking as I realized she'd gotten too far ahead of me.

She was getting away.

She jumped into the passenger seat of a silver truck. A man with very white-blond hair driving.

The license plate a candy cane stripe and mustard.

"VP," I said aloud. "The license plate was VP."

I'd known it this whole time but had been busy trying to put that night out of my mind entirely. I wasn't ready to recall anything about it. Too many terrifying images tried to crowd in on me—Vanessa on the floor, a hole appearing in Bill Hollis's head just when he was pointing the gun directly at me, so much blood, waking up on the floor of an empty van, and Jones. Oh God, Jones. But I especially wasn't ready to recall the fact that Luna got away.

Luna got away.

She got away.

She was insane and angry and now she had absolutely nothing to lose, and I was the one who had taken everything from her. And she got away.

I scrambled out from under the desk, my palms clammy and my heart pounding. I swallowed and swallowed, trying to get the taste of Tesori Antico out of my mouth. I backed against a filing cabinet and closed my eyes, resting my head on the cool cabinet, trying to calm my breathing. Soon Hue padded in and nosed my hand. I turned it over and let him lick my palm.

Get a grip, Nikki. Get a fucking grip.

I forced the image away. The car, the noise, the adrenaline of seeing Vanessa behind me with a knife. Everything except the license plate. VP. It was something. A clue to who was helping her; who she'd gone with. I had been fearing Luna for so long, had been waiting for her to find me and attack me, that it never even occurred to me that I could find her.

I. Could find. Her.

No. I *had* to find her. If I was ever going to get my life back—if I was ever going to be rid of Luna and Hollis Hell, I had to find her.

I had been waiting, fearing, cowering, for too long.

It was time to be done waiting, fearing, cowering. It was time to go on the offensive. Find Luna Fairchild and put an end to this once and for all.

But how, without Martinez? Having an unfinished police academy application did not make me a cop, by any stretch.

And if Chris didn't even remember what had gone down that night, how could he help me?

I raced up to my room and grabbed my cell phone.

It rang five times before he answered. I had started to worry that he wouldn't answer at all. He was out of breath.

"Hello?"

"Hey," I said. "It's Nikki. Miss Kill. Whatever. Nikki."

A couple of breaths. "You calling for career counseling? Because I don't really think I'm qualified."

A joke. I smiled. Maybe the old Chris was in there somewhere, after all. Beneath the anger and frustration and blank space. "Very funny. When does your comedy show go on tour?"

A couple more breaths.

"What are you doing, exactly?" I asked. "You're all out of breath."

"I'm at the gym, if you must know," he said.

"Didn't you just leave physical therapy? Aren't there, like, limits to what you should be doing right now? Like maybe you should be working on your daytime TV and potato chip consumption. Or maybe learning to knit."

"What do you want, Nikki?" And just like that, humor over. It wasn't terribly unlike him to get tired of my shit and shut me down, but these days it just seemed to happen . . . faster.

"Are you back at work yet?"

"No. Why?"

"I just . . . need some help finding something."

His voice got echoey, and I could hear water turn on in the background. "Finding what?"

I squeezed my eyes shut. "Luna Fairchild."

There was a pause. I heard the water turn off, and the sound of a paper towel being ripped. Finally, softly, "Why?"

"I know you don't remember," I said. "But you trusted me. Like, really trusted me. I need you to just trust me now."

A longer pause. "The last thing I remember about Luna Fairchild is that she was in juvenile detention. Now she's not?"

"No, she's definitely not."

"It sounds like you know what happened."

"Bill Hollis happened," I said. But I didn't know where to go from there. I didn't want to be the one to tell Chris all the horror that had happened at Tesori Antico. Surely he would learn that when he got back to work. "I'll give you the cheat-sheet version. Luna got out of juvie. She came after me. Well, *they* came after *us*. And we kind of went to them. But anyway, she got away again. She's disappeared. Nobody's heard anything from her, that I know of, since that night. But somebody helped her, and it's a guy I know I've seen before. I just can't figure out who he is or how he fits into this. And his license plate said VP. I'm thinking if we run that plate, maybe it can help us find Luna."

There was another pause, during which I imagined him trying to arrange everything I'd just said into a picture that made sense. "And then what?"

My voice rose. "And then put her away. Isn't that still your job?"

"Nikki, I'm not . . ." A long sigh. "Okay. Meet me at the station tomorrow morning. We'll see what we can find out."

I T DIDN'T MATTER how many times I'd been there; I would always feel like I was being stared at the moment I stepped foot into the police station. Like everyone thought I should be locked up but was slipping by because I had a friend to help me out.

They maybe wouldn't be too far off from the truth.

The last time I'd been in the station was the night of the Tesori Antico incident, after I'd been told to leave the hospital and go give a statement. I was barely even coherent. Fortunately, Chris had called it in before he'd walked out of the antique shop, so they had a pretty good idea of how all those bodies ended up not breathing inside that store.

What they didn't understand—and what I couldn't

help them with—was how their officer ended up mangled on the street. They were surprised to hear about the bullet holes in his car. Whatever he'd been mixed up in, he hadn't even told his colleagues. He'd been doing something off the record, and it had ended up almost killing him. And none of us could help him, as he lay on the operating table getting screws put into his pelvis and getting his collarbone reset.

They hadn't treated me like a criminal then, but I still felt like one. My hands had held the gun that killed Vanessa Hollis. I had taken a life, and I didn't know how to feel about that, especially since I mostly felt relief.

I didn't tell them about shooting Vanessa. Chris had taken the heat for it. For me.

And probably most of the officers I walked past suspected as much. And being the only one who knew for sure was making me crazy. I wished more than anything that Chris could remember. I wished I could tell him.

"He's in his office, waiting for you," the woman up front said, gesturing for me to head on back. This was the first time I'd walked through the station by myself. I tried to imagine doing it every day, on my way to my own desk, mulling over my own open cases. Yellow and brown pulsed in my temples, a relentless mix of determination and depression. Instant headache. No way could I work in this place. Never.

Martinez was standing behind his desk, sifting through a stack of papers. His cane was leaning against the wall, abandoned.

"Hey," I said, knocking lightly on the door frame.

He looked up. "Oh, hey. You're here. I was just trying to catch up." He shook his head. "Don't know if I ever will. Do you see this?" He gestured to the several piles of papers on his desk. Normally, his office was stark and overflowing with paperwork, but he'd seemed to know where everything was, even if it all looked like never-ending stacks of confusion to me. Having someone else dump a bunch of random things on his desk undoubtedly stressed him out.

"You're not technically back on the clock, are you?" I said, stepping through the doorway. "You don't have to catch up today."

"It's not going to get any better next week when I am back."

I raised my eyebrows. "Next week?"

He nodded. "I'm getting around without the cane. And I'm sick of hanging out in my apartment. If I can sit on a couch, I can sit at my desk. As long as I can concentrate." He narrowed his eyes at his computer, as if trying to remember what it was. Or maybe trying to remember what he'd been doing on it.

"Heriberto somebody," I said.

He shifted his gaze to me, eyes still narrowed.

"You were investigating someone named Heriberto. I can't remember his last name because words in other languages come to me in gr—" I caught myself again; felt my face flush. I tried out a shrug that felt fake as shit. I hoped it didn't look as phony as it felt. "It was an unusual last name," I said.

"Heriberto," he repeated.

I pointed to the stack of files on top of his filing cabinet. I'd seen him set open cases there before. "Maybe he's one of these?"

He shook his head. "I've been through those already." He sank into his chair and held his head in his hands. "This is so frustrating. I can look through those files and remember the names on most of them. But what I can't remember is exactly where I was in the investigations before . . ." He gestured weakly.

"You should have a partner," I said. "I mean, besides yours truly. Because we seem to get into some real shit when we partner up."

He turned his eyes to me. "I remember *you* getting into shit. Constant, unending shit. You telling me I got dragged into that nonsense with you?"

I pointed to my arm. "You have a scar there, right? That's from getting dragged into nonsense with me."

He held his palms out to his sides. "I got hit by a car. I

have scars everywhere."

True. I had forgotten what a bloody mess he'd been—scraped everywhere, it seemed. Kneeling on the road next to him, it had been impossible to figure out where the blood was coming from and how bad the wounds were, especially with my own colors going crazy. I just had to go on the assumption that the wounds were bad. Really bad. And they were. But he was not dead, and that was what mattered the most.

"Fine. You want to know about what we were doing?"

He studied me for a moment, chewing on his lower lip. "Maybe not," he said. "I can only handle so many of your emergencies at a time."

"Fair enough," I said, coming around the desk to stand beside him. The computer was on, but resting on the wallpaper screen. "But eventually we're going to have to address this whole someone-wanting-you-dead thing."

"Not we," he said. "Me. I have to figure this out. Myself. Since when does it involve both of us?"

Since I kissed you and you didn't pull away? Since I told you about my synesthesia and cried by your bedside just as Dru did at Peyton's? Since I came to you every time I needed help with anything, so I clearly came to trust you without even meaning to? Since I saw goddamn magenta almost strong enough to block out the crimson every time I walked into your hospital room? Since I agreed to believe in myself because you believed in me? Since I knelt next to your body in the street with tears streaking my face and terror coursing through me?

Since it hurts like hell to know that the rebooted version of Chris Martinez feels nothing for me. For us.

"Yeah. You're right," I said bitterly. "I was just offering. I'm not forcing myself onto you or anything."

"Well, I'll let you know if I need help," he said. "But don't hold your breath."

"Gosh, what will I do with my time? Actually live my own life?" I asked, trying to sound deadpan, but probably only sounding as sore as I felt. "Can we do this now?" I leaned over him and jiggled the mouse to wake up the computer. He turned and poised his fingers over the keyboard.

"So tell me what I'm doing exactly," he said.

"I need you to look up a license plate with the letters VP. If we can find out who owns that truck, maybe we can find Luna."

"We're back to 'we' now."

"Well, we were a 'we' the night she got away, which I would tell you, if you'd let me. I know you're the police, but I have an interest in finding her, too."

"Obviously. She shot at you."

"Right. And . . . she's done a lot more since then."

He was quiet for a minute. He leaned back in his chair; it squeaked under his weight. "Okay," he finally said, sitting forward and pulling up a database. "VP?"

"Right."

He did some more typing and then leaned back again. "There is no plate that's just VP. You sure there weren't numbers with it? Maybe more letters?"

I eased down on the corner of his desk. Candy cane and mustard. That was it. Candy cane and mustard. V and P. Nothing else. "That's not possible," I whispered.

"You sure it was a California plate?"

California. A radiant gold word with peach highlights. I hadn't realized I'd seen that—I was in too much of a panic—but now that I thought about it, it was there. The radiant gold with peach highlights, framing the V and P.

"Yes. It was definitely a California plate. Look again."

He turned his palms up near the keyboard. "I don't need to. It's right here. You must have seen it wrong."

I shook my head, disbelieving. Had I been seeing what I expected to see? Had my synesthesia gotten jumbled up, mixing the photo of the man with the VP belt buckle I'd found in my dad's desk with Luna's getaway car? It was possible. My synesthesia had steered me wrong before. But I had started to trust it—to really trust it—and it had been working for me. Was there nothing I could trust?

I closed my eyes. I had been trying to avoid remembering that night as much as I possibly could. It tried to push in on me during every quiet moment— my dreams, my shower, driving in my car, reading a book, watching TV. It was always there. The only times I even kind of let it in was during the few brief therapy sessions I'd gone to. When it became obvious that the therapist really wanted me to deal with that night, I quit going. I dealt by ignoring. That was how I did things. Who said you had to bawl into an entire box of Kleenex in order to come to terms with something horrible? Maybe your best way of getting over something was to push it away until it actually went away.

If only everyone would let that night go away.

God, I hated it, but I was going to have to try to remember.

"Well, I can't help you if I can't find—"

"Wait," I said, my eyes still closed. "Shhh."

I could hear my heartbeat, louder and louder, as I lifted the fog away from that night. Luna, holding me in a headlock. Bill Hollis's slithery voice and dead eyes. The noise, my God, the noise. The smoke and the smell and the yelling and the glass shattering. Vanessa, on the floor, crimson closing in. And Luna, running across the parking lot. Jumping into a truck. Candy cane and mustard. *VP.* Radiant gold with peach highlights. The truck fishtailing as it drove out of the parking lot.

Brown, brown, brown.

My eyes flew open. "One, one, one," I said. "There was brown. Three of them. One, one, one."

"Brown? What does—"

I motioned toward the monitor. "Just type." I was coursing with too much adrenaline to pay much attention to my slip.

He reached forward and typed: *VP 111.*

A result popped up, and we both leaned forward, my hair draping over his shoulder.

"Blaine Jones?" Chris read aloud. He glanced up at me, his eyes briefly pausing on my hair. He used one hand to brush it away. "Sound familiar at all?"

I had gone numb, my eyes glued to the name of the ghost on Chris's computer screen. "That's Jones," I said, not even feeling my lips move. He didn't respond, and I realized that he had no idea who Jones was if he didn't remember the months before the accident. I stood, blew a breath to the ceiling, my hands on my hips. "Jones was my"—*boyfriend* wasn't the right word, was it?—"a guy I used to hang out with."

"Used to? So you stopped hanging out with him. What happened?"

So much. So fucking much, I shook with the effort to keep it from bulldozing me. "He's dead," was all I said, pushing memories of falling into his blood out of my mind. There was only so much of that night that I could let in at one time. I was beginning to wonder if avoiding telling Chris the whole story was protecting him or protecting myself.

"Oh," he said. "I'm sorry." There was a pause. "So if she

got away with him, she's on her own now."

I shook my head. "No. He wasn't the one driving. He was already gone. He was . . . he was just helping Luna, so I guess that's why the plate was his."

I saw something in Chris's eyes go soft—a glimmer of a memory, maybe? I hoped so; this would be a lot easier if things just came back to him and I didn't continually have to worry about how much information to spoon-feed him.

He blinked a few times and went back to the screen. "Looks like the vehicle was abandoned about a month ago."

"Where is it now?"

"Impound. The family never picked it up."

Of course they hadn't. That wasn't Jones's car. There were so many things they didn't know. Jones's death was a tragic accident, as far as they were concerned. They were quoted in the news saying as much. *Wrong place at the wrong time. Got involved with a girl he shouldn't have.* They meant me; little did they know it was Luna who'd dragged him into the middle of everything. I'd been keeping him out. Now I wished I'd kept him close; maybe he wouldn't have betrayed me so easily if I had.

Chris clicked around a little. "Cosigner on the loan is Bill Hollis. Why would Bill Hollis help Jones buy a new truck, and why would Jones keep that truck a secret?"

I thought about it. The answer was simple. Luna wanted

Jones to do her dirty business for her. She wanted him to follow me, to steal and break my shit. But she wasn't stupid. "If he'd been following me around in his car, I would have noticed. Can we go?" I asked.

"Go?"

I pointed to the screen. "Can we get it out of impound?"

"No. I'm not authorized to do that. And if I pull out my badge and start demanding things, I'm going to have to have a reason. Do I have a reason? Am I even still on this case?" He gestured to the papers on his desk. "It doesn't look like I'm still on this case. And, no, before you ask, I don't know who is. I'm not technically—"

"Yes, I know, you're not technically back yet." I chewed on my thumbnail. "So if we can't get it out of impound, can we get ourselves in?"

He narrowed his eyes. "What do you mean?"

"I mean, can we get into the car while it's in impound?"

"They're not going to give it to us without ID and registration. Honestly, I'm surprised they haven't sold it at auction yet. Nobody coming forward to claim it—"

"Can we at least try?" He gave me a hesitant look, his mouth still open from being interrupted. I stood, paced around to the other side of his desk. "You have to understand," I said. "I can't just let this go. Luna isn't someone who broke probation and took off. She's dangerous." I placed my hands on his desk and leaned over him. "Trust me on this. You would have agreed to do it . . . before."

That was maybe not entirely true. Chris had never quite warmed up to my tactics. I basically had to force him into everything or do it on my own.

Like that was going to change now.

But he didn't have to know that.

He watched me a minute longer. I could feel low-level magenta and purple pulsing at my feet, and chose to ignore them as best I could.

"Okay. We can try. When?"

I reached over and grabbed his cane, shoved it across the desk at him. "How about now?"

THE IMPOUND LOT consisted of a grungy trailer surrounded by a tall chain-link fence covered with warning
signs. Behind the gate were rows upon rows of cars in various
states of disrepair. Chris pulled up outside the trailer and
parked.

"This is a waste of our time," he said.

"You never know until you try," I said, popping my door
open. I turned around and grabbed his cane out of the backseat.

"I actually do know. Impounding cars is something we
do every day." He took the cane from me, but I noticed he
didn't really need it to get out of the car. He was improving.

"Well, so it's registered to Jones. He's gone. His family

won't claim it because it wasn't his. I'm guessing it was actually Bill Hollis's, because everything in the free world belongs to Bill Hollis in one way or another, and he's not going to claim it, either."

Chris squinted. "Because he's gone, too," he said. I nodded. He seemed to search for a moment. "Shot?" I nodded again, my stomach dropping. What would he do when he finally remembered that night? When he finally remembered who shot Bill Hollis? And why? His forehead creased, and he rubbed it. "That's all I've got."

"It's something," I said. He shook his head, irritated. "So if nobody's going to claim it," I continued, ignoring him, "maybe they'll let us. It's better than letting it just sit there. Money is money, right?"

"So they'll prefer to make a hundred fifty on it from us—illegally—rather than sell it at auction—legally—and make a few thousand." He chuckled. "Nikki, you are impossible."

"So you've told me. Again and again. Can we?" I gestured toward the trailer.

He shrugged. "Why do I have a feeling that fighting you is futile?"

"Because I win," I said. "Or have you conveniently forgotten all the times I've kicked your ass in the *dojang*?"

"I let you win."

Our footsteps crunched over the gravel drive. "So you suddenly remember that?"

He grinned. "Don't need to remember it. I just know it. Like I know the sky is blue."

I rolled my eyes. "Wait until that leg heals, and we'll see who needs to let who win."

"Yes, we will."

He clomped up the two wooden steps that led to the trailer's door and opened it, stepping back to let me inside first.

"No, you go ahead," I said.

"Ladies first."

"You're injured. You should go first."

"Can you just make one thing easy? Please?" He opened the door wider. "Go."

I sighed. This didn't fit into my plan at all—which was, of course, never to actually ask someone if we could see the car. Asking almost never worked out well for me. Now I had to think of something on the fly. I walked into the trailer's lobby, my footsteps sounding hollow on the nubby carpet floor. There were a couple of beat-up chairs with stained cushions pushed against the wall, a dusty fake plant in the corner, and a counter with a window dominating one whole end. Next to the counter was a plain wooden door. Nobody was at the window. Instead, there was a note that instructed visitors to ring a bell for assistance. I pretended I didn't see the note so I could buy myself some time.

After a few long seconds, he sighed, reached around me,

and tapped the bell. We heard the noise of movement in what I guessed was a whole other room somewhere behind the counter. *Think, Nikki, think.*

I patted my jeans pockets, putting on what felt like the fakest panic look ever. "I forgot my phone," I said. I tugged down the hem of my shirt so he couldn't see the outline of my phone in my back pocket.

Chris's face screwed up. "So? I have mine." He held it out.

"No, I don't need your phone. I need mine. I think I might have lost it."

"Probably not. I'll call it." He started to punch numbers into his phone. Something I hadn't thought of. If my pocket started ringing, he was going to get suspicious. And for good reason. I pulled his arm, making him juggle his phone, a look of annoyance crossing his face. "Calm down. It's just a phone."

"You know what, it's probably in the car," I said. "I should look."

The movement behind the window got louder—hollow footsteps that matched ours—and a woman appeared at the counter.

"Right now?" he asked. "Can't it wait?"

"I won't be able to relax until I have it. It's got important things on it." I turned my back to the window and lowered my voice. "You can handle this until I get back, can't you?"

"Of course I can. The car's unlocked."

"I'll be right back, I swear," I said, heading for the door.

I wondered if he knew I was lying. Probably. He was pretty good at knowing what I was going to do even when I didn't know what I was going to do.

I shut the trailer door softly behind me, and then sprinted across the gravel. I didn't have all the time in the world; I had to get moving fast. I jogged along the fence line, looking for anywhere that might have some sort of breach. A hole, maybe, or a place near the ground where an animal had bent the wire pushing his way in. I ran all the way to the far end, where the fence turned into a small grove of trees, littered with rusty car parts and old tires. No holes, no breaches. I was going to have to climb.

Quickly, I scanned the lot for a watchdog or a person or a camera. Surely there was a camera somewhere, but I didn't see one, and I figured if I didn't see it, it probably didn't see me. The cars at the back looked like they'd been there a long time and had mostly been used for parts, so it was probably a safe bet that they didn't bother to monitor comings and goings. I glanced at the trailer—the door was shut, so Chris was either still waiting for me inside, or he was arguing his case. My case. Whatever. The case.

I had to move fast.

Ducking, I raced over to the cluster of trees—tall weeds slapping against my shins—while praying that I wouldn't step on a snake or a rabid animal's nest or a colony of ground hornets. I kept going deeper, until I reached a spot where the weeds and limbs were intertwined in the chain link. I couldn't get any more covered than this.

I stuffed my toes and looped my fingers into chain-link holes and pulled myself up, trying to move as quickly as possible, thanking God the whole way that there was no razor wire or even barbed wire to contend with at the top. The fence was tall and kind of unstable, and I swayed, gripping so hard my fingers were white, as I hoisted my leg over the top and stood, straddling the fence. I started to get dizzy from the height, but reminded myself I didn't have time for dizzy. And I sure as hell didn't have time to fall off this thing.

I swung over the fence and scurried down the other side, dropping into the dirt when I got about three feet off the ground.

I was in.

And now that I was in, it seemed like finding the truck would be an impossible task. Made even more impossible if Chris was actually successful in getting it released to us. I doubted he ever would, but he'd surprised me with his abilities before, and if they were bringing the truck out to the parking lot for him, I was screwed.

I walked several feet down the aisle I'd landed in. Like I'd thought, most of these cars were shells, missing tires and bumpers and engine parts, doors open to reveal gutted insides. The truck would not be back here.

I turned myself so that I was facing where the trailer had been—I could no longer see it from where I was—and started jogging between the cars, passing up aisle upon aisle, until I got to what looked like new stuff. Colors jumped out at me where license plates hung. I closed my eyes, trying to clear my mind and focus.

Candy cane and mustard. Brown, brown, brown. That was what I was looking for.

I opened them, and again the entire rainbow pushed in on me. Bits of candy cane here, mustard there, brown everywhere.

God, this seemed impossible.

I decided to look at trucks only. If it wasn't a truck, I let my eyes skip over it, flinging its plate colors out of my way. I'd thought that would make this easier, but practically every other vehicle there was a truck. *Red, blue, white, white, silver, red, red*—the colors of the vehicles themselves making it even harder to concentrate on the plates.

I wound my way down four aisles this way, until I heard voices coming from the direction of the trailer, which was much closer now. Time was running out. I pushed myself harder. *Run faster, concentrate better. Hug the cars, stay out of sight. Keep moving, but pay attention.* I was sweating. And my head was starting to throb

Just when I turned the final corner—taking me close

enough to the trailer that anyone who stepped out back for a smoke would see me—and thought I was going to have to backtrack and start all over again, I saw it.

Silver truck. Candy cane. Mustard. Brown, brown, brown.

VP 111.

Jones's license plate on a car that Luna got away in. I made a beeline for it.

Just as I reached for the door handle, my phone rang, startling the shit out of me. I snatched it out of my pocket before it could ring twice and spark someone's attention.

"Jesus, what?" I hissed into the phone.

"I don't know why I was surprised that you lied to me. Where are you?"

"Looking for my phone." My voice was cool, challenging.

"Bullshit. But nicely done. It worked. I can tell I'm still off my game."

Probably true. "I take it you weren't successful in getting the car released."

"How do you know I'm not sitting in it right now?"

I opened the driver's-side door with a soft click and slid onto the bench seat, keeping myself low so nobody could see my silhouette. "Because I am," I said.

"Damn it, Nikki. You're in there?" I heard a distant rattle of chain link, as if he'd tapped it or, more likely, pounded it with his fist. "Do you know how illegal this is? Now I have to arrest you."

"Can't," I said, opening and shutting every console door I could find. "You're technically not on the clock. Convenient for me, huh?"

"I doubt anyone would mind if I brought in a B and E."

"You don't have handcuffs." I pawed through rolls of mints and pens and a stack of fast-food napkins. Just like this was any old car.

"I can get creative."

I stopped what I was doing. "But we both know you won't. Plus, you'd have to catch me first, and that's not happening on that leg of yours. So, listen, get in your car and go. There's some sort of Laundromat or something on the street behind the lot. I saw the back side of it when I was climbing in. Go park there and wait for me. I won't be long."

There was a trademark Chris Martinez pause, where he wanted to appear to be mulling over his options but was actually just kicking himself for knowing that he was going to give in to whatever I wanted him to do. He may have forgotten me, but part of him still remembered us. "If you get arrested, it's on you. I won't bail you out this time."

I stopped, sat up, tucked the phone tighter between my ear and shoulder. "You remember?"

"Remember what?"

"Bailing me out of jail."

Another pause. "Yeah. I guess I do. You did something typically stupid like assault an officer or something. But you were set up, right? And somebody wanted me to let you go."

"Blake Willis," I said softly.

"That's right," he said. "Blake Willis." But it was as if he were repeating the name to only himself, trying it out to see if it jogged any memories.

I didn't want it to jog memories, and I couldn't explain why. It had to do with the magenta, with the kiss, with the way things had been between us after Blake, his gorgeous, totally-put-together ex-girlfriend, had left him. There was nothing wrong with Blake Willis. Actually, everything about her seemed absolutely perfect. Which was why I didn't want her back in his life. It was hard to compete with perfection.

You're not competing, Nikki. It never was a competition.

"Just wait for me at the Laundromat," I repeated, and hung up, quickly flicking the sound off so it couldn't ring again.

I couldn't be worrying about Blake Willis. I had to get through this truck and get out of here, because there was something about the way he said it that made me believe Chris really meant that he wouldn't bail me out again.

I stuffed the phone back into my pocket and continued rummaging. Nothing. Nothing on top of nothing. Whoever had abandoned this truck had made sure to clean it beforehand. Not surprising, given the professional criminals that Luna had for friends.

I grunted in frustration and sat back with my fists in my lap. Not that I was super hopeful that I would find someone's driver's license or a neon sign that would point the way to Luna's hideout, but I had been more hopeful than I realized that I would find something. Anything better than a wadded straw wrapper and the car manual.

Sighing, I opened the door and slid out, trying to keep low to avoid being seen. Just before I closed the door, something under the seat caught my eye. I reached in and pulled it out. Before I could really study it, I heard voices coming from the direction of the trailer. I popped up enough to see through the windshield. Two hulking men were stepping down the wooden stairs from the trailer onto the lot. They were talking loudly, gesturing, laughing. No idea they had a trespasser only about thirty feet away.

"Shit," I breathed, sinking down against the side of the truck. Did I shut the door and risk the noise attracting their attention, or did I leave it open and hope they didn't notice? In the end, I decided on a combination of both. I let the door gently swing closed and then pushed it slowly until it engaged the lock with a soft click. I pressed my lips together, perking my ears for any sense that the men had heard it. More laughter. Apparently they hadn't.

I shuffled forward a few feet and rose up again, peeking

over the hood. They were still there, still talking, only now they were moving toward me, one twirling an overstuffed key ring around one finger. If I stayed where I was, in two minutes they would be on top of me.

There was no way I was going to stay there.

I pushed away from the truck and, staying low, scurried across the aisle. I plunged in between a BMW and a Buick and crouched low again, pressing my back against the Buick and trying not to breathe. Didn't help.

"You hear something?" I heard one of the guys say.

"No."

"Sounded like footsteps right over there," the first one said. I chanced a glance over the trunk of the BMW, only to see them making a beeline for the silver truck I'd just been inside. I had to go, and go now.

I leaned against the door for a second longer, bracing myself, and then sprang into action. I popped up, turned toward the back fence, and started running with everything I had.

"Hey!" I heard one of them shout, and then, "Did you see that?"

I didn't wait around for an answer; just kicked up dirt and gravel behind me as I sprinted, then scrambled over a gutted SUV, which put me almost at the top of the fence. I hoisted myself up and over in three pulls.

The voices were too far away to be anywhere near

me—almost as if they'd given up halfway through the lot—but I still let go almost from the top of the fence, hitting the grass and tumbling backward onto my butt, my arms flailing out to catch my fall. My elbow lit up in pain, but I ignored it, turning to get myself back up on my feet and plowing through the tall grass and weeds until I came out at the back of the Laundromat.

My shoes slapped the asphalt hard as I raced to Chris's car, which was running, with him behind the wheel, waiting for me.

"Go," I said, breathless, as I dove in and shut the door.

He slammed the car into gear and backed out, his tires screeching. Typical Chris, driving without asking a single question.

Once we were on the highway and I'd caught my breath, he slowed down.

"Well?"

"Cleaned," I said, still trying to catch my breath.

He nodded. "Not surprising. I tried to get them to at least release the property to me, but they said there wasn't any. Wouldn't have even if there was. Just like I told you."

"Dude, I never doubted you. I just needed you to distract them while I went in. But I know you well enough to know that you would never agree to that, even if you knew I was going to bring back something."

"I thought you said there was nothing."

"I said it was clean. But there was this." I pulled what I'd found beneath the seat out of my waistband and held it up.

He eyed it skeptically. "An empty notepad."

"Correct."

"Is there something on the other pages?" he asked.

"Nope. Just this one."

He looked at the notepad harder, glancing back and forth between the road and the pad. "There's nothing there."

"Wrong," I said. I tipped it so the light could catch it just right. "There are indentations."

He pulled to the side of the highway, hit his hazard lights, and took the notepad from me. He studied it, turning it this way and that. He shook his head and handed it back to me.

"It's nonsense. So many pages going through that it looks like a jumble. This isn't a clue to anything, Nikki."

"You've said that to me before," I said. "And you were wrong before."

"I'll take your word for it."

"You have any other choice?"

He gave an eye roll and turned off his hazards, then pulled onto the highway. "Whatever you say. It's your wheels that you're spinning. Not mine." He drove for a moment, and then said, "It was a painting, wasn't it? The clue that you found before?"

I paused in surprise. "Among other things. And I bought

it. At an auction. You were with me. We almost got run over."

"I think I remember that," he said softly.

The air between us grew thick, and he seemed to be a million miles away as he navigated us along the highway. I tried to ignore my heartbeat, which sped up as I willed him to remember more. Remember everything. Remember how it felt to be there together, how it felt to be tangled on the ground, watching the van speed away. Not just recall the events that happened, but the way we felt when they were happening.

I clutched the notepad in my lap, wondering if maybe this time he was right. Maybe this time it really wasn't a clue.

But, then again, he didn't see the notepad the same way I saw the notepad. Pages upon pages of writing bled through in indentations, yes. But where he saw jumbled indentations, I saw each letter and number scratching itself out faintly in the correct hue, creating a blur of mixed colors. Orange As and purple threes and the lunch-meat pink and lemon chiffon of *Es* and *Hs* and the oxford blue of the word *Friday*. The mottled yellow-green word *Pear* and the velvety burgundy word *Magic*. Nothing that came together in anything that made sense.

Except two words—one midnight with star pops of light, the other sunshine yellow.

Celestial. Day.

But as I looked closer, I realized it was not *Celestial*; it was something shorter. *Celeste.*

Celeste Day.

I didn't know what Celeste Day was, or what it had to do with Jones, or Luna, or the white-blond-haired man driving the truck.

But I sure as hell intended to find out.

A FTER CHRIS AND I parted ways at the police station, I drove straight home, turning the two words over in my head as I went. Celeste Day. Celeste Day. It rang no bells. Was it a fair? A celebration of the moon and stars? One of those unofficial "holidays" that nobody but the person who created it celebrates, like National Hot Dog Day? Not one I'd ever heard of. Was it a person?

I was going to have to figure out who or what Celeste Day was.

Dad was downstairs in the basement when I got home. I could hear the metal clink of free weights hitting each other. He hardly ever worked out. Only when he was completely stressed or had something weighing on his mind.

Like guilt, maybe, Dad?

Like, maybe, the feeling that your daughter is figuring out that you had some sort of link to the family who has been trying to kill her? That maybe you suspect she might be this close to finding out you were somehow involved in your own wife's death?

The thought turned me icy.

I sat in the kitchen, turning up the TV to drown out Dad's grunts, and ate a sandwich, Hue sitting patiently at my feet waiting for me to drop something. I was staring at whatever dumb show was on, but my mind was everywhere else. Dad, Luna, Chris's memory loss, Celeste Day.

I was rinsing my plate when Dad appeared at the top of the basement stairs. He had a towel draped over his neck, and his hair was wet with sweat. He was cleaning his glasses with the bottom of his shirt.

"You're home."

"Yep. Going upstairs, though. Got some work to do."

He scrunched up his face. "What kind of work?"

"Research," I said. "Job research."

His eyebrows went up, and his lips curved into the meekest smile, wavering at the edges, as if he was afraid to let it completely loose, for fear of scaring me off. "Any particular job?"

I shook my head. "I'm still trying to figure that out."

He closed the basement door behind him and put the

glasses on, then pulled the towel off his neck and used it to wipe his forehead. "Have you thought about photography?" he said into the towel. He was acting nonchalant, but I knew the question was incredibly loaded. He would love nothing more than for me to follow in his—and in some ways, Mom's—footsteps.

"Not really." Truth, I had thought about it, and had immediately dismissed it. Mom's death, the way her life intertwined with the Hollises', Dad's deception, had all soured photography and film for me. I wasn't really sure what I would do if not policing, but I knew I didn't want to be involved in the tawdry shit my parents had been involved in.

"I was thinking maybe you could go on a shoot with me sometime," he said. "It's been a while."

Like, a really long while. I had been in middle school last time I joined Dad on a shoot. It was boring and hot and I got sick of being told to stop distracting the models and hold the light reflector steadier and, no, I couldn't swim, even though I was sweating and we were on the beach, because this wasn't a play day, it was business.

"What do you think?" he prompted when I didn't respond.

I shrugged. "I guess. Not, like, out of town, though, okay?"

He tossed the towel over the back of a kitchen chair. "Why not?"

Because I have answers to find. "Because I . . . have jobs to apply for."

He gave me a skeptical look—who would blame him?—but played along anyway. "Okay. I have one coming up. One of my models wants to do an updated urban shoot for her portfolio. I'll let you know." He walked to the kitchen sink and poured himself a glass of water. "So. Research for the rest of your day?"

Day. Celeste Day.

God, even if I figured out what Celeste Day was, who was to say it had anything to do with Jones, Luna, or the white-blond-haired man who helped her get away?

Well. It was all that I had. I had to go with it, because it was the only thing I could go with at all.

"Yep," I said.

"I was hoping you wouldn't hole yourself up in your room all day again." He set the glass down. "Look. I know you're scared. And I'm scared, too. And I would love nothing more than to wrap you up in bubble wrap and tuck you away somewhere safe forever. But I would be a horrible father if I let you waste your life away sitting in that window of yours smoking and ruminating about bad things." I must have made a face, because he raised his eyebrows. "Yes, I know about the smoking. I wish you wouldn't drop your butts in the flower garden, but that's a conversation for another day."

"I'm not ruminating," I said, feeling my face flush,

because of course we both knew rumination was something I specialized in. *Nikki Kill, Professional Brooder: Guaranteed depression in six sessions, or your money back!* If there was a market for that, I would be a rich woman. "Besides, I'm quitting smoking. And I'm not going to hole myself up. I'm going to the library." I could actually see him struggle to keep his surprise in check. I hated libraries. So many colors, so much silence, and the atmosphere of every damn one of them the same boring pencil-lead gray. When I was in elementary school, I would fake stomachaches on library day—not that the nurse's office was much better, but at least it was really only one color. "What? I can go to the library," I said.

"I know you can. I'm just surprised that you are." He came across the room and poked my ribs. I jumped, pushing his hands away a little too roughly, looking at my own hands with surprise, even as I did it. I didn't trust the man—I already knew that—but since when did I not let him touch me?

"Everything okay?" he asked, looking concerned, his finger still in the air pointing at my side.

I folded a dish towel in half and draped it over the oven door, doing everything I could to keep from meeting his gaze. If there was ever a time for me to bring up what was going on—Mom, the locked box, his lies about Bill Hollis—this was it. But I wasn't ready to confront him yet. I needed proof on my side. I needed to get into that damned box. If

I told him I was onto him, he could empty the box before I could ever get inside.

"I'm fine," I said. "Just . . . ruminating, I guess." I gave him a thin grin.

He grinned back. "You see? You can do it without filling your lungs with poison." Good God, if Martinez and Dad ever got together, they would hassle me about smoking until I quit, just to shut them up. He put his hand on my shoulder. I had to force myself not to flinch. "Listen, Nik. Everything will be fine. I know I keep bugging you about having future plans, but I understand why it's taking you a while. You'll get there. I believe in you."

I wish I could believe in you, was what I thought, while "That makes one of us" was what actually came out of my mouth.

I didn't give him a chance to argue with me again. I turned and hoofed it upstairs. I didn't want to go to the library when I had a perfectly good—and new, thanks to Jones killing my old one—laptop right in my bedroom. But I was locked in now. I grabbed my keys off the desk and headed out.

TAKING DEEP BREATHS to steady the colors in the library never did any good. It always just filled my nose with the smell of graphite that I knew wasn't really there, but was such a strong connection with the color of the atmosphere my senses fooled me into thinking it was there. Instead, I made a beeline for the computer bank and did my best to push away any color distractions.

Celeste Day. That was all I cared about. Figuring out who or what Celeste Day was. And if it was a what, then I needed to find out if it had already happened, or if it was something coming up that I could go to. The thought of going to some sort of carnival where Luna might be hiding made my hands shake, but that was why I was doing this, right? To find Luna and put an end to this once and for all. If my hands shook, so be it.

I sat at a computer and typed in my library card number to pull up the internet. An incredibly sweaty guy in a camouflage shirt sat at the computer next to me, and I inched my rolling chair away, turning the monitor so he couldn't see it. Another reason to hate the library—no fucking privacy. Letting out a breath, I typed in *Celeste Day*.

Nothing.

No calendar. No fair. No festival or carnival or even explanation. Just a few Whitepages entries, a couple of social media pages, and an IMDb page.

Wait. Not nothing.

I opened the IMDb page. Celeste Day, a teen actress. Born in Albany, New York. The word *Albany* lit up in eggplant, tickling the back of my mind with a memory. I couldn't quite pinpoint it, though. And I couldn't waste time trying to figure out why that eggplant color looked so familiar to me. I pushed it away and went back to Celeste's bio. She'd moved to Los Angeles to pursue her acting career when she was thirteen. She'd managed to land a few theater roles, a commercial voice-over, and one independent movie, currently being filmed at Pear Magic Studio. Mottled yellow-green *Pear*, velvety burgundy *Magic*. Those had been written on the pad by her name. I had thought they were nonsense, but apparently not. Whoever had written *Celeste Day* on that pad was talking about *this* Celeste Day.

There was only one photo attached to her profile; she wasn't a big enough star yet to have a gallery. But to read her bio, it seemed she was poised to take Hollywood by storm, and soon.

I leaned back, idly playing with a chunk of my hair. Celeste Day, actress. How was she connected to Luna? Was she one of Bill Hollis's protégées? More likely she was part of Hollywood Dreams. Young, aspiring actress. Beautiful in the same creamy, delicate way Peyton and Luna were beautiful, only with darker hair, softer cheekbones, and poutier lips. Definitely motivated.

Maybe motivated enough to help Luna get away.

God, it seemed like Luna knew everyone. Like the list continued to get longer and longer every time I thought I had a handle on everyone who could possibly be involved.

Luna was getting help. That much was for sure. A

sixteen-year-old orphan didn't just disappear from the face of the earth—breaking probation in the process—without somebody knowing where she was. Maybe that was why Celeste's name had been written in the notepad. Maybe Celeste Day was the one hiding her.

The only way to find out was to find Celeste Day myself.

THIS TIME I was the one waiting on Chris first thing
in the morning with a coffee in my hand. Well, two,
actually—one for each of us. It was a joke—I'd thrown away
every coffee he'd ever tried to give me—but it was also a
guilt offering. I figured I owed him.

I parked my car next to his and waited, hoping today
wasn't the day he planned to stay home and clean the apartment or watch a movie marathon or do an all-day physical
therapy blitz. Nah. I knew him too well. He was a restless
type. Always sniffing out a case or punching a heavy bag . . .
or following me around. Well. In the old days, following me
around. Not so much anymore.

I sipped my coffee until it was gone, ignoring the

unending stream of overplayed pop songs on the radio and anxiously bouncing my knee against the center console of my car. I was eager to get going; I couldn't wait on him forever. The old Nikki wouldn't have waited on him at all. The old Nikki wouldn't have even considered letting him in on her plans.

The old Nikki didn't watch him bounce off the hood of a Monte Carlo.

Albany. Why did the Monte Carlo make me think of Albany?

Just as I was deciding I'd been patient enough, and was about to go lean on his apartment buzzer until he got his limpy ass up off the couch, the front door opened and he came out. Limping, yes, but only slightly. And completely without his cane. He was wearing a pair of jeans and a T-shirt that advertised his gym. I had been so worried about his legs, I hadn't noticed how muscular his arms had gotten during physical therapy. The T-shirt sleeves strained against his biceps.

He was almost all the way to his car before he noticed me. He faltered a step, and then went back to his stride, maybe even looking a little more purposeful than before. I got out of my car and held up the full coffee.

"It's a little cold. I've been waiting for a while," I said. "But I didn't drink it So there's a plus."

He looked at the coffee, and then I saw the corners of

his mouth twitch up a little. "It's about time you did the buying," he said.

"You remember."

He nodded, took the coffee, tipped it up, made a face. "A little cold? It's like ice."

I shrugged. "It's warm outside anyway. Beggars can't be choosers, you know."

"I wasn't begging."

"Then stop being so choosy."

I let the car door shut and leaned against it. He was right, though. In all our time together, Chris had never asked anything of me other than to be honest, and to let him protect me. So far I'd done a shit job of both. Which was why I was here in the first place. I wasn't quite sure what had shifted between us, but I knew I had to do a better job of letting him in. Not so he could save me; so I could save myself.

He turned so he was leaning against the car next to me, his elbow lightly brushing my arm as he lifted his cup for a sip. "This is the second time you've just shown up. You trying to make some kind of statement, or are you just checking up on me?"

"I'm not checking up on you," I snapped, but actually, I hadn't realized it until just that moment, maybe I kind of was. I adopted an aloof tone, to try to play it off. "Besides, if I was, it would be fair payback, don't you think? You've checked on me until I wanted to jump off a bridge just to get rid of you, if I wasn't afraid you'd follow me down."

He winced. "Ouch."

"Just a joke," I mumbled, still feeling awkward. I hated having to explain my feelings. Gross. "Actually, it is kind of a new thing. I know you don't remember much, but we were kind of working as a team. I'm used to you, is all. You're like a . . . purse. Or a pair of shoes that I've broken in."

"I'm remembering more every day, just like they said I would," he said, ignoring the last. He set the coffee on the hood of my car and crossed his arms, staring intensely at the asphalt while he talked. "This morning, out of nowhere, I remembered doing some kind of photo shoot with you. And I remember being in a warehouse with you, and a safe full of cash." His brow furrowed. "And I remember you wearing a sexy black formal, but I don't know why."

I felt my face blush at the word *sexy*, the gravel around our feet rippling with violet. "Estate auction," I said. "Same one where I bought the painting. We were looking for the cane that killed Peyton."

He nodded. "Yeah. Okay, yeah. I think I remember that, too. You dropped the painting in the parking lot."

"Sort of." I hesitated, but then decided to go on. "I dropped it when Jones tried to run us over."

"And he's the one who owned the truck Luna got away in."

"Right. But he definitely wasn't the one driving. She was

using him," I said. "Which is why it's so important to me to find her now. If she's using my own people against me, who knows what she's capable of?" I thought of poor Jones, crumpling to the floor in Tesori Antico. "And she needs to pay for what she's done. I want this to be over. She should be in prison."

He nodded again, turning back to the asphalt, deep in thought. "So why are you here this morning, then?"

Albany.

What was it about Albany?

I took a breath. "So listen, the notepad I found in the truck."

He shook his head, stopping me. "You don't even know if it belonged to her."

"But I don't know that it didn't."

"There was nothing on it."

I pushed away from the car and faced him. "Just hear me out, okay? You told me to never give up on evidence. You said sometimes you have to ask the same questions over and over again until you have answers. So I'm looking for answers. It's the only thing I could find, Chris. I have to start somewhere."

He sighed, picked up his coffee again. "So tell me about it."

I started to pace in front of him. "There were indentations from things that were written on the notepad before.

Most of it was a jumble of nothing that I could make sense of. But there was one thing that I could read. Celeste Day."

"What is that?"

"Not a what. A who. She's an actress. She's from New York. . . ." *Albany.* Eggplant. Familiar eggplant. "But she lives here in L.A. She's shooting a horror movie over at Pear Magic Studio right now."

He looked lost. "Connect the dots here, Nikki."

"I don't know how they connect. I don't even know if they connect at all. But I'm thinking if I can find Celeste Day, maybe I can find Luna."

"Seems like a long shot."

I stopped, let my shoulders sag. "It's the only shot I have."

"Okay," he said, switching his coffee to the other hand so he could dig in his pocket for car keys. "So what's the plan? I know you have one. You always have one."

Relief flooded me. It felt like the old Chris was coming through. I could even see sparks of yellow fizz off him when I stared hard enough. "I'm going to Pear Magic."

"And you'll get in, how?"

"I'll figure that out when I get there. It's not difficult."

"For you, I believe that. So what's my part in this?"

"Go with me," I said, sheepish, and pissed off because I sounded sheepish. I squared my jaw. "I might have to move quickly, and four hands are better than two." He rolled his eyes and started to talk. I knew he was about to protest, so I interrupted him, placing my hand on his arm.

Ignore the rainbow. Ignore the violet stripe. Ignore the colors.

"You don't have to do anything until it's safe. I won't jeopardize your job, I promise. Everything will be on the up-and-up. And if it's not, I'll take the heat."

"I don't know. I'm just getting back into—"

"Please? Chris? I need you." My whole body burned with furious humiliation. I didn't need anyone. I prided myself on that. So why was I being such a needy sap now?

Because you do need him, Nikki. Because you've always needed him, even when you weren't willing to admit it. And because he was always there when he was needed.

Albany. Something about Albany.

What the hell?

He stared into my eyes for a long time, and I could see him soften. The old Chris, the one who wasn't angry about what had happened to him. He was still in there. The relief nearly buckled me.

"Okay," he said. "I'll go. But if anything looks like it's going to get stupid, we're out of there. Or at least I am."

I let out a breath and smiled. "Thank you. And you know me. How could anything get stupid?"

"It's *because* I know you that I know things likely will." He hit the unlock button on his key fob. "Get in."

* * *

FORTUNATELY, THE DRIVE to Pear Magic was relatively short. But the traffic was awful, and the sun baked in on us, leaving a hot stripe across my legs. He had donned his sunglasses, which was how I was used to seeing him. Cane free, sunglasses in place, anger softened by yellow. It was almost as if the hit-and-run had never happened.

Hit-and-run. Why had those words come to me in eggplant?

Albany eggplant.

I turned down the radio—muting the stupid talk station that he was always listening to. "Does Albany mean anything to you?"

He glanced in my direction. "No. Should it?"

"I don't know. It's that this actress is from Albany, and when I read that, it made me . . . well, I just sort of have a feeling Albany is important to us somehow."

"A feeling."

I nodded. "I can't quite place it. But there's some sort of connection between Albany and the guy who hit . . ."

I trailed off. My mind spiraled back and back and back to where I'd seen a similar eggplant color. On a computer screen. In Chris's office. The guy who hit him. A name that I couldn't connect because it had come to me in an unusual color. Albany. Eggplant.

Only not Albany. Something similar. Albania or Albano. Or . . .

"Abana," I said, incredulous excitement coursing through me.

"Excuse me?"

"Heriberto Abana. That's who you were searching for before you got hit. I was in your office and I got bored and started to look around. You had been looking for this guy. Heriberto Abana. Albany. Shit. I fucking knew it."

"Heriberto Abana," he repeated, trying to keep his eye on the road while also looking at me.

"Yeah."

He scratched his neck, thinking, then shook his head. Frustration came off him in pillowy green waves. "It's like the name sounds familiar, but I don't know why. What was I looking for?"

"Beats me," I said. "You wouldn't tell me. You said it was none of my business and you were all into some personal case. Like, it wasn't assigned to you officially or anything. Do you think . . . he could be the one who hit you?"

"I don't know. He could have been just about anyone. Maybe I was looking for him as part of another case and he wasn't important."

"For someone who wasn't important, you were sure searching the hell out of him."

We had come up on Pear Magic and he steered the car into the driveway. "Then I guess I should figure out why."

W HEN I WAS a kid, and I used to follow Dad around
on his shoots, I went to lots of the studios. None
of the huge ones, of course. But plenty of little ones like
Pear Magic, which were generally pretty underwhelming. A
few warehouse-looking buildings crammed with people and
props and cameras and pouty actresses who ordered my dad
around like he was their dog. And some doughy guy eating cookies in a tiny "security" building at the head of the
driveway, acting like he could do something if you wanted
to bust your way inside. One time, when I was fourteen, one
of the security guys at a studio I can't even remember the
name of tried to kiss me when I was hauling one of Dad's
anvil-like camera bags through the parking lot. Even though

he was kind of cute in a completely unkempt way, I was still skeeved out and elbowed him in the ribs to let him know I wasn't into older guys with neck beards. I tried not to go to too many studios after that.

Chris inched his car up to the security hut and rolled down his window. An impossibly short guard with a buzz cut ambled to the car, one thumb tucked into his waistband like he was some sort of Old West gunslinger.

"Help you?"

"Celeste on set today?" Chris asked.

The guard frowned, tapping his finger against the front of his pants just under the waistband. "She expecting you?"

Chris opened his mouth, and my world exploded with yellow. If I let him talk, he was going to blow everything. I lunged across the seat so the guard could see me.

"I'm late. Sorry," I blurted. Chris and the guard looked at me with equal amounts of surprise. I had to come up with something, fast. I tried not to think about it too hard. "Makeup?" I said, miming brushing something onto my cheeks. "I'm her makeup artist."

"I thought Jayelle was—" the guard started, but I shook my head to cut him off.

"Something about a situation at home? I don't know. The agency sent me to take her spot."

"And you are . . . ?" the guard asked Chris. I could see

the back of Chris's neck instantly redden.

"He just carries my kits." I stretched my lower back, the fact that the guard's eyes followed my breasts with his eyes when I did it not lost on me. I held the stretch a beat longer. "I'm recovering from a surgery. He stays in the car when he's done hauling stuff. The agency doesn't mind. It's not a problem for him to be here, is it?"

The guard narrowed his eyes. "I probably should double-check," he said. "I've got a number somewhere." He started toward the hut.

"Miss Day is waiting, though," I said. I tried to take the panic out of my voice and replace it with authority. "She can't go on set until I apply the . . ." I mimed some more motions around my face.

"Oh, you're the blood girl?" the guard asked. "They've been waiting."

I nodded frantically. "Yes! Exactly. They've been waiting for the blood. I'm the best the agency has. Honestly? I'm better than Jayelle. I've won awards."

"Okay. Yeah. You should get back there. The director doesn't like it when he has to wait for people. He's probably going to lay into you a little."

I hung my head, contrite. "I deserve it." I smacked Chris on the arm. "I told you we didn't have time to stop for that Cronut." Chris's eyebrows went up. His lips were parted, as if he wanted to speak but didn't have the first clue where to start. I had to bite the inside of my cheek to keep from laughing.

The guard stepped off the curb and gestured toward a small building. "Miss Day's in building three. You can park in the lot right next to it."

"Thanks," Chris finally said, and rolled up his window. It wasn't until we had driven forward a few feet that I finally let my laughter loose.

"Oh my God, you should see your face," I said. "You're a detective. Shouldn't you be better at playing along?"

"You're the blood girl?"

"You had a better plan?"

"Yeah, actually. Show him my badge and tell him we needed to talk to her."

I rolled my eyes.

"What? You'd be amazed what people will spill when they're confronted with a badge."

"Right," I said. "And this girl is just going to hand Luna over on a silver platter. Because Luna's friends are all so well-adjusted and cooperative. Give me a break."

He rounded the corner and parked the car. "You do real-ize you're going to be expected to actually"—he mimicked my hands flailing around my face—"do something with her makeup now, right?"

I shrugged. "It's all in the authority. You pretend you

know what you're doing, and people believe it."

"Do you know anything about theatrical makeup? Anything at all about blood?"

I flashed back eleven years. *Nikki . . . go.* Mom, lying in a pool of her own blood, her hand outstretched. Me, kneeling next to her, trying to get her to stay awake, to come back.

"You'd be surprised," I said as I got out of the car.

CELESTE DAY WAS not the type of actress to get a giant, luxury dressing room all to herself. But it appeared that, even if she was, Pear Magic was not the type of studio to give her that, anyway.

I stood in the doorway for a moment, blinking the purple after-sun shadows out of my eyes while they adjusted to the light change. When I could finally make out what I was seeing, I glanced around a sleepy studio trying to get ready to work. Off to my left was a set: what looked like a kitchen in a run-down, beat-up house with a red splash—meant, I assumed, to look like blood—up one wall. A large man in ripped clothes and shadowy eyes sat at the kitchen table, idly puffing on a cigar and talking to who I imagined to be some sort of assistant. She kept pushing her glasses up on her nose as she giggled at whatever he was saying.

Men and women wearing all black shifted around behind cameras and boom mics and lights, none of their movements looking particularly urgent. A woman wearing flannel and boots tromped around the set, softly fretting as she moved things a quarter of an inch here, a half inch there. She looked like every stressed-out director's assistant I'd ever seen when working with Dad.

I heard the rattle of plastic tubes and turned to my right, where there was a black wall with light radiating out from behind it. I peered around the corner to see a dressing area—about eight mirrors lined side by side with soft globe lightbulbs dotting the perimeter of each mirror. There were small stools in front of each station, and a handful of actors occupied them, leaning toward the mirrors to fix their ghostly faces or leaning back for a stylist to rat their hair or worry over their faces with makeup brushes.

It was easy to find Celeste Day. She looked just like her IMDb photo. Shoulder-length chestnut hair, stiff with curls, soft, wide brown eyes that looked like pure innocence, high "actress" cheekbones, full pink lips, and curves for miles. She was exactly what Hollywood was looking for in an actress, and I guessed it wouldn't be long before sneaking in on Celeste Day would be impossible due to all the bodyguards.

Celeste was absently rubbing lotion on her elbows, the chairs on either side of her unoccupied. She was dressed in a royal blue men's button-down shirt, her legs bare all the way up to a pair of very short, very tight boy shorts only visible when she shifted to uncross her legs. She snapped the lotion bottle closed, stood, and leaned toward the mirror, fiddling with blackheads across the bridge of her nose.

Now or never, Nikki. You will be noticed if you just keep standing around.

Definitely. I already stood out enough next to the bohemian styles of the artists working in their yellow-lensed glasses and smocks and combat boots.

I took a deep breath, walked into the dressing area, swiping a makeup box from a cart behind an actor whose artist was busy gluing on the ugliest toupee I'd ever seen. I disappeared behind a costume rack and rooted around until I found a ratty-looking knee-length cardigan. I pulled the hem of my T-shirt into a knot at my back, exposing my belly button, and shrugged into the cardigan. I quickly plaited my hair into two braids that hung down my shoulders and wrapped a silky orange scarf around my hair like a headband. I fumbled through the makeup kit and pulled out the liquid eyeliner. I was terrible at makeup. Always had been. Even as a little girl, fooling around with Mom's makeup in the bathroom, I never could quite figure out what was supposed to go where, and how. Mom always made it look so effortless— she never looked like she had makeup on; she just looked fresher somehow.

There was no mirror, so I moved where I could see myself in the long costume rack pole. My face was warped, convex, But good enough. I drew severe lines across my bottom lids, swooping them up into cat eyes, then found a tube of red lipstick. I was all eyes and lips when I was done. I felt ridiculous, but I fit in much better.

I rubbed my lips together, straightened my plaits, picked up my toolbox, and made a beeline to Celeste Day.

She saw me in the mirror and stopped poking her face. "Who are you?" she asked.

I held up the makeup kit, and she frowned.

"Where's Jayelle?"

That was a good question. A really good question, actually. Somehow I'd gotten lucky enough to pick a time when Jayelle was not around. But I had no idea when she would show up, so I decided to cover my bases.

"I'm just here to get things started while we wait. I'm sure she'll be here any minute."

Celeste gazed at me, her eyes uncertain. She licked her lips nervously. I pretended I didn't notice. I set the makeup kit on the table in front of her and opened it. In the light of the mirror, I was finally able to see everything inside. And I had no idea what half of it was for. I rooted around until I found a thick, pouffy brush and a canister of loose powder. At least I knew what to do with this. I held up the brush and looked at Celeste expectantly. She eased back in her chair, still eyeing me dubiously. I swirled the brush around in the powder and leaned forward, trying to surreptitiously look around her dressing area while I swept the brush across her forehead.

"That's not my color," she said.

I studied her in the mirror. Sure enough, the powder I'd just dusted her with was about two shades too dark for her. She watched me.

I checked the bottom of the canister. "Oh. Looks like someone put the wrong lid on it," I said, hoping I sounded convincing. "I hate when that happens." I rooted around in the kit, looking for something lighter. I came out holding another canister victoriously.

It was a matte foundation; something much closer to Celeste's skin color. At least as far as I could tell. I found a sponge and dabbed the cream-colored makeup onto it, then quickly—hoping I looked like an expert—smeared it across her forehead, taking extra care to smooth it in at her hair-line. I leaned back and studied my work. Not too bad. Maybe I could do this after all.

"That's not mine, either," she said. Her chair rippled with various shades of green. She didn't trust me.

I tried to smile, which wasn't something I'd normally do when being challenged. I hated looking stupid. But if I dropped into typical Nikki eat-or-be-eaten mode, I would give myself away for sure. My smile felt wobbly; a little on the grimace-y side, so I concentrated my acting skills on staring at my makeup kit, dumbfounded. "Sorry," I said. "I really do think someone must have messed with my kit."

She tilted her head to the side and studied what I'd

done in the mirror. "That's okay. It's close. You almost can't tell. But trust me, the director will notice." There was a soft twang to her voice—something I would usually associate with the South rather than upstate New York.

"I'm sorry," I repeated. "I think I'm just flustered today. Should I start with something else?"

"Maybe you should just straighten my hair. We can save the makeup for when Jayelle gets back."

"Of course." I closed my kit—glad to be rid of it—and began hunting around for a straightener, picking up things on the counter and bending to look underneath. All that was under the counter was a handbag. Not only was I not finding a straightener; I wasn't finding anything that could possibly link Celeste Day to Luna, either. There had to be something.

"It's over there," she said, pointing to a cart that held massive amounts of hair appliances and accessories. I went over, grabbed a straightener and a wide-toothed comb, brought them back, plugged in the straightener, and began softly combing out her springy curls. I wanted to ask her what she knew about Luna. Why her name was written on a pad in Luna's getaway car. But I had learned something about my usual tactics: they didn't work so great. I kept surviving by the skin of my teeth. Instead, I tried small talk.

"So, who's directing this?" I asked. "It's not, like, Steven Spielberg, is it?"

She looked up from her phone. "In a place like this? I don't think so. As you can see, there aren't exactly any megastars here."

"Hmm, I don't know. To me, you're a megastar." Barf, barf, barf. Gray, lying barf with a side of yellowy-olive disgust.

She didn't respond for a while, then said, to her phone, "You've never heard of him. It's his first film."

I dragged the straightener through a swatch of her hair, tugging her head backward slightly. She resisted a little but didn't complain. I straightened another.

"Do you think you'll ever get to work with someone like Steven Spielberg?" I asked.

She barked out a laugh. "Well, I guess anything is possible."

I smiled. She seemed comfortable with me. I decided to go the direct approach. "Speaking of directors, wasn't it crazy what happened with Bill Hollis? I mean, he was, like, a big deal when I was a kid. I personally think he was innocent. But nobody ever asks me what I think." I chuckled, hoping she couldn't hear the nerves behind it. "And his son," I said, my lips going numb. "He was superhot. Do you know who I'm talking about?"

"I mean, I saw the news, I guess." She was still fiddling with her phone. If she had a Hollis connection, she wasn't showing it.

I raced to think of another way to approach it. Somehow bring Luna into the conversation. But before I could gather a thought together, a woman whisked behind me. She threw a toolbox down on the counter and immediately began unpacking it. Vials and tubes and powders and brushes, all expertly placed in order.

"Oh. My. God. I can't even tell you. So sorry I'm late. The guard is freaking stupid. When are they going to fire him? He acted like I wasn't supposed to be here. Like I haven't been here every freaking day for the past month. I step out to grab a coffee and the moron doesn't want to let me back in? I swear, we need to call the staffing company about him. Get someone good out here. I mean, he's supposed to be security. We can't have some idiot in charge of who's—what the hell happened to you?"

She had finished unpacking and had turned to Celeste with brush in hand, but had stopped short and was staring at Celeste's forehead.

Celeste lowered her phone into her lap and blinked, confused. "Your replacement."

"My replacement?" The woman—obviously Jayelle—turned to take me in. "What replacement?"

"I don't know. You'll have to ask her."

"Not really a replacement," I said. "More like a floater." I bent to meet Celeste's eyes in the mirror. "Sorry, you must have misunderstood." I straightened. "I'm just supposed to fill in here and there when someone needs to step out or something. It's a new thing the agency is doing."

Jayelle stared at me with her mouth hanging open. My palms began to sweat, the straightener sliding against my skin. This was what Chris was always complaining about—that I dove headfirst into situations with no plans on how I would get myself out of them. He had a point. But somehow things always just seemed to work out for me. It was the synesthesia. It helped me read a room and know when to get out. Problem was, my synesthesia was telling me two conflicting things right now. The greens that radiated off Celeste also pooled around Jayelle's feet, but they were much weaker. And the longer she stared at me, the weaker they got. But as they got weaker, Celeste's got stronger, until I felt like I was in a forest. Celeste was pretending to be cool, but I was making her nervous as hell.

Jayelle broke the tension by abruptly tossing her brush into her kit and fumbling around for something else, turning her attention away from me completely, the greens evaporating.

"Just like the agency to make a change without filling everyone in. Whatever. I'm back, so I don't need you now." She turned to Celeste. "Why don't you go wash that nonsense off, and I'll just work fast when you get back."

Celeste hopped out of her chair and sped toward the ladies' room.

"Don't worry. They can't have the show without the star," Jayelle said to Celeste's back, still searching in her kit. "You won't miss anything. Now where is that blusher . . . ?"

Without even acknowledging that I was still standing there, she scurried back the way she'd come, patting her apron pockets bewilderedly.

I was left standing behind an empty chair, holding a hot straightener in my hand, looking absolutely ridiculous in my braids and headband. One thing was clear. It was time to move, or I was going to end up caught. Chris was going to be full of *I told you so*'s when I showed up at the car with nothing for my efforts once again. Maybe Celeste was just an actress who Luna admired. Or someone Jones wanted to hook up with. Or maybe the pad was already in the truck when they bought it and Celeste Day had nothing to do with them whatsoever. Without flat-out asking Celeste, I would never know. And I'd already managed to make myself look suspicious enough. The last thing I needed was to have some overzealous security dork call the cops on me. Then the *I told you so*'s would be full of laughter that I would never live down.

I stepped forward to put the straightener on the counter, my eyes landing on the bag that had been tucked beneath. It was a Givenchy—a little pricey for a B-list actress, if you asked me, but I would never understand the people of Hollywood, even if you gave me a billion years—and it was yawning open. Something inside the bag caught my eye. A familiar flicker of color.

Orange and lunch-meat pink. A and E. But it was the shape that they were in that triggered a memory.

Mom, proudly carrying a black canvas bag as she headed off to work. The bag was full of props and lights and cameras and odds and ends that she thought she might need on one of her locations. I loved that bag, because she always slipped a few toys into the very bottom of it, just in case I should be tagging along and she needed to keep me busy. When Mom was carrying that bag, it was a mix of emotions for me. She was leaving. But she was always so happy when she was carrying it, like she was in the middle of her own dream.

And I could clearly remember the colors that emanated from the side of that bag. Orange and pink. A and E, shaped into a couple of angry-looking eyebrows, over the swoosh of an elephant trunk.

Angry Elephant.

The studio where my mom worked all the way up until the day she was killed.

I did a double take, leaning closer to the bag. I was so confused at this point, my synesthesia wanted me to see things that maybe weren't even there. It was a matchbook. Why would Celeste Day be carrying a matchbook from my mom's studio? She couldn't be. No way.

But the closer I leaned, the more sure I was. The letters

swooped and swayed and dipped into the shape I was so familiar with. Angry Elephant.

I could hear Jayelle's voice. I peeked over my shoulder and saw her coming closer to the dressing table, still patting herself down and ranting about missing something that the star needed immediately.

Time to boogie.

I didn't give it any more thought. I reached into the bag and snatched out the matchbook, ignoring what felt like tingles of electricity shooting through my palm. I closed my fist around it and left, going the opposite way of where Jayelle was coming from and hoping that I wouldn't run into Celeste Day on my way out.

I stole around the costume rack and into a hallway that was painted all black, even the ceiling, and I felt like I'd been thrust into a tunnel. The walls felt very close. I could still hear Jayelle's voice, and then Celeste's too, and I thought maybe I heard the word *floater* and I hurried through the hall, one hand clutching the matchbook and the other running along the wall.

The hallway took a sharp turn and I could see a lobby at the end, which housed the front double doors. It let out onto a different parking lot from where Chris was waiting, but I felt like I could more easily get to the car unnoticed outside than in.

I picked up my pace and was almost at a run when I popped out the end of the hallway.

And right into a chest.

The matchbook flew out of my hands and skidded across the floor, bumping to a stop against the wall. "Shit," I breathed, scrambling for it.

I snatched it up, and it wasn't until I straightened that I saw who I'd run into.

It was the belt buckle I recognized first.

Mustard. Candy cane.

Holy crap.

I slowly raised my eyes, only to find myself staring into a pair of eyes so pale blue they almost looked light gray. The white-blond-haired man. The one who'd been driving the truck. My heart squeezed until I felt as if I couldn't breathe.

His jaw tightened, and then he said, in a cold, threatening voice, "Nikki," sending waves of chills up my spine that almost knocked me over. He started to reach for me, and I jumped back.

"Where is she?" I asked. My hand trembled around the matchbook, and I pressed my fingers in on it tighter. "Luna?" The word scraped out of my throat like shards of glass.

His lips curled up in a growl over his perfect and blindingly white teeth. "You shouldn't have follow—"

"Director?"

A young man wearing a headset had come into the lobby from a different hallway. We both jumped.

The man turned toward the voice and then back to me.

"I think we're about ready to shoot the sidewalk scene?" the young man said, clearly nervous to be talking to this man. This white-blond-haired man who looked like the devil in my eyes. This man who knew Luna and knew Jones and knew Celeste.

Director? He was the director?

"I'll be there in a minute, Corey," the white-blond-haired man said. "I've got—"

But I didn't give him the chance to finish the sentence. I shoved past him and bolted out the door.

I veered away from the front doors wildly, guessing at which would be the faster way to Chris's car. I'd lost my bearings in the dark building. I tried to jump over a low bush but was too nervous to clear it and tumbled. I let out a grunt as I hit the ground and rolled, my shoulder groaning under the blow. I thought I heard the swish of the door opening behind me but was too panicked to look back. I scrambled, pushing myself back up onto my feet and churning through the grass, cramming the matchbook into my pocket as I went. I turned a corner, nearly colliding with a Dumpster, and my feet hit asphalt. Thank God. I pushed harder, raced faster, until I saw Chris's car, which was already on the move, coming for me.

I dove into the car, breathing so hard I was gagging. Fucking cigarettes. I pulled the door shut, and Chris took off out of the lot. We were probably a mile down the road before one of us finally spoke.

"I would ask you what happened and why you're dressed like that," he said. "But I have a feeling I already know."

I was breathless from my run, and in no mood for his judgment. "Just keep driving," I said. The matchbook pressed into my hip, but I didn't tell him that.

8

WHILE I WAS inside Pear Magic, Chris had spent his time idly searching for Heriberto Abana on his cell phone. He had come up with nothing much. I remembered sitting in his office before the hit-and-run. Heriberto's name had been searched and searched on his work computer, but, other than some addresses, nothing had really come up. I told him I'd do some poking around when I got home, which, for some reason, pissed him off. *I got hit by a car, but I'm not dumb,* he'd said. I didn't point out to him that I never called him dumb. He was being sensitive. I guessed I couldn't blame him. If I'd lost a big chunk of my memory, I would be sensitive too.

I made a sandwich and poured myself a glass of iced tea,

dumping so much sugar in it, you could see a layer of white on the bottom quarter of the glass. I rummaged in the pantry until I found an old, likely stale bag of chips, and took it all up to my room.

I sat at my desk, the food spread out next to my open laptop, and wolfed down half my sandwich while checking the IMDb page for Celeste's movie. Of course, the director was still listed as TBA—it couldn't be that easy. So instead I pulled up my email. I'd been neglecting it since the night at Tesori Antico, only popping in every week or so to weed out my in-box. Most of the time, it was crammed with junk, but every so often there was a legit email that I wanted to ignore. This time there was an email from my grandma— pictures from my graduation. I looked sweaty and irritated. My shoulders were bunched up and tense, as if I was waiting for something bad to happen. And Peyton's chair shrine was in the background, turning the edges of every photo crimson. I closed the email and dragged it into the trash. Dad would be pissed that I didn't share the pictures with him, but he was a photographer, so I knew he had more than enough of his own. So many he wouldn't know what to do with them. Probably stuff them away somewhere and never look at them again.

I scrolled down, picking off emails and sending them to the trash, one e by one. A sale ad for a boutique. A postgrad questionnaire from the school. A reminder from our former class president to join some stupid classmate website so they could find us come reunion time. *Uh, no thanks.* Junk, junk, and more junk.

I drained my tea, pushed my empty plate over by the chips, and brushed off my hands. I didn't have time for pictures and questionnaires and websites. I had searching to do.

It took no time for me to learn that Chris had been right. Heriberto Abana didn't have much of an online footprint. In fact, if the internet was any indication, there didn't seem to be any existing person with that name at all. It was like he was a ghost. Maybe I had the name wrong. Maybe *Albany* came to me in eggplant for an entirely different reason. Maybe that was just the color of the word *Albany* and there was no connection behind it at all and I was totally giving my synesthesia too much credit. But no, I felt strongly that wasn't it. Because even if *Albany* was eggplant all on its own, so was *Abana*. I could see that clearly.

I also remembered some numbers. A five and two threes. An address that I'd seen when I'd been snooping in Chris's office. But no matter how hard I tried, I could not remember anything else. Just the colors, flashing at me like an OPEN sign. Ugh, was it possible to have amnesia by proxy?

Nothing in my life was adding up, even though it seemed like everything was so close. I remembered Heriberto's name, but he didn't exist. I got to search Jones's truck, but there was nothing in it. I found Celeste Day, but not Luna. So frustrating to be this close on so many levels, but continue to come up just short.

I dug the Angry Elephant matchbook out of my front pocket and turned it in my hand, studying it. I half expected to feel something—some sort of cosmic current that would link me with my mother. Maybe hear her voice, guiding me. But it just wasn't there. She was gone, and it was just a coincidence that I'd found something belonging to the studio where she used to work. Not really all that outside of reason, when I thought about it, for an actress to own something with a studio label on it. Especially an unknown actress and a small, independent studio. She probably owned loads of stuff from small studios. It would be much stranger for her to have something from a big studio, probably.

There was a knock on my door frame and I jumped, dropping the matchbook on my desk.

Dad was standing just inside my room.

"Sorry, didn't mean to startle you. You looked pretty deep in thought there." He gestured toward the matchbook. "Anything important?"

Because I couldn't trust him, I didn't want Dad to know about what I'd found or where I'd found it. If I told him I'd lifted it from an actress, he would undoubtedly want to know what I was doing at Pear Magic. And the truthful answer—trying to find the girl who'd twice tried to kill me—would not be a popular one.

"Nothing," I said, sliding it off the corner of my desk so that it fell into the trash can below. "Just some trash I found in my pocket. Been a while since I wore these jeans, I guess."

"Were those matches? I thought you were quitting smoking."

Just hearing the words made my jaw ache for a cigarette. I didn't know why I was still on the wagon if I wasn't planning to go to the academy. *Because Chris may not remember telling you to stop, but he doesn't like it, and you may not want to admit it, but you care.* I pressed my lips together, a sad attempt at a grin. "Like I said, it's been a while."

He looked unconvinced but apparently decided it wasn't worth pursuing. He scratched his chest, right next to his armpit, his shirt bunching up beneath his fingers. "You still thinking about joining me on a shoot?"

I resisted the urge to roll my eyes. "Sure. When?"

"Tomorrow? Taking Marisol downtown. You said you wanted to go on an urban shoot, yes?"

No. I didn't particularly want to go on any shoot, urban or ocean or out in the middle of a fucking cow field. I didn't have time to be "trying to find myself" in Dad's footsteps. Not to mention, I didn't want anything to do with him. Just looking at him made my heart ache.

But there was only one way to get him off my back.

"Yep. I'll be ready."

* * *

THE WORST THING about being a photographer is that you're a slave to the light. Photographers could work for themselves all they wanted, but that didn't mean they could mosey on out for a shoot anytime they felt like it. They had to be up before the sun, so they could get their things together, meet their model, find the perfect spot, and set up before the sun got to its best position in the sky.

I hated being up early for any reason, but especially for standing around while my dad fiddled with lenses and Marisol paced in stilettos with one arm pressed into her concave gut while her other hand held cigarette after chain-smoked cigarette.

Models weren't always as healthy as they looked.

Every so often, Dad would order me to kick some rocks away from a doorway or hold the reflector disc higher, no, not that high, a little lower, no, you've gone too low. You know what? You should be standing on the other side of her. . . .

Photography was some mind-numbing shit.

After what seemed like a lifetime, but had only been about four hours, and a miserably few photos, my stomach started growling.

"Can I get a coffee or something?" I asked.

"Good idea," Marisol said. "I swear I'm going to pass out if you have me jump in the air one more time, Milo."

"We're just getting something done," Dad said, not even

bothering to look up from behind the camera, which he'd spent the past twenty minutes painstakingly screwing onto a tripod and adjusting to whatever constituted the perfect height. "If we stop now, we'll lose the good light."

Jesus. The light.

Marisol cocked her hip to one side, her hand on it, and pouted, actually whimpering a little. Dad responded by snapping a picture. She probably looked amazing in it. Life was unfair that way.

"How about I'll get something for everyone and bring it back?" I asked. "I'll get sandwiches."

"Bread. I don't eat white food," Marisol said at the same time that Dad barked, "Don't move! You're in perfect position!"

"Then I'll bring you a salad," I said.

"I don't do lettuce or dressing."

I gave her an *are you fucking kidding me* look, but she was too busy posing to notice.

"I'll be back," I called to Dad. He gave me a sigh when I tossed the reflector disc on the ground, but simply went back to clicking the shutter on Marisol.

Starvation wasn't the only reason I was dead set on getting some food right away. The other reason was that the alleyway Dad had chosen for Marisol's backdrop by happenstance was across the street from Morning Glory, a peace-and-love-style café. I had seen two people who I was pretty sure were Vee and Gibson, two members of Peyton's band, haul all their crap inside. I hadn't seen them for months, but I would recognize Vee anywhere. She kind of stood out.

I jogged across the street and into Morning Glory.

"Can I help you?" a woman behind the counter asked the second I stepped foot in the door.

"Uh, yeah," I mumbled. "Three coffees and three turkeys on rye. To go." Screw Marisol and her white food. My eyes landed on a display of cookies the size of cake plates. I grabbed three of them and placed them on the counter. "And these." Hopefully—and likely—Marisol didn't eat sugar, either, and I would be forced to eat hers and mine both.

The woman rang up my order, and then slipped on some gloves and turned to make the sandwiches.

I took the opportunity to mosey over to the back corner, where Vee and Gib were setting up. Gib was tuning his guitar, sitting on a stool with his ear bent so close it was practically touching the wood, and Vee was plugging in a microphone. Her hair had been cut—shaved on one side and left long on the other, coming to a point at her chin. Not for the first time, I wished I could pull off the looks that Vee rocked. That was the kind of person she was, though. Not me. I didn't actually know what kind of person I was. Which was maybe why I had no look.

"No bass?" I asked. Her head whipped up. It seemed to

take a second for her to place me, but then she smiled.

"Nikki, long time no see." Ever since Peyton died, Vee had tried to forge some sort of bond with me. I was the only one who cared about Peyton as much as she did, which was weird since Peyton and I never actually spoke to each other out loud in her lifetime. And sometimes I wondered if Vee ever gave any thought to why I cared so much about Peyton. But somehow she just seemed to get it. I think she figured keeping me around was one way to keep Peyton alive.

But there was Shelby Gray to consider. She'd replaced Peyton as Viral Fanfare's lead singer. And she was friends with Luna. Last I talked to Shelby, she'd been hanging out with Luna, even as Luna was plotting to kill me. Tangling with Shelby Gray was about as fun—and about as productive—as beating my forehead against a wall. With Luna still out there, I had zero desire to bring Shelby back into my life. With Shelby came suspicions. With suspicions came trouble. I wasn't looking for trouble; I was looking for resolution.

Vee gestured to the mic. "Nah, acoustic bass is kind of outside my price range. Plus, somebody has to sing. That's the problem with your lead singer still being in high school."

"You sing?" I couldn't picture it.

She shrugged. "When I have to."

We both stood there awkwardly for a beat. A couple wound past us toward a table, holding plastic baskets heaped with salad, and I shuffled to the side to let them by. "So, regular gig? In a sandwich shop."

Vee laughed. "Wouldn't Peyton just die?" Her face flushed. "You know what I mean."

I chuckled. "She totally would. This place hardly screams glamour. Where are the rhinestones and fur?"

"Those are on my other shirt," she said. "I didn't want to start out too Hollywood, you know?" She stuck her fingers through a gaping hole near the bottom of her shirt.

"Order's ready," the woman behind the counter hollered. I turned. She was setting a paper sack and three paper cups on the counter.

"That's mine," I said to Vee. "I'm sort of working with my dad. Otherwise, I'd stay."

"That's cool. You can buy the album when it comes out." She winked. "So are you, like, working for your dad now? Everything's good?"

I shook my head. "Just for today. Helping out. But, yeah, I guess everything's good. Shelby say anything about Luna these days?"

"She wouldn't dare. Maybe to Gib, but not me. She knows how I feel about the whole thing. I wouldn't be surprised if Luna was somehow behind what happened to Peyton."

This time it was my turn to blush; my cheeks felt hot. She had no idea. But it was probably best kept that way.

"She hasn't talked about her at all, though," she continued. "For some reason, I was under the impression that Luna was gone. Like, left California completely."

"Yeah," I said. "That's what I'm hoping for, anyway." Too bad I couldn't be as convinced as Vee was.

"If I hear anything, I'll let you know. I don't think she'd be dumb enough to come around."

"No, Luna is definitely not dumb." Sometimes I wished she was dumber. She would have been a lot easier to defeat if she was.

Gibson cleared his throat, staring at me pointedly. Vee ducked her chin, going back to fiddling with the microphone stand.

"Well, my coffee's getting cold, I guess," I said.

"Yeah. Okay. You'll come back sometime? When you can stay, I mean."

"Definitely."

I grabbed my food and stacked the three coffee cups, balancing them by using my chin for support. Vee called my name. I turned.

"I just realized. Shelby's been hanging around at igNight a lot." She slid the microphone into the stand, glanced at Gibson, and came to me. "She has been for a few weeks. Acting really weird. Like she's going to quit the band or something. It may be nothing. Shelby's kind of a flake. She might have met another guy, or who knows what. But it's just weird that right when you're looking for Luna again, Shelby's . . . being like she was. Before."

"igNight?" I asked. The bottom cup was starting to burn my hand through the cardboard.

"Hookah dance club in the city. Full of dopeheads, mostly. But also rich girls like Shelby who think smoking orange-flavored tobacco makes them look sophisticated. Not really my kind of scene. She goes, like, every night." She leaned in and lowered her voice. "And she broke up with Gibson, so things are totally awkward right now. I'm not complaining when she doesn't show up to practice. She is constant drama. It's kind of nice not having her around, you know?"

"Vee," Gibson barked.

She checked the clock behind the counter. "I should get going."

"Yeah," I said. "Thanks for letting me know about igNight. I'll check it out."

She grinned, letting her hair point flop forward over her face. "Have fun with that."

She went back to their little nook and turned on the mic. There were a few muffled whumps as she tapped it to see if it was on. Gibson turned knobs on a small amplifier and then gave her a nod. He sat back on a stool and strummed out a few soft chords. Vee began to sing. Her voice was low and sultry, and while not exactly smooth, it was still coarse in the way waves are coarse crashing onto shore.

I recognized the opening lines of the song.

She was singing "Black Daisy."

"GOD, FINALLY," MARISOL breathed when she saw me with the food. She grabbed a coffee and pulled the lid off the top. "Ew, black?"

"Seriously?" I said, ready to punch her no-white-food-no-dressing-no-black-coffee face.

She rolled her eyes and sat on a box, hunkered over her coffee as if it was twenty below zero outside. Which it most definitely wasn't. The back of my neck was damp with sweat. I was kind of wishing I'd opted for soda. Though I wasn't sure a place like Morning Glory would be the kind of place to sell soda. Organic unsweetened fruit juices, yes. Pepsi, not so much.

I pulled out a sandwich and handed the bag to Dad, then opted to sit on the ground at the opposite end of the alley. That way I didn't have to listen to Princess Marisol bitch about the cheese being too cheesy or not eating mayo. Bonus: from where I was sitting, I could very faintly hear Vee's singing. She'd moved on to something even more mournful. I wouldn't have thought it was possible for a song to sound more mournful than "Black Daisy."

After a few minutes, there was a scuffling of shoes. Dad was coming toward me. He held out my coffee. I took it and set it next to me. I really, really wanted that soda now.

"Can I join you?" he asked.

I scooted over to make the slightest amount of room and kept eating wordlessly. All morning I'd been watching and listening for numbers. Anything that might tip Dad's hand as to what the code for that locked box might be. I noted the exact time that we got started, in case he started at the same time every session, or some weird superstition like that. I noted the serial numbers on his cameras and his tripod. I even noted the model number on the back of his car. Nothing seemed like it would be the one, but it was all I had.

"So what do you think?" he asked, groaning out the last couple of words as he lowered himself to the ground.

"Think about what?" I asked around a mouthful of sandwich.

"About this. You think you might want to follow in your parents' footsteps?"

I almost choked. Which footsteps would those be? The ones where my mother hid her prostitution-borne baby, or the ones where he lied and hid whatever it was he had to do with it? I chewed extra slowly to give me time to measure my words. "I don't know. I'm not very artistic."

"You can learn that."

"I don't like to get up early."

"Well, you'll have to get over that, no matter what you choose."

"I don't like Marisol," I said. I swallowed and ran my tongue over my front teeth, where a gummy piece of bread was stuck.

Dad glanced over his shoulder and then back at me. "Neither do I," he said, and laughed. "You don't have to be her best friend to take good pictures of her. Why don't you try snapping a few when we're done with lunch?"

I raised my eyebrows. "You're going to let me use your cameras? Those are your babies."

"No, you're my baby." He shrugged. "I let your mother use them."

"Mom was a photographer, too. She knew what she was doing."

He chewed, swallowed, pushed his glasses up on his nose. In this light, I could see his hair was beginning to thin. Before I knew it, Dad would be old and would still be alone. Why? Why, when his wife betrayed him, did he stay loyal to her, even after death?

Because he's guilty, Nikki, and he knows it.

I pushed the thought away.

"Mom was more of a director. She was good at telling people what to do."

Except for Bill Hollis. Nobody told Bill Hollis what to do. But Dad knew that already. He just didn't want me to know that he knew.

There was a long pause while we finished our sandwiches.

I didn't have a choice but to wash mine down with the coffee, which had gotten cold. Marisol was right; it was gross without cream and sugar. I peeked over at her. She had her sandwich open and spread out on one thigh and was picking through its contents with her long nails. At her feet was a small pile of refused food.

That would have been what Peyton would have captured on film, I thought. Dirty, discarded food, next to a shiny stiletto heel. A perfect commentary about this town, this life.

"Dad?" I asked.

"Hmm?" He was poking around on his phone.

"Why did you give up?"

He glanced at me. "Give up on what?"

"On Mom. Why did you stop trying to find her killer?"

He opened his mouth, stopped, let his phone rest on his lap. "Why are you asking this, Nikki?"

"Because I've been almost killed twice in the past year. And it just seems really odd to me that Mom was killed, too. Like, what are the odds that two people from the same family are murdered? It's almost like . . . like she had to know who it was. Like someone has a grudge against us."

Dad's face clouded over and he concentrated on tightening the laces of one shoe. I couldn't tell if that was because he knew I was on to something about Mom, or if it was because he hated talking about what had happened to her, and what had almost happened to me. Maybe it was a little of both.

He straightened, softened, and pushed my hair behind my ear. "I didn't give up. I just knew when it was hopeless. I couldn't make the police find her killer. As much as I would have liked to."

"But weren't there any suspects?"

"No."

"None at all? I find that really hard to believe, Dad."

I saw his jaw stiffen. "The police weren't motivated, I guess."

"That's bullshit," I said. His head whipped up.

"Nikki, you know I don't like that kind of lang—"

I interrupted him. "And you know I don't like being lied to. I think they had suspects and you knew about it. So why don't you just tell me? What is there to hide? Who were the suspects and why weren't they caught?"

His face turned red, starting with the tips of his ears and creeping all the way down his throat into the collar of his shirt. He stared hard at his hands, and I could practically feel the discomfort vibrating off him. "Okay, I suppose you're old enough now."

"You think?" I said.

"I didn't want to burden you with it when you were young. You had enough to deal with, losing your mother like that. You didn't need to know that they suspected . . ."

I was impatient and let him flounder for only a second. "Suspected who?"

He pressed the rim of his coffee cup in, fidgeting. "Me."

I felt the world around me pulse green and gold. I had suspected Dad had something to do with Mom's murder, but hearing him say it out loud was still a shock.

"They thought you did it?" My throat felt small and tight. Was this going to be the moment when I finally got honest answers? "Why?"

He shrugged. "They always suspect the husband first, right?" He shook his head at the ground and muttered, "Damn cops."

"So what happened?" I asked, not wanting him to stop talking. But also definitely wanting him to stop talking. If my dad confessed to me, would I have to do something? Would I be able to turn him in? It seemed so cut-and-dry, so easy, when it was all theory. But now, sitting next to him— the man who'd brushed my hair and fixed my lunches and took care of me when I was sick—it seemed so much more complicated than that.

Still. It didn't matter what he might have done to atone after the fact. If he was the one who had taken her from me, I would still hate him.

"They questioned me a few times and decided they had nothing on me. Then they let me go. And as far as I could tell, they closed the case. They were so certain that I'd done it and had just covered it up well enough that they couldn't bust me, they didn't even bother to really look at anyone else."

"It's getting hot," we heard, and both turned to see Marisol clomping toward us on her impractical heels, fanning her face with her hands. The tension between Dad and me snapped away in an instant. Damn it.

Dad checked his watch. "Oops!" He hopped up on his feet. "We're going to lose any semblance of good light if we keep sitting around. Nikki, you want to take the next few shots?"

That was it.

That was it?

He had been the one and only suspect in Mom's case, and he just casually slipped it into a conversation before getting back to work? There had to be more to the story.

Vee's voice floated across the street and into the alley. She'd moved on to a different song—one I'd never heard.

Seemed like everyone wanted to just move on.

Well, not me.

When was I ever like everyone else?

I stood and brushed the dirt off my butt. "Absolutely," I said. I hooked my elbow through Marisol's and marched her into position. "Let's finish this."

I LEANED ON Chris's apartment buzzer, imagining the sound dragging him away from whatever it was he was doing. Honestly, I didn't care if he was watching TV or asleep or on the freaking toilet. I needed his help, and I wasn't going to wait around in the parking lot this time.

A breeze kicked up behind me. The sun had gotten too harsh for Dad's photographing pleasure, causing shadows under Marisol's eyes, and he'd called it quits for the day, but only after making me take about a zillion shots of her. As if I could concentrate on lighting and composition after the bomb he'd dropped on me.

I let my thumb off the buzzer, but only for a second. I peered through the double doors at the stark, industrial-carpeted stairs. Nothing. I jammed my thumb into the buzzer again.

Soon there was a thumping noise, and I saw Chris coming down. He was in a pair of baggy sweats and a ratty, stained T-shirt. His hair looked funky, like maybe he'd been lying down on it. His expression looked like he wanted to slap whoever was ringing his buzzer.

I let off the button and waited for him to open the door.

"What are you—"

I pushed past him and started up the stairs. "We need to talk." I didn't wait to see if he was following me. I knew without even looking that he would. Why was he the first one I always went to when shit got real?

Because maybe he didn't remember, but I knew what we could accomplish as a pair. And I was sick of getting nowhere.

"You could have called. I was sleeping."

"I could have," I said, rounding up another flight of stairs. "But I didn't. No time." I jogged up that flight and threw open the door to his floor, my breath coming heavy. "God, would it kill your landlord to install an elevator?"

Chris took considerably longer to get up that second flight of stairs, and when he finally came through the door, he was limping a little, one hand protecting his ribs. Now that he was walking without his cane, it was easy to forget that he'd been mangled just a few months ago. I waited for him by his apartment.

"It's open," he said.

I went in.

The place was a wreck. Or at least for Chris it was. There were dirty dishes in the sink, a collection of empty beer bottles on the coffee table, lined up like soldiers, and several wadded, worn T-shirts taking up residence in front of the TV. And for the first time ever it didn't smell like cologne or cleaner. In my bedroom, this mess would look normal, but he was fastidious.

"You okay?" I asked, looking around.

"Yeah, why?"

"No reason. It's just . . . I'm used to it looking different in here." I kicked off my shoes at the door; dropped my keys inside one.

He picked up four beer bottles and carried them, clinking against one another, to the recycling bin, and dropped them in with a crash. "Well, you'll forgive me if I haven't really been into housecleaning lately." He rubbed his hand over his forehead a few times and then up through his hair. It stuck up. "Sorry. I . . . I have headaches. Bad ones. And I'm ready to get back to work."

"That's actually what I wanted to talk to you about." I climbed onto my favorite bar stool. It was here that I'd first found an application for the police force, meant for me. It was here that I'd first really known that Chris believed I could be something more than a fuckup.

He sat on the stool next to me. "I can't wait to hear how my going back to work will benefit you."

"Well, don't say it like that."

"What other way is there to say it? Isn't that why you're interested in me going back to work? So I can do something for you?"

I thought about it. He was right. And I hated that he was right. It made me feel like a self-centered jerk. But I didn't have time to coddle feelings. "I need you to find a file for me," I said.

"Nope."

"What do you mean, nope? You haven't even heard what it is yet."

He stood, walked to the fridge, and grabbed a beer. "I don't need to know what it is in order to know I can't do that for you." He twisted off the cap with the bottom of his T-shirt and tossed it into the sink. It rattled around a few times.

"Since when does 'can't' keep you from helping me out?"

"Since I don't remember pulling files for you before, and if I did, I was wrong to do it. You want to be able to pull files? Go to the academy. Get the job. Then you can pull all the files you want."

"We're not going through this again. I already told you I wasn't going to do that."

"Fine, and I never said you had to. But if you want inside access, you don't really have a choice."

I felt my face get hot. I imagined myself filling from bottom to top with ragey rusty starbursts. It was like he'd lost his personality when he lost his memory. I took a breath and pressed my palms onto the counter to calm myself. I did not do vulnerable well, but it was starting to look like I had no choice. "Please, Chris," I said. "I know you don't remember bending rules for me before. And I know you don't want to bend them now. But I'm desperate. I need your help. I think my dad might have had something to do with killing my mom. I have to know."

We locked eyes for a long moment, and I saw his resolve melt away, draining the rust out of the air and replacing it with the blue-gray of protection, the yellow of . . . well, of Chris Martinez. He came back and sat next to me again.

I took a chance and placed my hand over his. I instantly felt the blazing rainbow I always felt when I touched him— my body feeling light and floaty, like I was sliding down an indigo stripe.

"If you . . . if *we* find something, you can reopen the case. I won't stop you, even if he is my dad. Imagine how it would feel to come back to work after all you've been through and bust open an eleven-year-old case. You'd be a fucking hero."

He gave a disgusted headshake, but even I knew it was only for show. My heart thumped with happiness.

"Jesus, you pile it on when you're desperate. What do you need?"

Relief. "Eleven years ago, my mom was murdered. My dad was a suspect. He was questioned. I need you to find his file." Chris pulled on his beer, thinking. I leaned forward so I could look up into his face. "He was the *only* suspect, Chris. I need to know why." *I need to know if I can provide the missing evidence,* I didn't say, because the thought of those words leaving my mouth scared the hell out of me.

"Okay," he said. "I'll look."

I pumped my fist, celebratory, and he cut me off with one hand. "I'll look," he repeated. "I'm not promising anything."

"I never asked for promises," I said. When he turned to gulp his beer again, I wrapped my arms around him and gave him the quickest squeeze.

We hung out for a few more minutes, neither of us really knowing what to talk about. I didn't know about him, but I was too busy imagining what I might find in that file. Would it change everything? He loaded his dishwasher, his back to me most of the time. It felt awkward between us, and clearly it was time for me to go.

"Did you find anything about Heriberto Abana?" Chris asked as we made our way to the door.

"Not a thing."

"That makes two of us. I'm guessing you're just

remembering something wrong."

"Not possible." I grabbed my keys out of my shoe and slipped my foot inside.

"Why? Because Nikki Kill's hunches can't ever be wrong?" He was teasing, but the words came out feathery fern.

"Actually, no, they really aren't." He was mocking me. I felt stupid for sharing my synesthesia with him before, and was suddenly glad he didn't remember. I shoved my other foot into its shoe and straightened, clasping the doorknob. "You know what? It doesn't matter. The guy is Heriberto Abana. You were searching for him before, and one of the addresses you searched him under had a five and two threes in it."

"If you say so," he said.

"I do." I opened the door. When I turned to say good-bye, I noticed he had a piece of fuzz stuck to his stubble. I plucked it off. "You should probably shave before you go to work tomorrow. You look like a hobo." I flicked the fuzz to the floor.

He ran his hand over his jaw, smiling. "Thanks for the advice. See you tomorrow."

"Yes, you will." I turned and bounded down the stairs, my stomach in knots over what he might find between now and then.

10

I WOKE UP before the sun, on the heels of a nightmare I couldn't quite place. I had the feeling that Luna was in it, but I couldn't be sure, and I didn't want to scour my mind too hard to find her. Instead, I stared at the ceiling and listened to the water running in Dad's bathroom, wondering what I would do when I finally found the missing piece to the puzzle of Mom's death. I had pretty much convinced myself at this point that Dad was guilty of something. I'd given him so many chances to tell the truth, and he just wasn't doing it. Whatever he was hiding, I had only hours to decide what I would do with that information when I found out.

For the first time, my problem felt bigger than me. More

than I could handle on my own. I wasn't used to that feeling. I was Nikki Kill. I was ass-kicking, fearless, and, most of all, invincible.

Only I wasn't. Not all the time. Not now. And I knew it.

It would have been so nice to be able to talk to someone about everything. To come clean about Mom, about my suspicions of Dad, about my synesthesia, about my fears of Luna. Dru wouldn't have understood anything, but he would have listened. Peyton would have understood everything. Didn't matter. Neither of them was around anymore, anyway. Which left me with Chris to confide in.

How did I confide in a cop about how the cops had failed me my whole life?

How did I confide in him about my synesthesia after all this time?

Impossible. I got up and took a shower, taking as long as humanly possible to wash myself and get dressed. I heard Dad plod around the house, opening cabinets and shutting doors and turning faucets off and on. Eventually, I heard the front door open and close again, and then the sound of the garage door whining its way up and down. And then silence. It was just me.

Even with Hue around, it wasn't easy to be just me in the house ever since I had been attacked in my kitchen. Twice. I always felt unseen eyes on me; heard breathing that didn't exist in reality. Or maybe it did. Being home alone put me on edge. But then again, so did being home with Dad these days. So did everything.

I went downstairs and made myself a couple of pieces of toast, called Hue to my side, then spent half an hour or so trolling social media for Shelby Gray and any mention of Luna. Looked like Shelby had been busy being very Shelby—cavorting around the city in party mode, everything about her looking just a little bit better-than. Her black-hole eyes never smiled in any of the photographs—it was almost as if every smile was meant to convey power more than happiness. I scrolled through everything she had. No Luna. If they were hanging together, Shelby was being discreet about it.

Of course she was. Shelby Gray was no idiot. She knew that if Luna was found by authorities, it would be very bad for both of them. Luna would get sent back to juvie; Shelby would be locked up right along with her, and worse—she would be stuck being almost-but-never-quite-enough without Hollis fame to back her up.

I finished my toast and turned off my phone, and was just heading into Dad's office for yet another round of You Will Never Crack This Code on the locked box under his desk, when my phone rang.

It was Chris.

"You find something?" I asked, skipping all pleasantries.

"Hello to you, too."

I rolled my eyes. He could be a real baby sometimes. "Hi. How is your first day back going?"

"Going really, really good, actually. I remembered something."

My heartbeat sped up. What if he remembered us? What if he remembered our kiss? "Ah," I said, trying to sound cool. "You remembered where the good vending machine was. That's great. A day without potato chips is a day without sunshine. Crime-fighting fuel, in fact."

"Are you done?"

I smiled. He didn't sound cranky. In fact, he kind of sounded excited. "Probably not, but you can continue anyway."

"Meet me?"

"I was thinking of working out. You up for it?"

"I've been doing physical therapy since the day I woke up in the hospital."

I scoffed, "I mean a real workout."

"Okay. You try mending damn near every bone in your body. And your brain. And tell me how real it is."

I paused. I could hear irritation in his voice, seeping through the phone in ruby puffs like tiny clouds filled with anger. Leave it to me to kill his good mood instantly.

"Sorry," I said. "Just kidding. My gym or yours?"

"I could hit something," he said.

* * *

AS MUCH AS I loved my *kyo sa nim*, Gunner, I had to admit to myself that I missed Chris's smelly gym a little more. It was part gym, part zoo that housed grunting, thick-necked thug types. But there was something about it that drew me in. Maybe that nobody was judging me. Maybe that I could sweat and cuss and throw punches and it wouldn't be seen as weird or unladylike or gross.

Maybe it was that Chris was at this gym, and there was something about working out alongside each other, our sweat comingling on canvas, that made me like it.

I got out of my car. Chris was already there, waiting for me by the front door, gym bag in hand. He was still in dress pants and a tight polo shirt, his key card dangling from his belt. His hair was shiny from gel, and he was wearing his sunglasses.

"What took you so long?" he asked when I got to him.

"I don't know, maybe one of us has to drive the speed limit, and it's not you."

"Or maybe one of us is more excited about hitting the bag than the other one. You sure *you're* up to it?"

It had been a while since I'd been to Chris's gym. But it hadn't been long at all since I'd last pummeled an inanimate object. I'd been at the *dojang* twice in the past week alone, working on ducking and bobbing. I had always been bad at keeping it smooth and staying in a fighting stance while coming up from a crouch. Gunner thought it was the only real thing holding me back in tae kwon do now.

"Oh, I am so ready," I said, hooking my hand through his gym bag handle and swiping it on my way inside.

We sat on the bench where we'd sat before, the bag at our feet. There were two guys sparring in the center boxing ring. One was bleeding everywhere, but neither seemed to be letting up even a little bit. A couple of guys were leaning against some free weight equipment, chatting, their beer-and-burger bellies poking out in front of them like flags. The heavy bags were free.

Chris handed me a wrap and I started winding it around my hand. He didn't try to help.

Wait. He didn't try to help. Did that mean he knew I had done it before?

"So you remember bringing me here," I said. I wrapped fast, then finished and squeezed my fist, liking the way it felt taut and solid, like a stone.

He nodded. "It's been a good day."

I arched one eyebrow, paused midway through wrapping the other hand. "Oh, has it now?"

He didn't meet my eye, but I knew he could feel me staring at him. He messed up, had to unwrap a bit and rewrap. "I don't know, maybe it's being back at work. Jogged some things loose or something."

"What kind of things?" Both hands wrapped, I leaned down and tightened my shoelaces, then stood and pulled off my T-shirt, revealing a plain white ribbed tank top underneath. Chris's eyes flicked up, and then quickly down again. I could see little points of color dot the tops of his ears. I suppressed a smile.

He went back to wrapping his second hand, concentrating a little too much. Finished, he stood abruptly and shook out his arms before putting on his gloves. He hopped on his toes a few times, looking like the old Chris and not the beat-up hit-and-run victim Chris, put on his gloves, and smacked them together. "You ready?"

I had wriggled into my gloves. I liked the way they weighed down my hands, making my arms feel strong and anchored. "Always."

We found two bags, side by side, and laid into them at the same time. I noticed that Chris's bag moved less than mine, and when I glanced over, his teeth were gritted together with every punch. He seemed to especially favor his left side. I felt angry all over again at whoever had been behind the wheel of that Monte Carlo. They had taken something from him that he was struggling to get back, and it wasn't just his memory.

But then he caught me looking at him and smiled wide, his eyes crinkling at the corners. He was hurt and he was struggling, but he was happy to be back in the game.

He abandoned his bag, moved to the other side of mine, and steadied it. Sweat streamed down his temples to match the sweat that soaked the front of my shirt. "Come on," he said while I punched. "You can go harder than that. Harder. Why you holding back? You afraid of this thing?"

Every word spurred me on to whale harder and harder, my gloves meeting the bag in a frenzy of whumps, until my arms were noodles and my breath was ripping out of me. I sagged against the bag, leaning my temple against it. My hands were just above his, our faces inches apart.

"Wow," he said. "That was great."

"Your turn."

He shook his head. "I'm good. Don't want to overextend myself. Got to keep the energy up for chasing bad guys."

"Speaking of." I shook off one glove and wiped my forehead with the back of that hand, my breath slowing down but still labored. "You remembered something?"

He nodded, excited. His eyes were on fire, blazing at me. He leaned harder into the bag; I could feel his breath on my face. "A community center."

I waited for him to say more. When he didn't, I raised my eyebrows. "That's it? A community center?"

"Not just a community center," he said. "The Waller Recreational Center." He lowered his voice to a whisper, the breath coming at me so lightly it gave me the shivers. I felt goose bumps ripple up and down my arms, grapes and wine. "Address 15332 Dozier."

The numbers lit up in my mind when he said them. A

five and two threes, just like I'd said. I straightened. "Heriberto Abana?"

He shrugged, straightening too. "I don't know. Maybe. All I know is it's sure interesting that I remember being at that building and you remembered an address with those numbers in it. More than a coincidence, right? Has to be."

He had no idea how much more. I wasn't just remembering those numbers; I had seen them. My brain had remembered them, flashes of white and purple blinking off his computer screen, even when I wasn't trying to see them. Even when I didn't know I had.

"Way more," I said. "So now what?"

He pulled off one glove and tucked it into his armpit while he removed the other, then began unwinding his wraps as he walked back toward the bench. I bent to pick up the glove I'd dropped and followed him, my arms aching and too noodly to take off my other glove. I let my gloved hand dangle between my knees when I sat down.

"So I guess I visit the Waller Recreational Center," he said. He stuffed his equipment back into his bag.

"You mean *we* visit the Waller Recreational Center," I corrected.

Chris stared into my eyes for a moment. I gripped the seat of my chair with my one ungloved hand to keep the swooping, sweeping rainbow under me. He reached over and pulled the glove off my hand and began unwrapping it. "And you want to be there why?"

I looked at him incredulously. "Because I was there when you were run over. If this Heriberto Abana is behind it, I want to be there when you find him. Maybe seeing him will jog my memory." I had tried a million times to picture the person behind the wheel of that Monte Carlo. But it had all happened so fast, I'd never even had time to look. Still, maybe I'd looked without knowing. That had certainly happened before.

"Yeah," he said softly, turning back to my hand. His fingers brushed the inside of my wrist softly. I lit up with violet inside. I could feel my cheeks get hot. *Damn it, Nikki, don't blush.* "I guess you're right."

"Today?" I asked. "I mean, I'm not doing anything. That I know of."

"I probably should work until lunch at least before I bug out," he said. "You up for an afternoon swim?"

I pulled my hand away from his and unwrapped the rest of it myself, then pushed the wadded wrap into his chest. "How many times do I have to tell you? I'm up for anything."

He grinned. "I don't know if it's a good thing or a bad thing that I remember that."

I unwound the other wrap, my jelly arms starting to regain some feeling, and pulled my T-shirt back on. It was hot and my sticky hair felt trapped between the shirts. I would definitely need a shower before going anywhere with him.

"It's good, trust me," I said as we walked.

"I have something for you," he said as we pushed our way back out into the parking lot.

I followed him to his car. He opened a back door and tossed the gym bag inside, and then opened the front door and leaned in. He came back out with a fat manila envelope.

"What's this?" I asked. My eyes burned. I knew exactly what it was.

He held it out. "It's what you asked for. I told you I'd look." I stared at the file, suddenly afraid of what it could do to my life. He shook the envelope. "Take it."

"Did you look inside?" My voice was almost a whisper.

"No time." He started to pull it back. "We can look at it together, if you want."

"No." My arm shot out and grabbed the envelope from him. My dad's name, in its typical fuzzy tangerine, bounced around on the front of it. If there was something in there that implicated him in Mom's murder, I wanted to be alone when I found out.

Why, Nikki? Why keep so many secrets from him? Still keeping Chris at arm's length? Why? Don't trust him? Don't think he'll trust you?

Fuck that. It was personal. That was why. The only

reason why. It was personal and I wanted to be alone when I read it. Period.

And I supposed that was because part of me didn't know how I would handle it if I found out my dad was the murderer. As tough as I wanted to believe myself to be, I didn't know if I was tough enough to accept that kind of information. If it did me in, I didn't want anyone there to see it. Not even Chris.

I hugged the envelope around my middle. "What time today?"

He shut the car door. "Three o'clock? That give you enough time?"

"Sure."

More than enough time to find out if my dad was a murderer.

11

I STOOD IN my bathroom, palms pressed flat on the countertop, leaning over the envelope, staring at it. Fuzzy tangerine name, ringed with yellow, the whole envelope shading over into smooth slate, then rippling into asphalt gray and black. So many emotions. So many fears.

Did I really want to do this?

He had raised me. Alone. He had taken good care of me, even if he was a little more of a semi-interested roommate than a dad for most of my life. He'd tried. Until I'd found that box, and those photos with Bill Hollis in them—the ones that disappeared—I never would have even considered that my dad would be capable of hurting anyone. No way would I have considered he could hurt the love of his life. I couldn't believe I was considering it now.

My mind swirled around so many possibilities. It was an accident. It was revenge. It was rage. He'd found out about Hollywood Dreams. About Bill Hollis. About Peyton. He'd tried to be calm and rational. But his love for her was so fierce. A love that fierce could turn into rage without meaning to, right?

I couldn't open the envelope. My hands shook every time I touched it. My heart pounded so hard I felt breathless. Opening this envelope could change everything.

Wasn't that the point, though? Opening this envelope could change everything. It could solve everything. Every question I had. Gone. Finally.

I took a deep breath, made sure the bathroom door was locked, sat on the floor with the envelope, opened it, and pulled out the file.

Dad had been a suspect all right. There was his name, our address, a mug shot, Dad's eyes looking bloodshot and saggy, the tip of his nose red, his hair dirty-looking and mussed. I flipped through the pages, swimming through words and passages that looked important but I couldn't quite absorb.

No alibi.

Murder weapon in kitchen.

Disputes.

The words opened up a world I'd left behind long ago —a world with my mother newly gone, and questions and images and suspicions and grief. I felt like I'd stepped onto a stage, and the set was my life, circa ten years ago. And it was all colored over in crimson.

I saw the word *recordings*, maroon and royal blue. There were recordings of Dad's interviews. I laid the papers down and opened the envelope again, holding it up so I could peer inside. Sure enough, there were two tapes. I tipped the envelope over and dumped them into my lap. One slid off my thigh and landed with a rattle on the tile floor. I stared at it.

Dad's voice would be on that tape. Fresh after his wife was murdered. How would he sound? Devastated? Bewildered?

Guilty?

I picked up the cassette and turned it over in my hands. I didn't know what I expected—for it to feel strange, to feel telling? It felt like plastic. Plastic that I couldn't listen to because who owned a cassette player anymore?

Dad did.

As far as I knew, he still owned one. The question wasn't whether I could find anything to listen to them on; the question was whether I could force myself to listen at all. I felt light-headed and sweaty and a little bit gutted and oh so confused.

I stood, gathered up the file and cassettes, and took them out to my desk drawer, cramming them in with the black notebook where I'd kept Peyton's letter. I didn't want to listen when I knew I had to leave soon. What if it completely shattered me and I couldn't leave at all? I would want to be alone if I was a hot mess of tears and snot and bitterness, not at the community center with an audience. I would wait until I had some extended alone time, swipe Dad's cassette player, and listen until I had the answers I wanted.

I BEAT CHRIS to the Waller Recreational Center by ten minutes. He pulled up eating a sandwich.

I waited for him on a bench outside the center. I'd been watching the comings and goings, but because I had no idea who I was looking for, it was a pretty fruitless endeavor. Everyone could have been Heriberto Abana. Or no one could have been him, for all I knew.

Chris plopped onto the bench next to me, finishing up the final corner of his sandwich. "Sorry I'm late," he said. He uncapped a bottle of soda, swigged it, and stifled a belch. "You been here long?"

I shook my head. "Not really."

"What kind of trouble have you been into since I last saw you? Do I even want to know?"

I chewed the inside of my lip. "No trouble. Just hanging at home like a good girl. Aren't you proud?"

"Surprised is more like it. You go through that file yet?"

I shook my head again. He didn't press. I noticed the hair on his legs rubbing against mine. He was wearing a pair of orange-and-blue Hawaiian-style swim trunks. I'd never really gotten a look at his legs before. They were warm and brown and muscular. And now they were scarred, too, but the scars didn't make them look bad. He had a towel draped over his shoulders and was wearing his sunglasses.

"You ready to go in?"

I stood, picking up my bag, which had a beach towel and some sunscreen jammed into it. The towel was old—pink and frilly. It had been a while since I'd last gone swimming. My swimsuit was just as pink and frilly . . . and small. Or maybe it just felt small because I was in public. With Chris Martinez. And a lot of exposed skin.

I followed him into the center and waited while he paid our admission. I could smell the chlorine on the air, and for a minute it was almost as if we were on vacation, or maybe just relaxing for a day. God, I could use a day of relaxation. It felt like it had been forever since I'd had one. Would my life ever have another relaxing day? Had it ever had one? Mom was murdered when I was so young—how do you relax after that? The thought made me unreasonably tired.

"Let's go out to the pool," Chris said, "but keep your eyes open."

I quickened my pace to catch up with him. "What am I looking for?"

"Someone familiar, I guess."

I pulled his shirt until he stopped. "I never saw the guy."

He let that sink in for a moment. "Right. Look for him anyway." We kept walking, peering into every party room and locker area and weaving through the gym slowly, pointedly. A group of guys were playing basketball on the inside court, and Chris stopped and studied them for a while, absently rubbing the back of his head. Thinking. Trying to remember.

I stared at the guys, unable to decide if any of them looked like a Heriberto to me. It was hopeless.

A few minutes passed; then Chris shook his head and continued walking. After poking our heads into a custodian closet and a restroom, we finally found ourselves outside.

School was in session, so there was hardly anyone in the pool. A few little kids splashed around in the shallow end, their mothers sprawled out on towels nearby. A bored-looking lifeguard stared off into space. I elbowed Chris and pointed up to the guard, raising my eyebrows in a silent question.

He gazed at the guard and then shook his head. "Nothing."

We found two lounges in the corner, away from everyone else, but still with a view of the whole pool, and the entrance to the center beyond it. I spread my towel out on the chair and took off my cover-up, getting nervous goose bumps across my belly. I could feel Chris staring at me before I even got the cover-up over my head.

"What?" I asked, sharp, unfriendly.

"Nothing," he said. "Nice suit. I didn't really take you as a ruffle type of person."

"It's old, okay?" I snapped. I wished I had taken the time to go shopping this afternoon. Gotten a one-piece. A plain black one-piece. Ugly and boxy. With a skirt.

Chris stretched back on the lounge, then took off his shirt and draped it over his head to shield himself from the sun.

"You're going to get a stupid-looking tan line doing that," I warned.

"I'm not here to tan," he said.

"Fine. Look ridiculous. See if I care."

"Says the girl in a thirteen-year-old's bikini."

I felt myself blush and crossed my arms defensively. "I was fifteen, thank you."

He gestured toward my chest. "You're going to get a stupid-looking tan line doing that." I glared at him; he chuckled.

Slowly, I uncrossed my arms. "Whatever."

"Seriously, you look great. I'm just giving you trouble," he said. "Not that I'm looking. I know how you are about that. Especially when you're half-dressed in front of a camera."

"Funny how selective your memory loss is." I made air quotes around *memory loss*.

"I'm starting to remember a lot of things." He leaned

back in his chair again and crossed his arms behind his head. "Now I'm just hoping to remember why I was at this place. And what it has to do with that guy whose name you saw on my computer. If it has anything to do with him."

I sat back, too, and was silent. Several employees came and went, relieving the lifeguard, chatting with one another; there was a shift switch at the snack bar. Every time I saw a new person, I flicked a glance at Chris, who was watching, nearly motionless. Either that, or he was sleeping. Impossible to tell behind those glasses. The late afternoon sun warmed us, then baked us, and suddenly he stood up and tossed his shirt onto the lounge next to him.

"Hot," he said. He kicked off his flip-flops and headed toward the pool. I got a full view of the scars—surgery scars and some slick, pink spots where the road had ripped off his skin. I glanced away before he could notice I was looking. "Come on. I know you're hot. I can see you sweating."

Sure enough, beads of sweat stood out on my stomach. I was probably getting burnt, too. It was hot. But the idea of standing up and moving around in this ridiculous bikini made my nerves jump.

"I'm good. I'm watching. Which you should be doing, too."

"I can watch from inside the pool." He dipped a foot into the water and kicked a splash at me. It felt like ice, and I gasped when it hit my skin. "Come on."

"Stop." I sat up and pulled my knees into my chest.

He splashed me again, bigger this time. "You know you want to."

"Stop."

He didn't stop. He splashed me again and laughed when I squealed and splashed again until I jumped up—completely forgetting about how naked I felt—and rushed him, shoving him into the pool, which was easy, given his recent injuries. Of course, shoving him into the pool was a terrible idea if I wanted him to stop splashing me. It only got more intense, and soon we were both laughing and it was almost like we were just two people having fun at a pool instead of who we really were—an awkward love/hate couple brought together by murder.

The water did feel good, though. I jumped in and swam to the far side and back again in one breath.

"Look at you, mermaid," he said when I surfaced.

"Hardly," I said. "I used to swim a lot after my mom died, that's all." Truth. Some of my best memories of Mom were together in the pool or at the beach. Mom loved to swim, and she passed that love down to me. After she died, I came to the pool to feel closer to her. I loved the way the water blocked out the noise and let me think. For those few minutes underwater, I could hear her talk to me. It was like she wasn't gone; she was just in the water that we both loved. I tugged at my bikini bottom self-consciously.

"Never did much swimming in our neighborhood," he said. "And my mom couldn't afford to take us to someplace like this. Maybe that's why I was hanging out here. Maybe I was just swimming. Or running on a treadmill. Hell, I don't know. Who says I was chasing someone?"

"It was on your work computer."

He bent his legs and propped himself against the wall, letting the water come up to his neck. "There's a lot of things on my work computer. I looked up a restaurant menu today—does that mean I'm casing the restaurant? No."

"Okay. Jeez." I felt defensive. Like I had led him down a false path. Like if we didn't find the guy who hit him, it would be my fault. "Haven't you told me in the past that a bad lead is better than no lead at all?"

He thought it over. "Sounds like something I would say."

"Uh-huh." I sank down in the water next to him, aware of his shoulder brushing against mine. I drifted sideways a bit to break the connection. "So this was a dead end. What's next? I guess we could go back to—"

He stood up suddenly, tipping his sunglasses so he could see over the top of them.

"What?" I asked, following his gaze. A man pushing a cart full of basketballs had stopped and was talking through the fence to some middle-school-aged boys standing in a recessed corner of the building. "What is it?"

"I don't know," he said, but his voice said otherwise. "I think I know that guy."

"That guy?" I pointed, but Chris pushed my hand down into the water. I stood so I was shoulder to shoulder with him again. *Ignore the rainbow, Nikki. It is not a good time for the rainbow.* "That guy?" I repeated, in a softer voice.

He chewed his lip, still watching. The man opened his cart, handed something through the fence, closed the cart again, and moved on. Chris sighed, resigned. "I don't know. I thought maybe I knew him, but I guess not." He pressed his palm to his temple and rubbed in circles, a scowl forming on his face. "I'm so sick of this. The ringing ears, the headaches. Trying to recall something impossible." He gestured toward where the guy had been. "It's like it's all right in front of me, but I can't grab it. Every time I think I'm back to my old self, I'm reminded that I'm not."

I watched as the man with the cart came back into view. This time he was carrying an armload of foam kickboards, which he hauled to the shallow end and dropped onto the deck, scattering them about with his foot. As he started back inside, another kid—about the same age as the last ones— walked out onto the pool deck. The man stopped and talked to him.

"Wait, I definitely know that kid, though," Chris said. The guy shook the kid's hand, clapped him on the back, and they went into the shadows. A few seconds later, the kid came out, hopped on a bike, and sped away.

Chris pulled himself out of the water and stood on the deck, watching the boy go. I scrambled up the ladder and stood next to him, shading my eyes from the sun. "Who is it?"

"I'm not sure," he said. "I know him, though. I want to say his name is Sam."

We watched until the kid rode out of sight, then got our towels and dried off. "So maybe you do know that guy, then. Maybe he's Sam's dad. Or cousin. Or brother or . . . or uncle?"

He shook his head. "I don't know. Something in the back of my mind is telling me they're not related."

"Maybe he's a mentor." I pulled on my wrap and felt so much better covered up.

"Or maybe he's not," he said.

He slipped his shoes on, draped his towel over his neck again, and hustled back inside the center. The man was straightening the free weights on their shelves. Chris examined him, a pained look on his face.

"This is dumb," I mumbled.

I walked over to the check-in desk, where a bored-looking woman was doodling on a piece of notebook paper, her phone trapped between her ear and her shoulder.

"Excuse me," I said. She looked up. I tried pasting on my best fake Nice Nikki smile. "I'm wondering if you can tell me who that guy is over there." I pointed toward the man while trying to remain inconspicuous. "I think he's someone who used to live on my street. I want to say hi if he is, but it would be really embarrassing if he isn't. You know?" I let out a breathy laugh.

"Hang on," the woman said into her phone. She held it facedown on her shoulder. "What now?"

I fought the urge to snarl at her. "That guy," I said, pointing again. Chris had noticed I'd gone missing and was watching me, a look of horror on his face. "I think I know him, but I want to be sure before I'm all, 'Heeeey, how ya doing?'"

"Oh." She glanced at the man, who had moved on to refilling the disinfectant spray station. "That's our equipment manager. Heri."

I felt my stomach drop. "Heriberto?" I asked, though I was positive my faked persona had faded away.

She nodded. "Yeah, that's him. Heriberto. I haven't been working here very long, but I want to say his last name starts with an A."

"Thanks," I said. "Wrong guy." She went back to her phone call.

I turned to Chris. We had matching expressions on our faces.

I felt one side of my mouth pull up into a smile. "We found him."

I T WAS IMPOSSIBLE to watch Heriberto from the car
without being totally conspicuous, so instead we headed
back to the pool deck and situated ourselves so we could
see inside the building. Mostly, Heriberto carted equipment
from one place to another, wiped things down, checked
lockers, and sat at the check-in desk to give the receptionist
a break.

In other words, completely boring shit.

I was pretty sure from the sound of his breathing that
Chris had fallen asleep.

I slathered sunscreen on myself to keep from totally fry-
ing, but the sun was easing up as the afternoon began to be
pushed away by evening. Every so often, when the lifeguard

began eyeing me too suspiciously, I hopped around in the pool. As stakeouts went, this wasn't a particularly bad one.

Of course, the only other stakeout I'd ever been on had ended with the two of us totally lip-locked.

I had a hard time forgetting about that stakeout. I had a hard time forgetting about that kiss.

I started to get hungry, so I decided to wake Chris. I knelt down by the side of the pool, scooped up a handful of water, and flung it at him. His head jerked over toward me half a second before I released the water. He jumped, nearly toppling over his lounge chair with the movement.

"What the hell?"

I couldn't help laughing. "Time to wake up," I said.

"I wasn't asleep." He was brushing at the water on his chest, like he could dust it off. I could see goose bumps on his arms.

"Okay, sure. You were just resting your eyes."

He tipped his glasses down and peered at me over the top of them. "My eyes were wide open, for your information. I was relaxed."

"So relaxed you were snoring." I tied my towel around my waist and finger-combed my hair.

"I wasn't snoring." He got up, making a huge deal out of the fact that his towel was wet. He leaned over and said through his teeth, "I was trying to blend in."

I snorted and cocked my head to one side. "You blended in, all right. Blended in so well, if Heriberto noticed you, the only thing he'd be worried about is you boring him to death."

"Har-har," he said under his breath.

We were silent as we made our way out to our cars, which were parked near each other. "You want to get a burger or something? We can make a game plan for trying to figure out why you were searching for Her—"

"Shh," he said, grabbing my wrist.

"What are you—"

I didn't get to finish. He pulled me in, spun me so that my back was pressed against the sun-warmed door of his car, and leaned in so close our noses were touching. He caressed my cheek with one hand, the other planted on the door next to my shoulder. I could feel the warmth of him, and that, combined with the warmth of the car door, made me instantly start sweating.

"He's right behind us," Chris whispered, his breath puffing against my lips. I flicked a look over his shoulder. Heriberto was standing at the far corner of the building where there were no windows, smoking a cigarette. From this angle, I could see he had a tattoo snaking up his throat, but I couldn't tell what it was.

"He's just standing there," I said.

But he wasn't just standing there. He was staring in our direction, his hand absently raising and lowering the cigarette.

"He's watching us," I said.

Chris moved his palm around to the back of my neck, slipping his warm, dry hand up under my wet hair. "Put your arms around me," he said. I hooked them behind his neck, which pulled me up closer against him. Our hips were touching, my legs bursting into rainbows. I was suddenly aware of my breathing. I let my eyes drift shut as I momentarily melted into him. "He still watching?"

A glance, and then I nodded.

Chris let out a short sigh. He pressed his lips together, thinking. Heriberto had stubbed out his cigarette, but he wasn't moving. He continued watching us. "Oh, for crying out loud," Chris said. He pulled me in closer, resting his chin on the top of my head and swaying a little bit, as if we were just entangled in a long hug good-bye. My insides melted into a giant, swirling rainbow puddle at my feet. I felt completely engulfed by him. The hug lingered, and then he was reaching around me to open the car door. "Get in."

I hesitated, but not to be difficult. I just needed a minute to let the rainbow set me back down on the ground. I had so many feelings welling inside of me. Exasperation that it was always so difficult between us. Fear, because our lives were always in danger. Sadness that these moments between us always felt so right, even though I knew they were only out of necessity.

I stepped out of his way, then slid into the car. He shut the door behind me and came in through the other side.

"I drove myself," I reminded him.

"We've been here all day, and he was definitely watching us, ever since we got out into the parking lot."

"So? People have to go to the parking lot to get their cars."

"Think about it, Nikki. If we suspect Heriberto is the one behind the hit-and-run, he knows who I am already. And probably you, too."

I studied his face. A trickle of sweat was etching itself down one temple. "So maybe he wasn't behind it, then," I said. "He didn't even notice us until now. Could be you were looking for him for a totally unrelated reason."

He shrugged. "I don't know. I don't remember him at all. But I was searching for him and there's no official file for it. . . ." He trailed off.

"You knew he was coming for you."

"That would make sense. And somehow Sam is involved. I don't get it."

"Maybe he's, like, a mentor. Maybe you hooked them up."

We watched as Heriberto lit up another cigarette. He checked his watch.

"Why is he still just standing there?" I asked.

"Smoke break?" Chris responded.

But after another minute or two, a kid wheeled his bike up the sidewalk, jumping off just as he got near Heriberto and letting it fall into the grass. The kid was wearing a too-big jacket, a strange choice given how warm it was outside.

The kid looked over each shoulder, uneasy, then sauntered over to Heriberto, a put-on cocksure bounce in his step. They talked for a second, and then the kid glanced at us. Chris started the car and backed out of the space we were in.

"What are you doing?"

"We're making him nervous. I'm just moving, that's all. Don't stare at them."

But I couldn't help it. I waited for Chris to ease past them and then I turned in my seat, sinking down so I was peering out from under the headrest. Satisfied that we were gone, the two went back to talking. Then they shook hands and did one of those quick bro hugs, and if I hadn't been looking for it, I would have missed it altogether. In the handshake, the kid had pressed something into Heriberto's palm; in the hug Heriberto had shoved something into the kid's jacket pocket.

"Oh, wow," I said, turning to face forward again. "You were following a dealer. Heriberto is a dealer."

* * *

WE WATCHED FROM a side street. Which wasn't easy, given the distance. But we had no choice. We needed that distance.

Heriberto only stuck around for another half hour. But in that half hour, three more boys stopped and chatted with him. He pressed himself into the shadows every time. Once, when someone wearing the T-shirt of the community center uniform pulled into the parking lot, Heriberto quickly swiveled around and knelt in the grass, busily yanking at weeds.

He even waved at the guy in the community center T-shirt.

He was good.

Not good enough, apparently. But good.

I was starving, and just getting ready to suggest we leave, when Heriberto met with his last kid—one who approached from the passenger side of a silver Lincoln. That deal was short, with Heriberto casually leaning into the car, looking for all the world like someone who was just having a chat.

After the Lincoln pulled away, Heriberto tucked another cigarette into his mouth and walked to his car—a sweet yellow Mustang that shone like a mirror.

"Nice car for an equipment manager," I mumbled.

Chris grunted in agreement. He turned his key in the ignition.

"Let me guess."

"Yep," he said, waiting for the Mustang and two other

cars to pass, and then pulling out after him. "We're going to follow him."

Chris was amazingly good at following people. I should have known, since he'd spent so much time following me. Half the time I didn't even know he was there until he started pounding on a door or showing up at the *dojang* or hanging out in my driveway. It was creepy.

We followed the Mustang as it stopped to get gas, pulled into a drive-through, and paused while Heriberto talked to some girl who leaned inside the driver's open window, then popped out laughing and squealing. Heriberto was having an evening of it, and we were along for the ride.

Chris hardly spoke at all while driving. His mouth was pressed down into a grimace, and as the sun fell completely below the horizon, he took his sunglasses off and tossed them onto the dash.

I'd started the ride by saying things like, "He turned right," and, "He's slowing down," but quickly realized that wasn't necessary. Chris was in the zone. I might as well have not even been in the car with him.

Finally, Heriberto pulled into a neighborhood. It wasn't the worst-looking neighborhood I'd seen, but it wasn't anywhere I'd want to break down alone. There was a feeling of being watched, as if each window had eyes on the other side. As if every "regular" was memorized and catalogued. I'd never felt so much like an outsider in my life.

It was harder to keep a distance from Heriberto here. Chris went straight when he turned, and puttered around a few blocks to waste time. I kept my eyes open for a black Monte Carlo but saw none. Of course, I'd only ever seen that car parked somewhere near the Hollis warehouse hideout, so it wasn't too surprising not to find it here. Not surprising, but still disappointing. If that Monte Carlo didn't belong here, what did Heriberto have to do with the hit-and-run?

Short answer: maybe he had nothing to do with it.

Even shorter answer: waste of time.

After a few minutes that seemed like forever, Chris doubled back and turned down the side street Heriberto had turned down. He wound around until we saw the yellow Mustang, parked on a curb just outside an apartment building.

"There," I said, pointing. "Do you see it?"

"I think everyone sees it," Chris answered. Sure enough, there was a crowd on the front porch. Most of the people must have been from around there, because other than Heriberto's car, there was only one car sitting in the driveway.

There seemed to be a party going on, most of the people clutching drinks, loud laughter and faint music wafting through the warm evening air. Heriberto was sitting on the top step, a beer on the ground between his feet, a woman wrapped around him from behind.

He looked up when we passed, and we locked eyes.

I quickly looked away, sliding down in my seat a little and raising my hand to fiddle with my hair, obscuring my face with my arm. I was sure he'd seen me. And if he'd been paying attention at the community center, he would recognize me. He would recognize us. And our car. We shouldn't have followed him. But it was too late for that now.

Chris drove with purpose, but I could see his eyes flicking up to the rearview mirror every so often. When we were back on the highway, he hit the steering wheel with his fist.

I jumped. "What?"

"Waste of time," he said, mirroring my earlier thought.

"Did you recognize the house at all?"

He shook his head. "And I couldn't get a good enough look at anyone to see if I recognized any of them, either. Nothing." He sighed. "I've got nothing."

"That's not true," I said. *Bubble gum, pearl, blue. Bronze, silver, foamy sea green.* JSB946. "You have a license plate number. I have it memorized."

"What do I need his plate number for? I already know who he is, where he works, and what he drives."

"Not his," I said. "The plates on the car in the driveway."

CHRIS DROPPED ME off at my car in the community center parking lot, promising me he'd go home for the night, as one of his headaches was coming on again. The community center's evening programs were getting started—people were heading in with their workout bags and dance uniforms. It was dark outside. We'd been at this forever. No wonder he had a headache.

"The database isn't going anywhere," I said, writing down the license plate number on a napkin I found in his glove box. "You can check tomorrow."

He looked like he wanted to argue, but couldn't. The pain was so bad he was squinting one eye.

"I still can't believe you got the number. We drove by fast, and you barely looked out the window."

I didn't need to look too hard, I wanted to say. The number—the colors—came to me. As they always did. "Guess I'm just good," I said with a smirk.

"Yet you don't want to go into the police acad—"

I wadded up the napkin and held it up. "You say it out loud and I eat this. And you never get the number."

"As much as I'd like to see you eat that napkin, my head hurts too much to argue. Good night, Nikki."

He pulled the napkin from my hand, dropped it on his seat between his legs, and waved at me. I shut the door and watched him pull away. He was driving very fast. The headache must have been getting unbearable.

So we'd found Heriberto and it had meant nothing to him. We'd also found some kid possibly named Sam who

Chris knew, which was weird, especially since old Heri was obviously a dealer. We'd found a house full of people, and if any of them meant anything to Chris, he didn't have a chance to see them. Maybe the license plate we'd found would be helpful.

13

BRIGHT AND EARLY the next morning, I was at Light-ningKick, waiting for Gunner before it even opened. He showed up carrying a giant Thermos of green smoothie, and I had to wait what seemed like forever for him to finish it up, the whole time trying to chat with me about crap I didn't care about.

The four-year-old class was getting canceled. An irate mom had broken one of the lockers when her kid complained about being sore from practice. The sparring dummy had a split in the neck and needed to be replaced and it was prob-ably my fault, ha-ha-ha. The landlord wouldn't fix the back door. Blah, blah, blah.

I sat on a metal folding chair in my *dobok*, nervously

pumping one leg while chewing on my thumbnail. I'd driven home the evening before with one eye in the rearview mirror the entire way. I'd hardly gotten any sleep; every time Dad moved around downstairs or Hue sighed on the floor next to my bed, I was certain Heriberto was going to pull a Basile brother act on me and bust into my kitchen—only this time I wouldn't get away with just a few bruises and a cut on my chest.

By the time morning came, practicing with Gunner seemed like the best possible use of my time. Not that I was afraid I was getting rusty or anything; I just needed to expend some of this nervous energy before it made me crazy.

Finally, Gunner rinsed out his cup in the tiny restroom and turned it upside down on a paper towel on the front desk to dry. He disappeared into the locker room, then reappeared in his *dobok*.

"You ready?" He stepped to one side by the mat and gestured for me to go first.

I stood, walked to the mat, and bowed. "Definitely ready."

"Want to work on anything in particular?" he asked, following me to the heavy bag. I gave it a few tentative kicks.

Something I could use to defend myself from crazy Hollis wannabes and potential drug dealers. Something that could be used to defend myself from my own father, or any other murderer, for that matter. "Anything," I said.

Gunner loped over to the equipment box and dug out a kicking pad. He held it in front of him and I worked on my power, gaining steam and momentum with every kick. *Snap, snap, snap.* Barely stopping to take breaths between, my hands balled up in front of my chin, my focus laser-sharp on the pads. *Snap, snap, snap.* After a while, Gunner had to change hands, shaking out the one that had been holding the pad.

"You haven't lost your touch," he said when I finally took a break. I was sitting on the folding chair again, sucking down a bottle of water as fast as I could. Sweat poured off me. It felt good. I was calming down, anyway. "How are your evasion techniques coming?"

I almost laughed out loud. I thought about running away from the man with white-blond hair at Pear Magic. If there was anything I was good at, it was evasion.

"I could probably work on that," I said, tossing the empty bottle into recycling and heading back to the mat.

After a bow, Gunner settled into a fighting stance and moved to strike. I stopped him with a high block. He tried again and I used a middle knife hand. He reared back and threw a kick at me. Quick as lightning, I blocked him low. He threw some combinations and I blocked them all, taking the force of his kicks and strikes with my forearms, sending jolty thuds of pain up into my biceps, my chest. I ignored it, I had too much at stake to feel pain.

After a few minutes, he let his stance down. "Your blocks are great, but you need to work on getting out of the way," he said. "Here, let me show you. Give me a forefist."

I planted one foot behind me and punched. He ducked out of the way and I punched the air.

"Palm heel," he said, straightening up again. I thrust my palm at him and he moved to the side. Again, my attack hit air. "Try a combination."

"Sir?"

"Anything you'd like. Kicks, punches, whatever. Just go for it. You're going to beat the snot out of me."

I took a deep breath, steadied myself, and then unleashed two punches into the air, becoming so off balance I couldn't even finish the combination.

"Yep, see, blocks are fine," he said, taking my arm and smacking it solidly into his palm. "But it takes a lot of energy away from your next offensive move. Not to mention, it hurts. You evade"—he bent at the knees and moved side to side, like he was ducking under something—"and your opponent is the only one expending energy. You've thrown him off by not being where he thinks you're going to be. He can't even figure out where to punch next, and he's off balance. It is almost impossible to beat someone who is evading you. If they're good at it, that is. Let's try it again. I'm going to attack you slowly."

He began throwing slow-motion punches and kicks, and I swerved and bobbed and swiveled and shifted, at first too slow and getting hit anyway, but eventually getting better. Gunner was mostly punching air, even at moderate speed.

But all I could think about was Dad. He had been evading me for over ten years. It was going to be impossible to beat him as long as I kept letting him duck out of the way. He was throwing me off by never being where I thought he would be.

In other words, I'd put it off long enough. I had to listen to those tapes.

I DIDN'T WASTE any time when I got home. I was pretty sure Dad was out for the day, doing some freelance work for a travel magazine, but what I didn't know was when he'd left or how long exactly he would be gone.

But what Gunner had said had made so much sense. Dad was evading. And I was done letting it throw me off balance.

I went straight up to my room and dug the manila envelope Chris had given me out of my desk drawer. I shook the tapes onto my desk. At first, all I could do was stare at them. I reached out to touch one, but my fingers shook slightly, almost like I was afraid.

No, Nikki. You have been afraid of too many things for too long. Time to step up. They're tapes. What's the big deal?

Oh, I could just find out that my dad killed my mom. No big deal there.

Still, I had to know.

I scooped up the tapes and took them to Dad's room. Last I had seen his recorder, it was on a shelf in his closet. He never used it anymore, but I was pretty sure it would still be there anyway. I was suddenly glad the man was such a hoarder. I flipped on the closet light and stepped inside. It smelled like Dad. Cologne and aftershave and something chemical, like camera oil or lens cleaner or gasoline. And underneath it all, the faint scent of flowers that I associated with my mom. There was nothing left of her in this closet, so there was no way I was actually smelling anything. But the scent was there regardless—always there, always beckoning me, always making me feel hugged from the inside out. If Mom was watching right now, was she sad that I had found out the truth about her, about Peyton? Was she hoping I didn't bust Dad? Or was she happy that I was finally going to get answers?

Putting the cart a little before the horse there, Nikki. You don't actually know if he killed anyone, do you? You have to listen to the tapes. Save your judgment.

Yeah, but my judgment was telling me he was definitely lying about something. I'd seen the photos with my own eyes.

I could barely reach the shelf above Dad's suit jackets—the one where he kept all kinds of odds and ends, along with a box of medicines and bandages and wraps—the things I was constantly needing when I was new to tae kwon do but we hardly ever used anymore. Pushed behind it all was a boxy cassette recorder—the old-fashioned kind that would have had a microphone that you plugged into it. He probably still had the microphone lying around somewhere, too.

I pulled it down, shoved everything back in its place, and brought the recorder to my bedroom. If he came home before I was finished with the recorder, I would just hide it under my bed. He would never know it was missing. He probably hadn't used it in twenty years.

I crawled onto the middle of my bed and sat cross-legged, staring at the recorder and the cassettes and wondering if I was strong enough to handle whatever I found out. I would have to be.

My phone went off, making me jump. A text from Chris.

Looked up the plate.

And??? I texted.

The name sounds familiar. No record on her, though.

Her?

I waited for him to respond, but he never did. If there was a way to hear frustration in someone's text voice, I was definitely hearing it in Chris's. It had to be maddening to remember bits and pieces of things, but have the most random information wiped from your mind. Especially if the random information helped you figure out who was trying to kill you.

Address match? I asked.

Yes was all he responded. Translation: *I'm done talking about it. I know nothing more than I did before.*

I tossed my phone to the side and chewed my lip. If we didn't have Luna or Heriberto, we might as well get my dad.

I put the cassette marked with a big *1* into the machine and pressed play.

At first there was nothing. Just the hiss of the tape and some faraway clicks and dragging noises. Then there was some mumbling—something garbled—and my dad's voice came in, so loud and clear and close to the microphone it sounded like he was actually in the room with me. It made my heart skip.

"Uh, Milo Kill. M-I-L-O K-I-L-L."

More mumbling, then a rustling and the voice coming in clearer. ". . . Thursday night?"

There was a pause. "Uh. I was home? I don't know, maybe I was out. I . . . can I get a drink of water?" There was the sound of liquid being poured, and then, "Thanks." A pause. "I mean, the whole week has been such a blur. I'm not sure what I remember. What's real and what's fake, you know?" A breath.

"So you don't remember anything about the night your wife was murdered? Not even where you were?"

"I . . . I was with my daughter. With Nikki."

I sat up straighter, staring at the recorder, which was bursting with gold fireworks, dripping gray contrails, and melting into a deep indigo sky. I pressed rewind and listened again. ". . . I was with my daughter."

"Fucking liar," I said out loud. I clicked off the tape, my entire room blotted out with inky rage. I had been at my friend Wendy's house. Her mom had given me Tootsie Rolls in a bag. I'd dropped them in Mom's blood. I remembered everything. Everything, down to the warmth of the blood as it soaked into the knees of my jeans. Down to the look in Mom's eyes when she told me to run. And he couldn't even remember that he wasn't with me that night? "Bullshit," I said to the recorder, hopping off my bed and pacing the length of my room a few times, my thumbnail jammed in my mouth. I looked longingly at my desk drawer, where I knew I'd stashed an old, stale pack of cigarettes. If there ever was a time I was saving them for . . .

Instead, I took several deep breaths and hit play again. "Well, now, see, we've been told your daughter was at a friend's house, Milo. Were you with her at that house, or . . . ?"

"I . . ." A sigh. "I guess I must have been. I must have picked her up, dropped her off. That's . . . I mean, I don't know where else I would be."

"Mrs. Coughlin—your daughter's friend's mother—has given a statement that she picked up your daughter and brought her home that day. She said you and your wife were going out on a date, and she'd agreed to do the driving so you two could be alone."

A long pause. "She did?"

"Yep. So how about we start over. Do you know what you were doing . . ." On and on it went. A faceless officer asking Dad where he'd been the night Mom was killed, and Dad giving him every transparent lie in the book. At one point, Dad broke down, his tears sounding angry and frustrated. Calculated? Yes, maybe even measured.

I listened to both tapes, and never did Dad offer a believable story. And he'd offered so many unbelievable ones it was impossible to think that a believable one existed. Why? Why would he lie unless he was guilty?

"Am I being arrested?" he'd asked at one point, and the officer had sounded brusque when he responded, "No, sir. We're just trying to get a sense of what happened that night. We don't have anything to arrest you for, do we?"

Dad's response had been chilling. His voice flat, impassive. "No. You don't have anything."

I let the second tape run until it reached the end. The machine gave a squeak and then clicked off, and I was left sitting in bloated silence in my room, my legs drawn up and my arms wrapped around them.

Not, *No, I didn't do it*. Not, *Whatever it takes to find my wife's killer*. Just, *No, you don't have anything*. Which was definitely not the same as saying there was nothing to have.

He didn't come out and say that he'd done it. He didn't confess and throw himself on the mercy of the court. But he'd lied. He'd done nothing to convince me that he hadn't done it.

I popped the cassette out of the machine and put it back in the manila envelope, then took the recorder back downstairs to Dad's closet.

But when I moved the bandage box to put it back, I noticed a stack of yellowed, clipped newspaper articles under where the recorder had been sitting. I pulled them down. The headline on the very top one caught my eye.

PRODUCER PAIRS WITH UP-AND-COMER FOR HOT NEW THRILLER

Hollywood, CA—Noted producer Bill Hollis has announced his newest film venture—an as-yet-unnamed cat-and-mouse thriller about a professional football player who is hiding the fact that he's a serial killer, and the young journalist who is next on his hit list. Hollis, best known for the 1994 Academy Award–winning *Penelope*, has paired with fledgling director Carrie Kill, in what he is calling his best work yet.

The article went on to name a short list of actors who were speculated to be in the film, and talked about Mom's work at Angry Elephant. Below, there were two head shots—one of my mom and one of Bill Hollis. Seeing his face filled me with a familiar mix of anxiety and hatred, while Mom's picture made me sad and nostalgic. The emotions swelled into a soup of colors that swam across the paper.

I flipped to the article beneath: *BILL HOLLIS INTRO-DUCES NEW DIRECTOR TO HOLLYWOOD SCENE.* Another photo of my mom, beaming into the camera. I kept flipping through the articles, all of them with similar headlines—wildly famous producer gives a shot to a nobody director, and wasn't she lucky to be making what would be such a smash hit movie?

So . . . what had happened to this movie? As far as I knew, Mom was never part of anything that actually made it to the big screen. She was amateur until the day she died. I checked the dates of the articles. They were all written about two years before she died. Something had happened in those two years. Something that made the movie go south.

Dad? Had Dad happened?

I flipped to the last article and froze. The headline was similar to the others. Nothing new about the story. It was the photo that sent my stomach to my feet. The first photo that showed them together. Mom and Bill Hollis, arms around each other jovially. Off to one side, my dad, unaware that he was being caught on camera, a scowl driving down the corners of his mouth.

And behind him, the white-blond man.

Luna's getaway driver. The director at Pear Magic. The guy with the VP belt buckle.

The man in one of the photos in Dad's desk drawer. The ones that went missing.

14

COULDN'T TELL if things were falling into place or getting more confusing. I didn't understand why the blond man kept popping up in so many places. He was connected to Luna. He was connected to the Hollises. He was connected to my parents.

Who the hell was he?

There was one way to find out.

I gathered the articles together, picking up the ones that had fallen on the floor, and crammed all but one of them back where they had been, then settled the cassette recorder on top of them and repositioned the bandage box. As far as Dad knew, nothing had been disturbed. Exactly the way I wanted it.

I couldn't even begin to wrap my head around the fact that my dad was standing right next to the man who'd rushed Luna away from Tesori Antico. There was no denying it now—Dad had something to do with the Hollises. He had something to do with Luna's getaway driver.

Goose bumps raced up and down my arms and my stomach knotted. I swallowed and swallowed, as the once-familiar scent of my father's closet began to choke me. Ink. The air felt thick as ink to me. Even if, by some miracle, my father hadn't betrayed my mother, he had betrayed me.

I stumbled out of the closet, my feet getting tangled on each other. I landed on my butt, sucking in fresh air, starting to feel swimmy. *Don't pass out, Nikki. Don't pass out.*

Oh, I had no intention of passing out.

I had every intention of figuring out how this guy was linked to my family.

DAD WOULD PROBABLY be pissed that I didn't leave a note. But at this point I was just trying to avoid him as much as humanly possible. Besides, what was there to say? *I've gone to get to the bottom of your lies, and hopefully find Luna along the way, all while avoiding the drug dealer who probably wants my cop friend dead.* Something told me he wouldn't be in love with that idea.

I was just glad to get out of the house before he got home.

I wanted to confront him with what I knew. I wanted to make him come clean. But what if he didn't? What if he still clung to his story, called me crazy, refused to admit anything?

I tried to call Chris again, to tell him I was headed to Pear Magic. But he didn't answer. **Meeting,** he texted as soon as I hung up. For the briefest moment, I considered waiting for him to get out of the meeting. But I guessed he wouldn't be too excited about going back to the studio, given how it went last time we were there. It was best for me to go alone.

I grabbed a bandanna and rummaged through the kitchen drawers until I found an old apron that Dad used to wear when he was going through his weekend cookout phase. It was plain black, and still dirty from years-old food grime that had never been washed out. I put on a black T-shirt and jeans and tied the bandanna around my hair like I'd seen cooks on TV do. I tied the apron around my waist, knotting it in front, and headed out.

The timing couldn't have been more perfect. It was just before one o'clock. Lunchtime. I drove to Fat Sal's and ordered random items—a couple of heroes, a couple of wraps, some fries—enough to fill two sacks—then made a beeline to Pear Magic.

The same security guard was working. He waved me through without even questioning me—apparently nobody had alerted him about my previous visit being bogus. This time I pulled into a parking spot right in front of the studio. My palms were sweating, but I had to act like I belonged here if I was going to pull off getting inside again. I was already counting on nobody recognizing me, and on avoiding the blond man, who definitely would. I pulled down the visor and gave myself one last look, tucking loose strands of hair up into the bandanna, took two deep breaths, grabbed the Fat Sal's sacks, and got out.

You can do this, Nikki.

A young man was standing behind the front desk. He barely looked up when I walked inside. I had a whole spiel practiced in my head about getting a lunch order and wanting to deliver it in person to make sure I hadn't made any errors, but it turned out I didn't even need to. I had just opened my mouth when he motioned over his shoulder with his pencil, not tearing his eyes away from the magazine open on the desk in front of him. "Go ahead," he said.

I closed my mouth, paused for the tiniest second—seriously, my luck was never that good—and walked past him, ducking my head so I didn't accidentally make eye contact with anyone.

Once I was inside, I realized I had no idea what I was really looking for. Something, anything that would tell me who the blond man was. That would be a start, anyway.

As luck would have it, they were mid-take, the set full of extras, with Celeste Day in the center of the crowd. The white-blond man was sitting in a tall chair with his legs crossed, looking completely bored as he tapped on a tablet. A handful of people stood around the edges of the set, at the ready should their services be needed. But nobody was really hanging around the dressing area.

I snuck back through the area where I'd pretended to be Celeste's makeup artist and set the bags on a chair. I had to move fast, so I tried hard to focus on colors as I scanned the dressing tables, nudging bottles and tubes and hairbrushes aside so I could riffle through any papers I found. Mostly scripts, the occasional memo or printed list, a press pass. Nothing useful. I crouched and duckwalked to check under each table, looking for open bags or purses. I pawed through what I recognized as Celeste Day's bag, where I'd found the matchbook before. Nothing. Less than nothing, actually. Nothing, with a side of not having a clue what something would look like even if I found it.

"What are you doing?" I heard. I jerked upright so quickly I nearly smacked the back of my head on the underside of the table. I slapped one hand over my heart.

"Oh my gosh, you scared me," I said, trying to give myself a southern accent, with no idea why. I pinched my finger and thumb together and held them up like I was holding something tiny between them. "My contact lens." I gave a nervous, breathy laugh. "They're new and I don't really know what I'm doing. They keep popping right out."

The woman, who was adjusting her zombie costume, appeared to have just come out of the bathroom. She looked unconvinced, but she also looked like she didn't have time to press it.

"Can I use the mirror to put it back in?" I asked. "It might take me a while."

"I guess," she said. She leaned down to check her reflection, pressing her fingers gently under her eyes to smooth her makeup. Satisfied, she started to head toward the set.

"I'm supposed to drop this in the director's office?" I said, pointing to the Fat Sal's bags. She looked at the bags and then took a few steps back to look at the blond man, and for a moment I feared she was going to call him over. But instead she just pointed in the direction of the set.

"That guy right there," she said.

"Yeah, but I have strict instructions not to bother him on set. I'm supposed to leave it on his desk. He already paid." This was the sketchiest-sounding story, even to myself, but fortunately, the zombie girl was too worried about getting back to filming to think it through. Part of me wanted to just ask her who he was, if she'd ever heard of Luna Fairchild, if she had any idea what his connection was to her. But she looked impatient and annoyed to even be talking to some sandwich delivery girl, and the last thing I wanted to do was arouse suspicion again—or worse, make her call him over. I felt lucky enough to have gotten away from him last time.

"Down that hall," she said, pointing toward the dark hallway where the blond man had caught me before. "Go left. His is the first door."

"Thanks," I said. I leaned over and pulled down my lower lid, bringing one finger up to my eye like I was getting ready to insert a contact. She wasted no time hurrying away, and I wasted no time grabbing my shit and getting out of there.

The hallway was quiet. My footsteps sounded loud in comparison. Every wrinkle of the bags I was holding sounded like a crack of thunder. I could hear my heartbeat. I chewed my bottom lip as I scurried to the left, and then stopped and gave a quick look around before I pushed open the door.

Please, God, let there be no one inside.

There wasn't. I flipped on the light and eased the door closed. Frightened gold fireworks painted the ceiling, but then gave way to rolling oranges and yellows. I couldn't feel my feet. It was so silent I could almost hear my own blood rushing.

I dropped the bags in the center of his desk and then stood there for a second, glancing around, hoping something would jump out at me. Fuzzy tangerine—my dad's name, maybe. Or lavender—my mom's. Glittery purple—the color of Hollywood Dreams—that I'd come to associate with the Hollis name without even realizing it. Even ice-blue *Luna* would be a welcome sight. Just something to let me know I wasn't crazy. That I was on the right track.

Nothing. Not a single loose paper on the pristine desk; only a bookshelf full of books. Random colors popped out at me, like flashbulbs and balloons and floating bubbles, but most of them with the beige edges of boring business. Was it weird for a director's desk to be such a void?

Frantically, I began opening drawers and scanning shelves. Nothing. Nothing, nothing, nothing.

God. No. I could not come away with nothing. Not again.

I dropped down, flipped to my back, and checked the undersides of the desk and chair. Nope.

I stood, cursing, and was just about to give up, when a black-and-white word streaked across my consciousness. *Journal.* Tucked in with all the books and binders on the shelves, a thin red notebook with the word *Journal* printed down the spine.

I pulled it out.

Pay dirt. Where there were journals, there were secrets, right? At least that was always how it was in the movies.

Curious, I opened it, thumbing through the pages. It was more diary, or even activity log, than journal. Weird. Nothing personal. Just line after line of recorded activities. And there was something off about it that I couldn't quite place.

8:10 A.M. AWAKE

8:22 A.M. SHOWER, DOOR CLOSED

9:10 A.M. BREAKFAST, CEREAL, DRY, COFFEE, CREAM, SUGAR, DIDN'T FINISH

9:30 A.M. STUDYING, OPEN TEXTBOOK, GEOGRAPHY

9:56 A.M. CIGARETTE BREAK 1, COMPLETE TO FILTER, NO BRAND CHANGE, DISCARDED BUTT SAVED, RETRIEVED, AND LOGGED

Damn, the blond man kept a boring-as-shit schedule.

But maybe knowing the kind of schedule he kept would be handy. Maybe there would be clues in later entries to tell me who he was. Maybe knowing his schedule would help me know exactly when his house would be empty. If I could ever find his house, that was. Either way, leaving with a boring journal that might or might not be useful was better than leaving with nothing.

I pulled up my apron, tucked the journal into my waistband, and scurried out of Pear Magic, leaving the Fat Sal's bags on the blond man's desk.

I liked the idea of him feeling watched. Of getting back to his office and wondering who was after him.

AS SOON AS I got out of the Pear Magic lot, I pulled off the bandanna and shook my hair out. At the first stoplight, I untied and shimmied out of my apron. I tossed them both into the backseat and stuck the journal in the glove box.

I didn't know what I had—if I had anything at all—but I felt like I had made maybe the tiniest bit of progress. Who knew—maybe I would find something in the journal that would open Dad's locked box. It was such a long shot it was basically impossible, but if I didn't stay optimistic, I would never get anywhere, right? I called Chris's phone twice more, to no answer, and when I buzzed past his gym, I could see why. His car was there, so he was likely inside, working out. I swung into the lot and parked.

Chris was doing sit-ups on a mat in the corner, sweating so hard his head was leaving a wet, circular blotch on the mat. I walked past the front desk like I owned the place, grabbed a light medicine ball off a shelf, and waited for him to pull himself upright. When he did, I tossed the ball.

"Shit!" He caught the ball half an inch before it hit his face, and held it in the curve of his stomach. "What the hell?"

"I can see your reflexes are still in working order," I said. "A little sluggish, but . . ." I shrugged sarcastically.

"And what if they weren't?"

"You'd have a broken nose right now, I guess."

"Real sensitive, Nikki." He tossed the ball back at me and lowered himself back to the mat. "You know"—he sat up and went back down again—"you are always"—*up, down*—"everywhere I don't"—*up, down*—"want you to be."

This time when he sat up, I threw the ball again. He caught it much quicker. "Your throw's a little sluggish, but . . ." He shrugged and lobbed it to me, then went back to his sit-ups. "To what . . . do I owe the . . . extreme plea-sure . . . of having you in my gym?" He sat up and let his arms rest on his knees, his hands dangling between his legs. "On a day when I thought I made it pretty clear I didn't want to be bothered."

I shifted the ball to my hip, holding it there with my forearm. "So now I'm a bother?" I acted like he was being ridiculous, but the truth was his words stung a little. Since when did he want to avoid me? Usually I was the one trying to avoid him.

He tipped his head to wipe his temple and cheek on his shoulder. "No, you're not a bother," he said. "You're just always demanding something. And before you ask, no. I don't remember anybody with the name on that license plate."

"I wasn't going to ask you about the name," I said. *But only because I completely forgot about it*, I didn't add.

"Good."

"But since you brought it up . . . ," I said.

He rolled his eyes and went back to his sit-ups. "What do you want, Nikki?"

I tossed the ball. He caught it and threw it back to me immediately. "What's her name?"

He grunted, ignoring me.

"Oh, come on. What's the big deal about you telling me?"

He stopped again. "The big deal is I tell you the name and next thing I know I'm having to rush to her house to either apologize to her or bail your ass out of trouble. Or, most likely, both."

"Funny," I said. "I thought I was bailing your ass out of trouble this time. You know, unless you don't consider getting run over to be trouble." I dropped the ball onto the mat and propped one foot on it. "I promise I won't—"

"Dear God, you are relentless. Fine. Her name is Rebecca Moreno. The name sounds familiar, but I can't remember why. And it's making me crazy to constantly have all these things almost making sense, but not making sense. I just need a day to think, Nikki. I need a day for this to be my problem. Not ours. Mine."

"Fine," I said. "It's your problem." Part of me wanted to be offended that he was shutting me out so completely, but then again, how many problems was I hiding from him at any given moment?

"Thank you." He did another three sit-ups.

"Now, to the reason I'm here," I said.

He laughed. "I knew it."

"No, this will be fun. I promise."

"Fun?" He stood, grabbed a towel from a nearby table, and wiped his face and neck. "When have your plans ever been fun?"

I ignored him. "Have you ever been to igNight?"

He thought, then squinted through the sweat. "The hookah place?"

I nodded. "Hookah *club* is what they call it."

He pitched the used towel across the room; it landed in a laundry basket, on top of a pile of other dirty towels. "Why on earth would I want to go to a hookah club? Or any kind of club, for that matter."

"Because you're not eighty," I said, kicking his shoe. "Even if you constantly insist on acting like you are." I hunched over and made a grumpy face.

"I don't really see you as a big dancer, Nikki," he said.

"I could be." He was right; I wasn't. Dancing felt too uncontrolled and vulnerable, and I felt like a fool when I tried. Mom used to dance. All the time. She was constantly turning up the radio, then picking me up and whirling me around the kitchen. I loved it. Maybe that was why I hated dancing so much now. It was just another thing that died with Mom.

God, that was pathetic.

"But you're not. So what's the real reason we're going to igNight?"

I beamed. "Does that mean you'll go?"

He zipped his duffel and stood, looping the strap over one shoulder. He raised his eyebrows at me like he was waiting for my response.

"Okay. Don't get mad." He rolled his eyes, still wordless. "Luna—"

"No way." He started out the door.

"No, listen," I said, following him.

"No."

He was limping a little, giving me a chance to catch up as he loped across the parking lot. "I have to—"

"It's not happening," he said over his shoulder.

I stopped. "I'm going with or without you. I'd rather it be with, but it's your choice. I'm not giving up this time, Chris. As long as she's out there, I'm not safe. Maybe you can ignore that, but I can't."

He stopped, a few feet ahead of me. He let his bag drop to the ground and sighed loudly. Finally, he turned. "So where does the club come in?"

"Vee told me that Shelby Gray has been hanging out at igNight a lot. She broke up with Gibson and is acting super sketchy, and if I were a betting woman, I would bet that she's going there to meet up with a certain psychotic friend of hers. It's worth a shot, anyway. I can't let this go, Chris. And the old Chris would have totally gotten that."

He seemed to think this over, his jaw working. "Yeah," he finally said. "I get it."

"Good. Meet me there at ten."

15

TONIGHT WAS PACKED. Like, wall-to-wall, elbow-to-elbow, shoulder-to-shoulder, hip-to-hip packed. A DJ worked in a high booth, buzzing techno music at us so loud you could feel it vibrate through the soles of your feet. Everything was black light and neon and sleek. Leather couches in the corners, high-top tables scattered everywhere, a long bar that stretched the perimeter of the entire room, an ornate hookah placed on it every two feet or so. It was hazy and loud and hot. Condensation ran down the windows, and our shoes felt squeaky and slick against the tile. People didn't dance so much as writhe, mixing sweat and smoke and breath.

I didn't know how I was ever going to find Shelby in there.

I turned to look at Chris; he appeared to be even more off-kilter than I felt. I laced my fingers through his and pulled him behind me toward an empty spot at the bar, on the dark end of the room.

"This is insane," he said, when we finally found a place. He gazed at the hookah as if it were going to bite him. I laughed.

"Relax, jeez. You have cop written all over you."

"Because I am one. I would rather be that than—"

"What're you having, hon?" A waitress had appeared out of nowhere, wearing a tight hot pink romper and thigh-high black hose with a pair of combat boots. Her hair was pulled back slick on one side and dangled to her chin on the other in a flat black waterfall. She handed me a card with the shisha menu printed on it.

"Oh. Uh . . ." I leaned over. I had never smoked shisha. I knew this wasn't exactly the same as smoking cigarettes, but it was a slippery enough slope that my palms started to itch. At the same time, my senses came to attention with craving. "Double apple," I said, choosing the first thing on the menu.

"ID?" she asked, holding her palm out, looking bored. I dug for my license and gave it to her. She scanned it, nodded, looked Chris up and down, and then moved on.

"Apple-flavored smoke? Sounds delicious," he said, deadpan.

"You never know until you try it." I picked up the hose and slithered it at him like a snake.

"Can we just get to what we came here for?" he asked, turning his eyes back to the room. I dropped the hose. He was determined to make this suck as much as humanly possible.

I concentrated. Words came out at me in their usual colors, which got confused among the neon and made my eyes wonky. The room felt salmon to me. Peaceful. Not at all the kind of place I would expect to find someone like Luna.

The waitress returned with tobacco, foil, and lit coals, and we watched while she expertly filled the bowl. "Fifteen dollars," she said in a voice equally as bored as everything else she did. I paid her and she disappeared into the crowd.

I picked up the hose and held it out to Chris. "You want to go first?"

He shook his head. "No desire, actually."

His Mr. Straightface routine was getting old. "Whatever. Up to you." I took a pull off the hose and felt the smoke roil through me, my whole world lighting up in apple green. "You should give it a try," I yelled over the music, holding out the hose again.

"No, thanks," he said. "I'm getting enough secondhand smoke to last me a lifetime."

That was it. I was done with this nonsense. I brought the hose to my lips, took a deep pull, then stepped in close to Chris, backing him up against the bar. I angled my leg between his and pushed in until every part of me was brushing up against every part of him. The green apple burst and stretched until it was part of a brilliant rainbow, a curtain of color between us. I snaked my hands up over his shoulders, cupped the back of his neck, and leaned in. With my mouth only centimeters from his skin, I exhaled. I could feel him relax around me, and then, with effort, straighten up again.

"You should at least try to loosen up a little," I said. But before I could say any more, I was distracted by a familiar laugh. I whipped around and saw Shelby Gray puffing on a hookah in a barely there backless halter and painted-on jeans. She was sitting on the couch, draped over the lap of some guy I didn't recognize. Definitely not Gibson. Guess Vee was right—they were Split City. Shelby tilted her head back and the guy nuzzled her bare shoulder.

I forgot all about the green and the rainbow and the smell of Chris's aftershave. My heart sped up and I felt a little tingly and dizzy. Probably part adrenaline and part green apple. Well, and part Chris, if I was being really honest.

"I'll be right back," I said. I started to weave through the crowd. Chris was saying something to my back, but I was singularly focused on one thing and one thing only: getting to Shelby Gray. Finding out where Luna was.

To get to Shelby, though, meant I had to cross the dance floor, which was like trying to swim upstream, if upstream was filled with flailing arms and whipping hair. The DJ had just started a new song—a grinding remix of something familiar—and people were flooding the floor like crazy. I lost sight of the couch and caught myself balling up my fists at my sides, my shoulders tensing. If Luna was here, there would be no better place to shank me and take off.

The DJ yelled into the microphone about partying, and ratcheted up the volume another notch, which I wouldn't have thought was possible. I turned to plead for help from Chris with my eyes, but I'd been cut off from him too. The crowd had closed in, and all I could see were the people surrounding me.

I didn't like being surrounded.

I began to get disoriented as the lights went crazy, flashing and strobing and zipping colors up walls and across faces and clawing across the darkness of the ceiling like meteorites. My head began to pound from trying to keep it all straight.

Suddenly, a hand reached through the crowd and grabbed my wrist, tight. Startled, I yanked back, but I was too distracted to be strong, and I found myself being pulled through the knot of bodies. I slipped on someone's spilled drink and almost went down, but the hand gripped tighter and I found myself being pulled back up again.

I had the thought that maybe I should scream for help.

Try to get Chris's attention. That I should fight back. But I was having too much difficulty getting my bearings. I couldn't see through the haze and the lights and the panic. My voice felt locked inside.

Finally, I burst from the crowd, shocked to find myself spit out on the other side of the room. I could see Chris across the room. He had found a stool and was slouched on it, playing with his phone. So glad to know he had my back.

The hand let go and I spun around.

And found myself nose to nose with a familiar face. Familiar heavily painted cat-eyes. A familiar wave of blue. A familiar corseted body. The girl who had given me the key to Dom Distribution. The girl who lived in, and went missing from, Bill Hollis's apartment building. The girl who I'd thought I'd never see again.

"Blue?"

"I thought that was you," she answered. Her eyes were huge and sparkly in this light. Her chin came to a severe point. She looked like manga come to life. "I wasn't sure what I would have done if I'd gotten you all the way over here and it wasn't you." She laughed. Tendrils of blue hair stuck to her forehead in sweat.

"I thought you were . . ." I struggled for words. "Bill Hollis said you were dead."

"Dead to him, maybe. But alive and well. A little bit homeless, but whatever. That's a detail."

I was aware of my mouth hanging open, of my hand hovering in midair between us, as if there was a force field around Blue that kept me from touching her. "What about Ruby?" I asked.

She pressed her lips together and then let them spring apart again. "Hollis actually did try to kill her. Came to her apartment and tried to, like . . ." She wrapped both hands around her neck and stuck out her tongue. "He was trying to find out what she had told you. But Ruby fought him off and that was the end of that. She went home. Texas. One day there, next day gone. Day after that, he kicked the rest of us out. Said we were 'too talkative' and 'dangerous.'" She made air quotes. "I've been here and there since. Mostly here. I know the owner. He doesn't charge me to hang out. And usually I can find someone to go home with."

"Does this mean Brandi is still alive too?" I asked, feeling a surge of hope that my mom's friend—Dru's real mother— had also somehow escaped Bill Hollis alive.

Her brow crinkled. "I don't know anything about anyone named Brandi. Was she one of Vanessa's?"

"Never mind." I'd never checked the news to see if Bill Hollis had been bluffing about burning Brandi's trailer down, but if he'd lied about killing Blue and Ruby, he could have lied about pretty much anything. Maybe it was time for me to do some looking around to see if I could find her.

Or maybe it's time for you to let her live her own fucking life, Nikki. Since you're toxic as hell.

"So what are you doing here?" Blue yelled. "This doesn't seem like your kind of place at all."

"It's not," I said. I gestured around me. "Too many people. I'm looking for Luna."

Her eyes widened. "Fairchild?" She shook her head. "I haven't seen her, and I've been here every night for months. I thought she was locked up."

"Got out a few months ago," I said. "She's disappeared. And you know as well as I do, Luna doesn't stay disappeared for long."

Blue shrugged. "Maybe this time she will. She doesn't really have anything to come home to, does she?"

Only me, I thought. *Only me and my buddy, Revenge.*

"I saw her friend, though. I was trying to get to her when you grabbed me."

Blue turned and we scanned the crowd, both of us pulling up onto our tiptoes. "What does she look like? Do you see her now?"

"She was on a couch." The music changed to something less frantic, and the lights settled down. The waitresses took advantage of the lull and were hurrying back and forth over the dance floor, holding drinks and tapas and trays with hookah supplies on them.

Blue grabbed my hand again and we pushed through the thinning crowd, but when we popped out next to the couch, the boy was still there, but Shelby was gone.

"Hey, where's that girl you were with?" Blue asked, tapping the guy's leg with her knee. He turned his eyes slowly toward us, and it was easy to see that he was completely stoned. I guessed Vee was right; igNight was full of potheads who wanted to dance and smoke.

"Left," he said. He cleared his throat and said it again, louder. "She left."

"Left, like, gone?" I asked, pointing toward the door.

He nodded, then leaned his head back against the couch and closed his eyes.

"Thanks, you were a ton of help," I said sarcastically. "Come on, let's go after her."

It took us a solid ten minutes to fight our way to the front door, and I knew by the time we heaved ourselves into the fresh night air that Shelby would be long gone. Just to be safe, I asked the doorman if he'd seen where she went. Of course, he couldn't remember anything. *Lots of people come and go, sweetheart*, he told me. I'd told him not to fucking call me sweetheart.

"Sorry you missed her," Blue said. "It was probably my fault. If I hadn't grabbed you . . ."

"That's okay," I said. I leaned against the wall. Now that I was outside, it was obvious how much of a rabbit hole igNight was. Impossible not to lose track of where you were, and even who you were. "It probably would have been like always. Nobody knows anything. Nobody ever does."

Blue reached out and touched my shoulder. "Maybe it's possible that she really did leave," she said. "I mean, she hasn't bothered you yet. Maybe she's not going to. It doesn't seem to go very well for her when she does mess with you. You should just let it go. Focus on something else."

I tried to imagine a life where Luna was still out there somewhere and I was living normally, focusing on other things. Forgetting that she existed. Forgetting that she'd tried to kill me twice and had failed. Forgetting that I had caused the deaths of everyone in her family.

Not possible. Not in a million years.

But it would be stupid to try to convince Blue of that.

But she was right about one thing—I did have other things to focus on.

I reached into my back pocket and pulled out the newspaper clipping I'd found in Dad's closet. I had pocketed it on the off chance that I would be able to work up the courage to tell Chris about my parents' connection to the Hollises, but the time had never seemed right. It was hard to let someone in when they desperately wanted to stay out. It was hard to let someone in, period.

I'd let him in once before. And he didn't remember any of it. I would be stupid to try it again.

I unfolded the clipping and showed it to Blue. "You see that guy right there?" I pointed at the man with white-blond hair. She nodded. "Have you ever seen him before? Like, with the Hollises?" She nodded again. "Who is he?" I asked eagerly.

She shook her head. "I don't really know. All I know is he's some sort of director or something, and he was always hanging around Vanessa. And Bill too, but more Vanessa. He always kind of creeped me out, so I stayed away from him. I think Ruby called him Mr. F once, but she said it stood for Mr. Fuckface." She giggled. "I doubt that's his real name. Why do you ask?"

I let out the breath I hadn't realized I'd been holding. "No reason. I think he knows my parents or something."

"Your parents are friends with the Hollises?"

Yes. No. Depends on who you ask and when.

"I don't know. I don't think so."

"I would tell you to ask Jetta about him. She seemed to know him a little better. I think sometimes he was her john."

"Jetta?"

"New girl. Came around after Dreams shut down. We figured she was one of the girls and we just didn't know her. She's not around here anymore either, though." Blue pulled a cigarette out of her pocket and tucked it, unlit, into her mouth. It seemed strange to me that she would come outside to smoke in front of a hookah lounge. "I think Mr. Fu—Mr. F got her a job at some film studio in Vegas or something," she said around the cigarette. She pulled it from her mouth and held it between her fingers as she scratched her head. "Something like Mad Cow?" I jolted as orange and pink lit up in my mind. Totally not the colors I would associate with *Mad Cow*. But I knew what colors I did associate them with.

"Angry Elephant?"

She snapped her fingers. "Yeah. That's it. Angry Elephant. I think he must have connections there or something."

So maybe that was why the man was always in the background of the photos with my mom and dad. He was connected to the studio Mom worked for. But he was also Luna's accomplice—of that, I was positive. Which could only mean one thing.

I had to go to Vegas.

16

LAS VEGAS WAS a four-and-a-half-hour drive from Brentwood. That meant four and a half hours of either trying to entertain myself, or of trying to get Mr. Personality to entertain me. The old Nikki would have preferred to entertain herself a thousand times over spending that length of time trapped in a confined space with sunshine-yellow Detective Martinez.

So I had no real explanation for why I asked him to go with me.

"Why?" He was already irritated that I'd dragged him to igNight and had left him inside wondering where I'd gone while I went outside to talk with Blue. Suggesting an impromptu road trip only served to exacerbate his bad mood. Fortunately, I was really good with exacerbation.

"The guy who Luna escaped Tesori Antico with is connected to a film studio out there."

His eyebrows knit together. "Wait, I thought you said the guy at Pear Magic was the guy who drove Luna away that night."

"Same guy." He gave his head a quick shake, confused. "Look, it's a long story, and I'll have four hours to tell it to you. You in?"

"I just got back to work. I can't ask for time off to run to Vegas."

"Good point," I said. "That's okay. I'm sure I'll be fine. It's only four hours."

I really meant that, but I wasn't at all upset when he gave a long sigh and smacked the steering wheel with the palm of his hand. "When do you want to leave?"

I smiled, victorious. "Tomorrow morning?"

"How about afternoon?"

"Whatever works."

WE MET AT the police station. He tossed a backpack into the trunk of my car and got in.

"I'm driving?" I asked.

"It's your trip," he said. "I would hate to deprive you of the pleasure of taking charge."

"I know when I'm being manipulated. Fine. I'll drive. I've

got gas. I'm rested. I'm sick of your crappy driving anyway."

He slid down in the seat, rested his head on the seat back, and closed his eyes. "You keep telling yourself that."

We drove for a few minutes—long enough to get on I-15—before I broke the silence. "Did you have a hard time getting away?"

He shook his head but didn't open his eyes. "I told them I was having some migraines and needed to take a few more days to rest."

"Good one."

He turned his head slightly and opened one eye. "It was the truth."

"Oh."

He slept, his mouth slightly open, the back of his hair getting messed up. It was the sleep of someone who hadn't been getting much. I knew the headaches were bad, but maybe I didn't know how frequent they were, or what other effects he was still feeling from the accident. Maybe he was sore, tired. Maybe the confusion and forgetfulness bothered him more than I realized.

I turned on the radio but kept the volume low. It was like I was driving alone after all. But not. There was something about Chris's presence in the car that centered me. The car felt yellow and a color I'd once heard described as Alice blue. So pale it was more a hint or feeling of blue than actual blueness. The color of safety.

I used to see that color when I was alone in a room with Dad.

Not anymore.

He finally woke up, and we stopped in Beacon Station to devour a late lunch—cheeseburgers at a bustling little gas station. We sat on a bench, enjoying the breeze while we let grease run down our arms and ketchup dot our fingertips.

After we were finished, Chris wadded up his napkin and tossed it at a garbage can. It bounced off the side and rolled into the parking lot. He scowled. I retrieved the napkin and threw it away for him.

"I kind of remember," he said, the wind nearly whisking away the words before they were out of his mouth.

I tried not to look as excited by this news as I felt. If I'd learned one thing, it was that pressure didn't tend to put him in a very good place these days. "Yeah?" Disinterested Nikki picked at a splintered piece of wood on the bench seat.

He nodded. "Rebecca. And Sam. The kid from the community center? She's his mom."

"So that's where you knew that kid from. You obviously knew Rebecca. And it makes sense that Heriberto would go to her house. Maybe he's, like, her husband, and Sam's their kid. Or something." We both knew that wasn't true. We'd seen the exchanges between Heriberto and the boys. Sam was no stranger to Heriberto, but he definitely wasn't his kid. If anything, he appeared to be a colleague. "Or maybe he's—"

"Sam is Rebecca's son," Chris said, interrupting me. "That's all I know for sure."

"And how do you know that?"

He rubbed his forehead; I wondered if another headache was coming on. "I think I used to date her."

My eyes grew wide. "You remember dating her?"

"Not really." He squinted, rubbed harder. "Maybe. I mean, I think so, sure. It's still fuzzy. I looked her up. I recognized her face. I know it goes with that kid, Sam. And when I saw her, I had a feeling that I knew her. *Knew her,* knew her." He gave me an embarrassed glance. "It's like it's on the tip of my tongue. Same feeling."

"Were you dating her, like, recently?"

"I don't know."

"Like, since I've known you?"

"I don't know, Nikki." Irritation. "How am I supposed to know what I'm not remembering and from when? Could have been six months ago or it could have been six years ago. But for some reason I think it was a long time ago."

"It'll come to you," I said. But there was a part of me that hoped it didn't. And that sincerely pissed me off, that I suddenly didn't want him remembering past girlfriends, because why, exactly?

Because of the magenta that you are firmly ignoring,

Nikki. The magenta that shines the brightest in that rainbow you keep feeling every time he touches you.

He slurped his soda. "I guess."

I dangled the car key in front of Chris's face. "My turn to sleep."

He took the key, reluctantly.

"Don't look so butt-hurt about it. You can listen to your riveting talk radio for company."

I popped open the trunk and rummaged around in the junk until I found an old hoodie. I slipped it over my shirt, and when I got in the front seat, I promptly pulled it so far over my head it was obscuring my eyes. If there was more to the Mystery Girlfriend conversation, I didn't want to be part of it.

CHRIS SHOOK ME awake when we got to the hotel. I was completely out and for a minute, I was totally confused. Where was I and why was I here with Chris? But then I recognized the building we were in front of, and it all came back to me.

"The Luxor?" I asked, groggy, as I looked up at the pyramid I'd seen a million times on TV but never in person. "I can't afford this place."

"Don't worry about it," Chris mumbled, unbuckling his seat belt. "I've got it taken care of."

I pulled myself to sitting. I was sweaty inside my hoodie.

I battled with it to get it off. "I'm not going to let you pay for my hotel. Just take me to a cheap motel off the strip or something."

"It's one night," he said. "And I'm not staying in a cheap hotel off the strip. And you're not staying in a hotel I'm not staying in." I started to say more, but he gave me a look. "I got two rooms, okay?"

I didn't know how to argue with that. Plus, there was the tiniest bit of me that was excited about getting to stay in a really nice hotel in Vegas. This was the kind of place Peyton would have stayed in. It was the kind of place Dru was known to stay in. Somehow I felt closer to them, even if I had no idea if they'd ever actually walked the halls of the Luxor.

We checked in and went to our rooms, our footsteps soft on the carpet. I felt self-conscious about my backpack, the hole in the knee of my jeans, my ratty sleep-hair.

Chris stuck his key card in his door and opened it. "Dinner? Seven o'clock?"

"Sure," I said. I opened the door and breathed in the money of my room.

I HADN'T REALIZED we were going to be staying in such style, so I hadn't brought anything particularly nice to wear. Chris called me and told me to do some shopping. *Just take my credit card*, he said, so I did.

I hated shopping.

I especially hated shopping in Vegas, where I felt like I was the only one with no money. It was a little bit like walking through the hallways at my school. I kept my eyes firmly planted on the ground as I passed from store to store, and when I was forced to look at someone, my eyes shot daggers at them. *What are you looking at?* I wanted to say about a thousand times.

I approached buying something nice the same way

I approached buying anything: by getting it over with as quickly and painlessly as possible.

I walked into a shop that had some fancy-looking clothes and pawed through the racks at breakneck speed. There had to be something there.

That something turned out to be a pair of black, flowy silk pants and a shimmery silver top that only skimmed the waist of the pants, so that a strip of bare skin showed when I moved. The cloth felt like water on my skin when I tried it on. An hour later I had it hanging in my room while I showered and blew my hair dry, using a rolling brush to give it waves.

Chris knocked on my door at exactly seven. Just like him to be so punctual it was obnoxious. Instead of answering the door, I simply stepped out and let the door shut behind me. I didn't know why I was being so territorial about my space— it wasn't like he was begging to get into my room.

Maybe you're afraid you'll *beg* him.

No. Our relationship wasn't like that.

Yes, but not because you don't want it to be. Ignore, ignore, ignore.

Chris was wearing a navy blue suit that hugged his biceps and quads. His striped shirt underneath was unbuttoned at the top, and he had a silver chain draped around his neck. He smelled like money. His shoes shone like mirrors.

He grinned. "You actually followed orders for once."

I raised my eyebrows at him. "If I'd known they were orders, I wouldn't have."

"You look amazing, by the way."

"Whatever." I started to walk down the hall. He didn't follow me.

"What the hell is that, Nikki?" Exasperation.

I turned and looked down at myself, brushing off my shirt, my pants, looking for missed tags. "What?"

He pointed at the Chucks on my feet. "Really?"

"You can't see them," I said. Truth. The pants grazed the ground when I walked. For all anyone knew, I was wearing diamonds on my feet.

"Then how did I see them?"

Good point. "They're black, anyway," I said. "And they're comfortable. And I saved you some money. You should be happy I'm so low maintenance. Can we go now?"

He didn't respond. Didn't move. Just stood there with a cocky half grin on his cocky face.

"Piss off. I wear what I want," I said, my mood already soured. I took off for the elevator.

I wasn't too surprised to see him hurrying for the elevator before the door closed. A part of me loved that he was going to have to suck it up and go to dinner on my terms. I resisted the urge to push the close-door button at the last minute, but I didn't bother to push the open-door button, either. He stuck his arm out and let the door bounce on it before getting on.

"Sure you can live with my tacky style?" I asked sarcastically as the elevator sank to ground level.

"I wouldn't call that a style," he said. He checked himself out in the mirrored wall, straightening his collar. "And I wouldn't call you low maintenance, either."

"You look fine," I snapped. "You can stop admiring yourself."

"You don't want me admiring you; you don't want me admiring myself. What do you want?"

The doors opened and I stepped through. "Food. That's what I want. I'm starving."

He grabbed my wrist at the last second. I was on the hotel side of the elevator door and he was inside the elevator. It felt like the door would never be able to close, with the brilliant fog of color that burst from his hand onto my arm. "Hey," he said. "You really do look beautiful."

I felt myself blush, and then bit the inside of my cheek to stop it. Blushing was for idiots. Blushing was for saps like . . . *Jones?* . . . No, I would not think about Jones. Not here. Not tonight. Not at all.

"Let's eat before I starve to death right here on the hallway floor," I said.

We got to the restaurant and were seated right away.

The table reminded me a little too much of the table I'd sat at with Stefan the Gross. I shivered.

"You okay?" Chris asked, studying me over his menu.

"Just cold," I answered.

We ordered, and I gazed around the room, suddenly feeling very self-conscious about my shoe choice. I imagined everyone looking at them under the table and thinking I was some sort of trashy girl Chris had picked up on the Strip. I dared people to meet my eyes. Nobody did.

The waiter brought our drinks and a basket of bread. I immediately grabbed a hunk and buttered it, just to give myself something to do. Peyton was definitely the right sister to be in the Hollis mix. I was not cut out for the fancy life.

"So," Chris said, taking a sip of his drink and setting it back down on the napkin. He watched me butter my bread. "Tell me about this studio. Why are we here, exactly?"

"Luna's getaway driver," I said, the bite of bread I'd just taken crammed into one cheek.

"Right. The guy you ran away from at Pear Magic."

I nodded. "He's got some sort of connection to Angry Elephant, too."

"Angry Elephant?" There was laughter in his voice.

I stopped chewing. "Don't look at me like that. Yes, Angry Elephant."

"So you think Luna could be out here?"

I put my bread down on the bread plate. Did I? This

was a question I had not yet asked myself. Was I out here for Luna? Was I out here to bust my dad? Or, when I looked down deep, was I simply out here to feel closer to my mom? I tried to imagine Mom in this city, with its bright lights and noise and constant bustle of people. Mom liked a simpler life. She liked the beach. She liked painting my nails to match hers. She liked cooking and reading and . . . *and Bill Hollis. Don't forget that, Nikki. She liked Bill Hollis an awful lot.*

"Hello?" Chris snapped his fingers in front of my face. "Earth to Nikki. Everything okay?"

I swallowed, wiped my mouth with my napkin, my appetite suddenly gone. "Yeah, I'm fine," I mumbled.

He leaned over the table. "You're not." I didn't answer. My pulse crashed in my ears as the reality about my mom really sank in. All this time I had been looking at her as a victim. But the truth was, she was a hooker. She'd had an affair with Bill Hollis. She had lied to Dad, to me, to the whole world. And now Peyton and Dru were dead. Mom was the cause of it all. Not just Bill Hollis. I felt my hands curl into fists. "What am I missing here?" Chris asked.

I blinked away some of the anger and saw him sitting there, looking vulnerable and tired. In some ways, Chris was a victim of Mom, too. If she hadn't had the affair with Bill, Peyton wouldn't have existed. Chris wouldn't have been with me at Tesori Antico that night. He wouldn't have been punched and shot at and creamed by a Monte Carlo. It wasn't fair. He followed me everywhere. He put his life on the line for me. Not once or twice, but over and over. In a world full of people I couldn't trust, I knew I could rely on Chris Martinez. He believed in me. He challenged me. And I kept him in the dark.

Why? Why did I shut out the one person in this world who proved to me over and over again that I could trust him? It wasn't fair to let him keep putting himself in danger and giving no skin of my own.

So let him in, Nikki.

It was hard. So hard to let him in. I'd almost lost him once. What if I actually did lose him? Letting people in meant heartbreak. Trust led to disappointment. Love led to loss. Always.

Except maybe sometimes it doesn't.

"You're yellow," I said in a small voice.

He flicked a glance at his hands, then concentrated his stare at me again, confused. "What?"

I took a deep breath. "You're yellow. Like, sunshine-bright yellow. That means you're trustworthy. You believe in saving the world. You're yellow. But you're also a little bit gray. Or you were. That has been kind of going away for a while now. Gray means you were hiding something. But I'm pretty sure that something had to do with Leon and Javi and that mess with Leon's sister."

His lips parted. The air between us felt full and heavy. He had told me in a moment of vulnerability about the gang war that resulted in his sister's death and his brother's incarceration. Maybe he'd forgotten telling me. Maybe he'd hoped I would forget.

"This restaurant is swanky as fuck, so it's off-white swirling with lots of pastels. Like an opal." He looked around, his mouth still open. "Not the actual restaurant itself," I said. "The air. It's pearl air. And you leave yellow on the tablecloth and sometimes when you're really mad at me, I can see rusty starbursts try to break through the yellow on your forehead, but they can't, because you're *that* yellow."

"I don't—" he started, but his voice was soft, husky, and I didn't let him finish.

"I see colors." I gave an impatient head shake. "I mean, everyone sees colors, but I see them in places where other people don't." The waiter came with our food, and I sat back, pressed my lips together until he left. As soon as he'd gone, I pointed to my lobster. "The word 'lobster' is like a speckled blue and black. Blue because it lives in the ocean, and everything related to the ocean comes at me in blue. Except for the actual ocean. It's pink. I can't explain it. Black speckles because lobsters aren't too pretty. Um, 'three' is purple. The word 'restaurant' is the color of bread." My confession was coming fast now, my heartbeat speeding up. I suddenly wanted him to know everything, all at once. "Rebecca Moreno's license plate is bubble gum, pearl, blue, bronze, silver, foamy sea green. JSB946. It's easy for me to remember because I remember the colors."

"Oh my God," he said, his voice almost a whisper now. "Your hunches."

I nodded, tears filling my eyes. "Peyton had it too. That's how I found all those clues. She was leaving them for me in colors. They weren't hunches. They were just hard to explain without sounding crazy."

He sat back, laying his napkin on the table next to his untouched plate. I could practically see his mind spinning. "And that's why Peyton had your number in her phone." I nodded. "Why didn't you tell me?"

"I tried. Peyton had my school file, and I left it in her car for you. But you didn't read it like you were supposed to. And then there was the accident and you couldn't remember anything, and it just felt like a bad time." We locked eyes. "I've never told anyone except my dad and doctors. I've never trusted anyone to understand."

"Peyton was your sister. That woman in the trailer told us. I do remember that. But . . . help me out here, Nikki. What aren't you telling me?"

My lips felt dry. I licked them twice. I hated feeling vulnerable, and this had me feeling like I might as well be standing nude in the middle of the casino. At the same time, it felt exciting. To finally let someone in—something I'd battled my entire life.

"We're not just here to find Luna's getaway driver. I mean, we are. But the reason we came here is because my mom worked at the studio we're going to tomorrow. She knew him. She worked for Vanessa. She had Bill's baby. And . . . and my dad is lying to me. He says he never met any of them. But I've seen pictures. I've read articles. He knew them all, too. They were like a big, happy family. Celebrating some movie they were going to make together. And then it never happened. The movie went away. My mom ended up dead. And my dad was a suspect. And I'm pretty sure he . . . no. I *know* he lied to the cops."

"The file you had me pull," he said. "And you want to prove that he didn't do it."

I opened my mouth to answer, but no answer would come. I wasn't sure, actually. Was I out here to prove that my dad didn't do it? Or was I out to prove that he did?

I DIDN'T FINISH dinner. I was too revved up. Too emotional. Chris kept staring at me, like he couldn't process
what I had just told him. The waiter had arrived, asking if
everything was okay with the food. Chris picked up his fork
and began prodding at it guiltily, but I scooted away from
the table and asked for a box.

"I'm not feeling well," I said. "I'm sorry."

"Nikki," Chris called after me, but I didn't turn back. I
couldn't. I didn't do vulnerable, and while it didn't feel as
bad as I'd expected it to, it felt too intense to call it good,
either. It mostly felt like my whole life was at risk of blowing up now. Which was funny when I thought about it—my
life had a habit of blowing up on a regular basis, and I was

somehow surprised about it every single time.

When I got back to my room, I saw that Dad had called. He left a message, wondering where I was. I couldn't talk to him. I sent him a text.

I took a road trip with a friend. In Vegas. Be home tomorrow late.

He immediately texted back: Vegas??? We need to talk?

I sent a laughing emoji back at him, and then, thinking it over, followed that immediately with: Just for fun. No need to talk.

Translation: *Please, for the love of God, do not make me talk.* With all that had come out of my mouth this evening, I was afraid of what I might say if I was pressed to talk.

I felt guilty taking off my expensive clothes. I'd hardly worn them at all, and Chris didn't have the kind of money to just go throwing it away like that. I hung my things in the closet, thinking I would leave them there. Maybe the housekeeper and I were the same size. Maybe she could sell them. It didn't matter. I was much more tees and jeans than silk and shimmer. I unrolled a pair of yoga pants and a T-shirt from my backpack and put them on, then climbed into bed and thumbed the TV on.

I was forty minutes into a movie that I couldn't pay attention to when there was a knock at my door.

Chris.

I opened the door and he held out a Styrofoam box for me to take. My stomach growled. Now that my nerves had calmed, I actually was a little hungry.

"Thanks," I said. "Sorry I left. I just . . ." I didn't know how to finish. "Should we meet tomorrow at ten? Go over to Angry Elephant then?"

"Can I come in?" he asked.

I didn't want him to. Actually, I wanted to rewind. To go back to dinner and cram all the words back into my mouth. Then he could come in. *You can't avoid him forever, Nikki. You have to ride in a car with him for half a day tomorrow.* I stepped aside.

"You should put that in the fridge," he said, shrugging out of his jacket. He opened the closet and hung it next to my clothes. I pretended I didn't see him pause to touch the fabric of my shirt. It was cloth. Just cloth. But somehow the gesture felt intimate. "Can I sit?"

I nodded and stepped around him to put the box in the refrigerator. I turned off the TV and sat on the bed, pulling myself up so I was sitting cross-legged on the mattress. He sat in the easy chair next to the bed and leaned forward, his fingers pressed together between his knees, like he was getting ready to pray.

"You think your dad might be guilty," he said. Quietly, gently.

I nodded.

"How long have you thought this?"

"A few months. Before Tesori Antico."

"And you didn't tell the police because . . . ?"

"Because . . ." I took a breath. I didn't want to say it aloud. I didn't want to hurt Chris. I didn't want to get into an argument with him. I wanted this to be all mine again, and I regretted ever opening my mouth. But I'd been honest with him up to this point. No need to stop that now. "Because I don't trust cops. Or I didn't. I don't know. I guess I still don't. It's confusing. They botched my mom's case. They only interviewed my dad one time and then they let it go. My whole life I've been waiting for them to solve this crime, and nobody cares. I'm guessing you had to dig a little to even find the file."

He closed his eyes and dipped his head briefly—a nod. "The case is cold."

I let out a sarcastic grunt. "See, they don't care. They've given up on Mom's case, and the Hollises got away with no trouble and Luna is still out there. Nothing ever happens to the bad guys. That's why I can't trust the police."

"You trust me." His voice was like a cloud, enveloping me. He got up, moved to the side of the bed, knelt, and put his hand on my cheek. My hair fell over it, a curtain concealing his touch, concealing my deep, deep blush. The violet spread over me so thick I almost expected him to see it, too. "You trust me," he repeated. He'd gotten so close I could feel his breath mingle with mine.

"Because you're yellow," I whispered. A wide chasm of fear opened up beneath me. He was right. I trusted him, when I never trusted anyone. Well, anyone except my dad, and look where that got me. Trust was bullshit. Trust could get a person killed. I pushed his hand away to break the connection before it melted me completely. I swallowed, trying to get my bearings. "And I wouldn't say I trust you so much as I'm stuck with you."

He chuckled softly and backed away, settling in the chair again. But it was an ugly chuckle. A scornful one. Bitter. "You're something else, you know that?"

"So I've been told."

"You shouldn't shut down on me like this."

I forced myself to meet his gaze. "I'm not shutting down. If you don't like what I'm saying, you can go. Actually, you should probably go anyway. I need to get some sleep."

He seemed to hesitate for a long time, and then finally got up. I sat still as stone while he went to the closet and pulled his coat off the hanger. "Right. I thought we made a connection tonight, but I forgot who I was dealing with."

"Yep," I said. A tear came out of nowhere and soaked into the bedspread.

He dropped his jacket onto the suitcase rack. "I actually had another reason for coming over here tonight."

I gave a sharp bark of a laugh. "You're going to have to

find another girl for that, Detective. I'm not into you." Purple fizzled and popped in my peripheral vision, arguing with me, then faded away on a sad brown mist.

"No. Nikki." He paused. I saw him place his hands on his hips, tipping his head down. I knew this to be his aggravated pose. A part of me was pleased as hell that I'd brought him to that pose. Another part was sad and scared and wanted to say I was sorry. "I came to tell you I remembered something. Maybe something very important."

My head whipped up. "What?"

"When you said Leon's name tonight at dinner. And Javi's. It . . . I don't know, it just connected. Rebecca Moreno is Leon's sister."

"Sister? *The* sister? The one things 'got complicated' with?"

He nodded. "I'm not proud of that, but yes. Heriberto was Leon's . . . I don't know what you'd call him . . . lackey? Right-hand man?"

"And he's selling for the gang?" I said.

"Yeah. Probably. Only he's not doing the selling. Too much of a chickenshit. He's got the kids doing it. Those boys we saw at the community center. They aren't buying the drugs for themselves. They're selling them and bringing the money to Heriberto. He gives them more and off they go. Including Rebecca's son, Sam."

"That's disgusting."

He nodded. "Yeah, well, gangs aren't really known for how kind and upstanding they are."

"And how do you figure in all of this?" I had forgotten all about being mad at Chris. I was sitting on my knees, wishing I hadn't worked so hard on chasing him out. "You're saying Heriberto wants you dead? Why? Revenge for what your brother did to Leon? Why now, after all this time?"

He frowned, like it was painful to remember. "That, I don't know. I only know that it was most likely Leon's boys—now Heriberto's—who ran me down."

"So why don't you just bust the dude?" I asked. "He's obviously dealing, and right there at the community center. And to kids. You're a cop. Get some video on your phone and take him down."

He shook his head. "It's not that easy."

"Of course it is!"

"No, it's not. I don't know what I was in the middle of doing, Nikki. And until I figure it out, this stays open. I leave Heriberto alone."

I rolled my eyes and threw my hands up in the air. "See? This is it. Right here. This is why I don't trust cops. You have the bad guy. You know who he is and where he lives—or at least where he's hanging out—you know he wants you dead, and yet you let him stay out there to fuck up more lives. Maybe you're not so yellow after all, Detective." As if in response to my words, the gray edging that always outlined him grew into more of a shadow.

His lips pulled into a straight line. His shoulders slumped and his stomach hollowed out, as if I'd delivered a physical blow. "I guess you're right," he said. "See you at ten."

He didn't even wait for me to respond. Just left, letting the door fall shut behind him.

With him gone, I got up and paced the room a few times. Why? Why was I so mean to him? Why did I shit on everyone I could potentially lo—no, I wouldn't even think the word. The truth was, he was letting a drug dealer sell to kids and was doing nothing about it. To be sworn to fight crime and turning a blind eye to it . . . in my eyes, that wasn't much better than being the dealer himself.

I went into the bathroom and got a drink, trying to calm myself so I could eat.

I was halfway to the refrigerator when I heard footsteps approach my door and stop, the shadow of feet visible in the crack between the door and the floor. My eyes landed on his jacket, still lying over the luggage rack. I marched over to it, snatched it up, and took it to the door.

"Here, your stupid j—"

But when I opened the door, there was no one there. I had heard footsteps. I hadn't been imagining that. There had been someone outside my room. I was sure of it.

Distantly, from down the hall, I heard the ding of the elevator arriving. Whoever had been there was leaving.

Tossing Chris's jacket on the floor, I raced down the hall to see who was getting on the elevator. But I was too late. The door slid closed just as I rounded the corner. It was just me and the humming, buzzing soda and ice machines.

My hands and feet went cold. Maybe it was nothing. Maybe it was someone mistaking my room for theirs.

Or maybe it was Luna.

The elevator was descending; I could see the numbers ticking down. I ran to the stairs and flew down them, my bare feet making slapping sounds on the concrete floors. I was instantly sucking wind, but I couldn't let the elevator outpace me. I pushed myself to run harder, faster.

When I got to the ground floor, I slammed through the stairwell door and sprinted for the bank of elevators, nearly colliding with a kissing couple along the way.

But when the elevator door slowly opened, I stopped cold, my feet nearly sliding out from under me. I reached back and caught myself with one hand on the wall, and then backed up and pressed myself into a room doorway, making myself as thin as I could get, so I wouldn't be seen. I poked my head around the corner and watched, my legs weakened by what I saw.

The white-blond man stepped off the elevator and slowly, deliberately, stalked out of the hotel.

19

THINGS WERE PRETTY strained between Chris and me on the way to Angry Elephant. He sipped on his coffee petulantly, and I silently seethed that he hadn't brought me one. Even though we both knew I wouldn't drink it. Couldn't, after all this time of rejecting his coffees. It was my thing.

Most of our sentences were logistics-related. *Do you know where you're going? I've got the GPS programmed. Watch out for that car. Do you see that pothole? Do you mind if I turn on the radio? Nope. Do whatever you want.*

It was so uncomfortable, the giant cinnamon roll I'd gotten from room service balled up into an angry wad in my stomach.

I didn't tell Chris about seeing the white-blond man back at the Luxor. I didn't, mostly because I was afraid of where my mind would take me if I began to consider what might have happened if he'd still been standing there when I foolishly threw open the door, thinking it was Chris looking for his jacket. Plus, I didn't really get the best look at him. He could have been any number of blond men, and the only reason I saw him as *the* blond man was because he was on my mind. After all, that was part of why I was here in the first place, wasn't it? To find out who he was and what he had to do with my parents.

I yawned. I hadn't slept well the night before. I'd been too busy tossing and turning, thinking about Heriberto and Leon and Rebecca and how Chris fit into all this. Why he didn't arrest Heriberto and be done with it. At some point just shy of dawn, it occurred to me.

Just a few minutes before reaching our destination, the thought got the better of me and I couldn't keep from saying it any longer. "It's because you were in love with her, isn't it?" I asked.

Chris, who had been staring out the passenger window, turned. "What? Who?"

"Rebecca Moreno. You haven't busted Heriberto because you were in love with her and you're afraid that if Heriberto goes down, so will Sam." He made a *pssh* noise and went back to staring out the window. "Were you selling, too?"

The question seemed ludicrous, even to me, but it had to be asked. "Were you helping? Was the hit-and-run maybe just a drug deal gone bad?"

"Of course not," he said, dropping his empty cup into the cup holder in the center console. The scent of coffee wafted up to my nose and made me salivate. I needed a cigarette, bad. "I wasn't selling anything. And I was never in love with her, Nikki."

"You were just, what? Getting revenge?"

"At first, yeah. It was about the fact that she was Leon's sister. But after a little while, it just didn't feel right to use her like that. We were more like . . ."

"Friends with bennies. Charming." Although, after how I'd treated my relationship with Jones, I supposed I couldn't get too uppity about it.

"Big sister, little brother," he corrected. "She worried about me. She knew the things the gang was trying to have done to me. She tipped me off, over and over again, and I managed to stay alive somehow, and I started to realize how stupid it all was. People dying all the time, and what for? She got me out of that world, Nikki. She is the reason I'm a cop today. I haven't even talked to her since I moved out of the neighborhood. But I've seen her around. I knew about Sam. I still cared, and sometimes the best way to care about somebody is not busting them when you really want to bust someone bigger than them."

"So that's what you were doing? Waiting to bust the big guy? And it never occurred to you that the big guy could also be the one who ran you over?" The Angry Elephant logo appeared on my right—orange, lunch-meat pink—and I pulled into the lot.

"I think I was buying," he said as I parked the car.

"You were what?"

"I think I was buying. I have little pieces of memories, and in them, I'm buying. From Sam. From some other boys."

I shook my head. "No way. I don't believe it. It's wrong. It's a wrong memory."

He opened his door and got out. "You don't have to believe it for it to be true." I got out, too, and he eyed me over the roof of the car. "I wasn't taking them, Nikki. Or selling them. I was putting them somewhere. I just can't remember where. Or why."

ASIDE FROM BEING orange and meaty pink everywhere I looked, Angry Elephant was pretty disappointing. Nothing like the studios in Hollywood. Not even like Pear Magic. It was a crackerbox of a building, tucked back in a neighborhood with no personality. Nothing at all that said movies.

I'd grabbed a file folder from the backseat. Inside were the clippings from Dad's closet, which I had taken before leaving for Vegas, along with photos of Luna. We went inside, where two women sat, side by side, behind a tiny desk. They were gazing at a computer screen and laughing, like they were watching something funny online. They both looked up when we walked in.

"Hi," one of them said. "Can I help you?"

I had rehearsed what I was going to say about a billion times between Brentwood and here, and also in my hotel room last night and this morning. Still, my mind went blank for a second. The woman shifted her gaze from me to Chris, her smile fading a little.

Chris cleared his throat. He dipped into his back pocket and pulled out his wallet, then opened it and showed it to the women.

"I'm Detective Chris Martinez. I'm wondering if I can ask you a few questions."

One of the ladies placed her hand on her chest, a worried look overtaking her. "Oh, I don't know if we should—"

Chris held out a hand to silence her. "Nobody's in trouble," he said. "We're just trying to find someone. Have you heard of Luna Fairchild?"

The two women looked at each other questioningly, and then shook their heads in unison.

"What about Jetta? Is Jetta here?" I asked, finally finding my voice.

"Jetta?" one of the ladies repeated. The nameplate on the desk read *Barb Jones*.

"I was told Jetta was working here."

"Never heard of anyone named Jetta," the other woman said. She had scooted her chair back over behind a second desk. The nameplate on that one read *Deb Thurston*. She tapped a few keys on her keyboard, then shook her head again. "No, there's no record of a Jetta ever working here."

This time Chris and I exchanged glances. Blue had been wrong. "Is the owner here, by any chance?" Chris asked.

Barb's eyes lit up. Finally a question she could answer. "Mr. Weers? No, I'm afraid he's out for the day. On location."

On location, meaning spying on me at the Luxor? I wanted to ask. Instead, I opened my file and pulled out the article and pointed to the photo. "This is him, though, right?"

Barb leaned over the photo, her brow creased as she studied it. She shook her head as she gently took it from me and passed it to Deb. "No, that's not him. Mr. Weers is completely bald. And much shorter than this man."

Strike two.

"But I have seen that guy before," Deb said. My ears perked up. "He came in several months ago trying to get a job for a girl. Said he was an agent."

An agent? The white-blond man was an agent, too? I was beginning to understand that he was a chameleon, able to do anything as long as it benefited him.

Deb had passed the photo back to Barb, who held it under her lamp to study it again. "Oh, yes, now that you say that. She was the girl with those creepy eyes."

I practically lunged over the desk at her. "Creepy how?"

Deb and Barb looked at each other for silent confirmation again, and then Barb wiggled her fingers in front of her face and said, "I don't know, they seemed really . . . dull. Like serial-killer flat, if that makes sense. We both noticed it."

Or like a reptile, I thought. I dug through the file and came out with a photo of Luna, taken from one of the tabloid pages. She was quite a bit younger, but it was the best I could find. I handed it to Barb. "Was this the girl?"

"No," she said right away. "I mean, she looks kind of like her in the face, but the girl had long black hair. Jet-black." She pantomimed long hair flowing. "We joked that it was so long it had to be a wig." A wig. Of course. Jet-black hair. Jetta. It made sense now. The new girl at Hollywood Dreams suddenly leaving, the blond man looking for a place for a girl with a jet-black wig.

"Oh, it was way too shiny to be real hair," Deb said. She held up her hand. "Not that there's anything wrong with that. We see all types here."

"So what happened to the girl?" Chris asked.

"We didn't have anything for her," Deb said. "We're pretty small. We thought it was odd that he would come all the way from California to try and find something with us here. We moved out of California long ago. No more ties there."

Barb was still gazing at the photo from the clipped

article about the movie. She tapped it. "I do remember this, though. It was right before we relocated. Do you remember, Deborah?"

Deb scooted her chair close to Barb again and stared at the photo over her shoulder. Now that they had gossip to spread, they seemed much more relaxed. "Oh, yes, of course. That was a sad, sad deal, huh."

Barb handed the article back to me. "That movie was supposed to be the big movie of the year. The director they chose—that Carrie Kill—was one of ours. She was so excited about it."

"What happened to it?" I asked, staring at the photo as if I didn't know it by heart. As if I didn't know the people in it. "I couldn't find it anywhere."

"Didn't ever happen," Barb said. "They were about halfway through filming and there was an accident. A big fire. Somehow a spotlight fell onto some props and *whoosh.*" She bloomed an invisible fire with her hands. I saw it in the usual reds and oranges I associated with the word *fire.* "That producer was so angry, he pulled the whole project. And eventually we left California altogether."

Deb was shaking her head sadly. "He had so many other movies to make, but it was really the end for poor Carrie. She died a couple years later, if I'm not mistaken. *Eleven* would have been her only film."

My heart thumped hearing it from someone else. *No, she didn't die,* I wanted to snap. *She was murdered.*

"*Eleven?*" Chris asked.

"Wasn't that what it was called, Barb? It was a number, anyway."

Barb snapped her fingers. "Yes, that was it. Eleven on his jersey. Ten people dead. Will anyone catch him before he kills number eleven?" She said the last in a deep voice meant to sound like a commercial voice-over. "Not my kind of movie." The phone rang and she jumped to answer it.

Deb stood and smoothed out her slacks. "Is there anything else, Detective?"

"No," Chris said. "I think that was all."

She stuck out her hand; Chris shook it. "Sorry we couldn't be more help."

But she had no idea how much help she'd actually been.

20

IT WAS A long four and a half hours home. We weren't really speaking anymore. There was just too much to talk about. Too many revelations. Too many secrets. Too much confusion. Talk seemed dangerous.

I couldn't tell if we trusted each other more now, or less. I couldn't tell if I was relieved to have someone know about the synesthesia or if I hated it. My gut told me I hated it. I just maybe didn't so much hate that it was him.

God, it was so confusing. Why was he so damned confusing?

Not to mention there was the whole drug thing. I believed with every fiber of my being that he was not taking or selling them. I knew he had a plan, because Chris Martinez always had a plan, and his plans were always For the Greater Good. My plans were usually to save my own ass.

Mostly, I spent the time under my hoodie, working out what might have been his reason for buying drugs from those kids. And the rest of the time was spent rehashing what Barb and Deb had said, and how my mind had lit up like crazy every time they said one word: *Eleven*.

A tomato-colored word, juicy and smooth and warm from the sun. Tomato, tomato, tomato.

I drove the last hour, and Chris slept. Or at least he pretended to sleep. He didn't look particularly comfortable or restful. Maybe he, too, was working things out in his head. I dropped him off at the station, and we went our separate ways.

I couldn't wait to get home.

"JESUS, YOU HAD me worried," were the very first words out of Dad's mouth when I walked into the house. He came eagerly downstairs as soon as he heard the door open. He was carrying an armload of laundry, but dropped it on the landing when he saw me.

"Sorry," I said.

He wrapped me in a hug, and then held me out at arm's distance. "What in the hell were you thinking? What friend? What was in Vegas? You're eighteen, for Christ's sake."

"Almost nineteen," I muttered, breaking away from him and taking my backpack upstairs. "And just a friend. It was a spontaneous thing."

"Nikki." Sharp. I turned. The backpack bounced softly against my leg. "I know you. Spontaneous and Nikki do not go together. Not without trouble. What was going on in Vegas? Who were you with?"

"Fun, Dad. Fun was going on in Vegas. Maybe you wouldn't recognize it, since you seem to have dedicated your whole life to swearing it off." I knew I was pushing it, but after everything I'd learned, I was in no place to play nice with Dad. Not anymore.

He pushed his glasses up on his nose. He looked stunned.

"I'm sorry," I said. "But I'm young and I want to have a good time. And obviously I can't have any fun here without having to look over my shoulder all the time. So I went to Vegas with my friend and we had one night of fun and now I'm back. And everyone is safe and everything is fine." That last part was a bit of a stretch. Everything was so far away from fine I couldn't even recognize fine anymore.

"And was this friend that guy Chris you were hanging out with before?"

I felt my face burn. "We stayed in separate hotel rooms, if that's what you're asking. Dad, we're just friends. No sex, I promise." Truth. That seemed like a barrier Chris and I would never, ever cross. "We wouldn't even think about that. Not with each other." *Lie, Nikki. You know that's such a fucking lie.*

"I still don't like it," Dad said. But I could feel Concerned Dad retreating, to be replaced by the usual—Friend Dad. The dad who didn't really want to be a dad. "Next time, just tell me beforehand, okay?"

"Sure," I said. It was impossible for me to keep the sourness out of my voice these days, especially when it came to being honest and my dad. I continued up the stairs, but he stopped me.

"You want me to wash your clothes?"

The backpack brushed my leg again. I knew what was inside—a file folder filled with stolen newspaper articles. He would never understand why I had those.

"No, thanks. I'll take care of things."

IT SEEMED LIKE the man would never give me space now that I'd come back from an unapproved mini vacation. Everywhere I turned, he was lurking just behind, looking at me over his glasses, passing me in the hallway, asking me through the bathroom door if I wanted a snack. He did it under the guise of "cleaning house," but it felt like more than that to me.

It felt like surveillance.

Did he already know? Had he seen that the articles were

gone? How could he? What reason would he possibly have for noticing they were missing? Had Angry Elephant called him, told him there was a couple snooping around the studio, asking questions about *Eleven*?

I tried to keep myself busy to take my mind off it. I popped a bag of popcorn and parked myself on the couch and watched TV, every single show reminding me somehow of Chris.

That actor looks like Chris, only with blue eyes.

That police station doesn't look anything like Chris's station.

That girl is eating her fries in clusters of three. Just like Chris does.

It was disgusting, and the carpet began to puff up in brick-brown shame. I was such a hopeless freak. *Introducing new Crush Nikki!* A Confused Asshole Doll with Trust Issues. *Understanding and kindness not included.*

After what seemed like forever, Dad finally disappeared into his bedroom, and a few minutes later, I heard the shower turn on. I bolted from the couch to his office.

Tomato, tomato, tomato.

Eleven.

The number that never was.

I lowered myself to the floor and scooted on my belly under Dad's desk until I could reach the black box. A part of me was surprised it was still there. Things had a way of disappearing—or dying—the minute I got a handle on them. I spun the dial.

Problem.

Eleven was one number. A tomatoey, juicy, delicious number, but still. One number.

Maybe if I split it up. Brown, brown. 1-1. Nope, I still needed a third number. I tried a third 1. The box didn't open. Damn it. I put a zero in front of the eleven. Still nothing.

I heard the pipe rattle of Dad turning the shower off. Shit. Now I had to really move. *Think, Nikki, think.* Honeydew nagged at the back of my mind.

Ten. Of course. Ten. The player had murdered ten, but was working on eleven. What if the number was a combination of those two?

I tried 1-0-1. Still the damn box wouldn't budge.

1-1-0. Nothing.

I spun the dial three times, thinking hard to remember what Barb had said about the movie. Eleven on his jersey. Ten people dead. Trying to catch him before he makes it eleven.

I dialed 11, spun to 10, and then back to 11.

It opened.

At first I just lay there staring in stunned silence. Then I almost cried out, I was so excited, but I could hear Dad's footsteps upstairs as he dried off and got dressed. No time for celebration.

I reached into the box and pulled out . . . papers. No, not papers. Envelopes. A whole stack of them. I held up the first one. It was to my mother. From B. Carter.

Letters? Why would Dad lock up letters? Why would he even keep them in the first place?

I started to pull the letter out of the envelope but heard Dad's footsteps hit the stairs.

"Nikki?" he called.

Jesus. Leave for one night and you become a prisoner. I stuffed the partially opened letter back into its envelope, shut the box and spun the dial to lock it again, gathered all the envelopes together, and stood. I had barely gotten back on my feet when Dad poked his head in the doorway. I was holding the letters behind my back.

"What are you doing in here?" he asked.

I smiled, trying to come off as nonchalant—my least believable act. "Looking for a pen," I said.

"A pen," he repeated, looking unconvinced. "For . . . ?"

"Does it matter?" I rolled my eyes. My fingers shook on the envelopes. "God. Okay, I was thinking about filling out some job applications. I didn't want to tell you because you get all up in my business about it." Fortunately, Dad was old-school enough to believe that filling out job applications was something you still did with a pen and paper.

"I'll believe it when I see it," he muttered. But he moved toward the desk anyway. I sidestepped out of his way, and while he was busy opening and fumbling around in drawers, I slipped the letters into my waistband, then pulled my shirt over them to conceal them. Finally, he handed me a pen. I smiled thinly.

"Thanks. Maybe a little faith in me next time?"

"I always have faith in you," he said. "It's you who doesn't have faith in you."

Ouch. That was a little too close to home.

Not true, I thought. *It's you I don't have faith in anymore, Dad.* That one was even closer.

I backed out of the room and hurried upstairs. I was halfway up when Dad called my name. I froze, my hand involuntarily going to the back of my shirt to make sure the letters weren't peeking out. They weren't; he was standing at the bottom of the stairs, holding the remote and the half-empty bowl of popcorn. "I just cleaned," he said. "You could at least pick up after yourself."

"Sorry," I said, relieved. "I forgot."

He grumbled and turned back to the living room. I heard the TV snap off as I hustled my way to my room, locked the door, and flopped belly-first down on my bed.

I had some reading to do.

Dear Carrie,

I was both happy and sad to hear from you this weekend. Happy because it's been too long and I missed you. Sad because of what your letter told me. He has sucked you back in. I would say I don't know how, but I guess that would be wrong. I do know how. He is who he is. Nobody says no to him. Well, nobody says no to him without paying for it, anyway.

Maybe there is a way for you to get out. It can't be as bleak as it seems.

Come to Oildale. I have found a wonderful church home. You could live with me. You and Milo and little

Nikki. We could be a family. I know it's not impossible to get out, because I did it, Carrie.

Think about it. Please?

B

I had opened all the letters and ordered them according to their postmarks. There had been many of them, over a period of about six months. I wasn't able to understand everything they talked about—it would have been really helpful if I'd had Mom's letters to Brandi, too—but I was able to piece together a few things.

Mom had reached out to Brandi. She'd confided in her about going back to Hollywood Dreams. She'd felt trapped. Brandi had offered her a way out, but it wasn't until she was pregnant and had nowhere else to go that she finally took Brandi up on her offer.

What Bill Hollis had over Mom was a bit of a mystery. But by reading Brandi's letters, it became clearer what Mom had done.

Dear Carrie,

Yes, I heard about the fire. I had no idea, honey. I'm so sorry. Accidents happen, and you can't take all the blame for that. It wasn't your fault. You didn't drop the spotlight. You didn't leave the props lying around.

*It is a shame—although not at all surprising—that he
is using the accident as a way to get you back into the
business.*

*You don't have to do this. You have Milo and little
Nikki to think of. What can he really do to you if you just
refuse? Surely you're not worried about him ruining your
film career. With the failure of* Eleven, *it seems that it's
already been ruined. I hate to say that, but I'm afraid you
need truth right now. And the truth is, that man isn't
your key to salvation.*

You know who is.

Come see me.

B

I read them all. Every sentence begging Mom to come
to Oildale. Begging Mom to get out of Hollywood Dreams.
Begging Mom to get away from Bill Hollis before she ended
up broken or dead.

Begging Mom to think—just, please, think—about Milo
and Nikki. She was supposed to love us. She was getting
seduced by Hollis power. She was too scared to see her way
out. Brandi offered her a way out, over and over and over
again.

And she chose to stay.

Why?

I found a letter dated about four months before Peyton's birthday.

Dear Carrie,

Thank you for meeting me for lunch. It was so great to see you! Little Dru absolutely loves the race car you brought him.

I paused, touching the word *Dru*. Imagining him as a two-year-old sitting on my mother's lap—another link between us—chewing on his fingers. Imagining him sitting on the floor of Brandi's trailer, pushing Hot Wheels around the floor, making zooming noises. If he had been allowed to stay with Brandi, what would have been different? Would we have still crossed paths? Would there have been something more there?

I read on.

I hate to see you cry, honey. You know that. It tears me up inside. I wish you could see how strong and beautiful and perfect you are. I wish you could see that God's plan for you does not include Bill Hollis. I tried to tell you when you argued that what you're doing isn't hooking—that what you're doing is only seeing him— that it was a bad idea. I know firsthand what happens when Bill Hollis decides you're one of his special ones. A lot of us know, Carrie. I'm just the only one who had the strength to keep my baby.

I understand you wanting this pregnancy to be a secret. I really do. Why jeopardize things with Milo when he's the one you actually love? And I think you're right—he wouldn't understand that you can't terminate. But I understand. I obviously couldn't do it either, no matter who fathered my Dru. And I'm so glad I didn't. Dru is the light of my life.

Come to Oildale. Let me help you. Let me raise this baby. You can go back to Milo and Nikki. You will be able to see your baby as often as you like, and I will have the side benefit of getting to see you. It's a win-win. I promise to treat the baby like my own until you're able to make a break from Bill Hollis. We can worry about what to tell Milo then.

I know you don't feel ready to make a decision yet, but like I said at lunch, you're showing. Pretty soon both Milo and Bill will know that you're pregnant, and I'm afraid that would be very bad for you. You need to decide right away.

The offer always stands.

B

The letters stopped then, for about six months. When Brandi commenced writing again, she was writing to a shattered version of my mom. Stroking her from miles away, telling her everything would be okay, telling her that she did the right thing for her beautiful daughter, Peyton, even if it didn't seem like it just now.

Warning her to stay strong and stay far away from Bill Hollis.

Surely Mom had learned her lesson. Surely she understood that messing with Bill Hollis was something that could ruin your life. She'd had to give up a child, for God's sake. She knew that he was dangerous.

The letters continued. Peyton had smiled for the first time. She was saying *mama*. She crawled. She walked. She loved the birthday gifts Mom sent. And then a curious one.

> Dear Carrie,
>
> I can't believe the news. He married Vanessa? Who does that? She is so crazy, I can't believe even he would fall for it. Does he know about the little girl she left behind with her ex-husband? Probably not. God help that child. If it isn't demon possessed, I would be shocked.

I would have laughed if it hadn't been so prophetic. Luna wasn't demon possessed, but she was about as close as someone could be.

The letter went on to talk about Peyton and referenced

an included photo that I didn't see in the envelope. Mom must have taken it out and kept it somewhere. Hidden it from Dad. Only Dad had all these letters, so nothing was hidden. Or maybe he didn't find them until after she died. Either way, the question remained: Why did he keep them?

The last letter in the pile wasn't from Brandi. And it wasn't addressed to Mom, either. It had come to Dad. And had no return address.

But as soon as I pulled it out of the envelope, the slanted words lit up, not in their usual colors, but in a sunset orange with brown spots. A color memory. Africa. Kenya, to be specific. I went cold as I was taken back to the day in Bill Hollis's office, when I found his hollow globe, a split across Kenya, stuffed with handwritten star ratings of his conquests. Notes. And invoices for abortions.

I would recognize Bill Hollis's handwriting anywhere.

And he had written to Dad, a month before Brandi's first letter to Mom.

Dear Mr. Kill,

I have received your message regarding your inability to pay for the damages you have caused my studio. You are correct that insurance will cover much of the accident. But insurance won't cover it all. Your actions have cost more than a set and props. Your actions—no,

your negligence has cost me the movie of a lifetime.
It is an immeasurable loss. Your refusal to pay is
unacceptable.

Let me be clear about one thing. You were only
involved in the project at all because your wife insisted on
it. If I wanted her, I'd have to use your subpar services,
too. Had I known you were going to send my movie
quite literally up in smoke, I would have gotten another
director.

You should be very careful what enemies you make in
this town, Mr. Kill. I do not lose. Remember, you are not
the only one indebted to me. I will get my money from
you, or from your wife, one way or another. I have other
jobs for her. Jobs she performed for me long before you
came along. She is quite good at what she does. Although
I doubt very much you would want to see her in action.

My lawyer will be in touch with you regarding a
payment plan.

The letter was finished with a scribble that was mostly illegible but came at me in glittery purple. The Hollis name.

I read the letter a second time, and then a third, and then let it fall to the bed. The orange and brown, the sparkly lilac pulsed up at me, taunting me. All these years, I'd thought my life was relatively normal, save for this one thing. My mom's murder. A huge thing, yes, but in my mind it had always been random. It had always been the bad luck of the Kill family.

But now I was beginning to grasp the truth: that Mom was caught up in something bigger than she'd ever imagined. That she wanted out but felt trapped. That she was paying for someone else's mistake.

That someone else was my father.

Angrily, I brushed the letters off the bed. They fluttered to the floor, appearing no more threatening than any other piece of paper. They turned the carpet around them an inky, rusty boil of betrayal and outrage. It smoldered, making me feel physically ill. I could hear my dad puttering around downstairs, opening and closing the refrigerator, scooting chairs around, whistling. As if his life had never been anything but perfect.

I flopped back onto my pillow, trying to get the letters out of my range of vision, and stared at the ceiling. My eyes burned and watered, not with sadness or disappointment, but with anger.

I understood what had happened now.

My father found out about my mom's past. He found out she was sleeping with Bill Hollis. He found out she was pregnant, and that she had hidden the pregnancy from him and given the baby to Brandi. He found out everything. He burned down the movie set to ruin her. Only that didn't work.

And now she was gone and he was the only one who knew everything. The *only* one. Not even Bill Hollis knew everything. Not at the time she was killed.

The police had a statement that I had gone to my friend's house and he and Mom were going out on a date night.

Dad had lied about where he'd been when my mother was murdered. Why? And why would he pretend to know nothing about Bill Hollis when they actually had a lengthy history? Why wouldn't he point the police to the Hollises, who had threatened them both?

Maybe because he knew Bill Hollis wasn't the one who did it. Maybe because he knew how guilty he looked, and pretending to be in the dark about her affair was the one thing he hoped would keep the police from discovering the missing motive that they needed to bring charges.

You don't have anything.

Maybe he really had killed my mother.

And he'd kept the evidence like a sick, murdering freak.

I KNEW IT was getting late, and Chris and I had spent entirely too much time together over the past two days, and things were weird between us now, but I was going crazy, pacing my room and scouring the letters over and over, all the while becoming more and more furious. It was the deepest betrayal I could think of—murdering your wife, keeping it from your daughter, pretending like you loved the woman all this time. I wanted him out of my life. I wanted him locked up forever. I wanted him gone. Mom never got a chance to live her life; why should he?

It felt like someone was sitting on my chest. As far as I was concerned, I was an orphan now. My entire life a lie. I had nobody.

I needed to talk to Chris.

Can I come over?

Why?

I need to talk.

You had 2 days to talk. What's different now?

I'm going to take that as a yes.

I drove to Chris's at record speed, only remotely worrying that I might get pulled over. A part of me would welcome the trouble. I would welcome the chance to have a normal person's problems for even just five minutes.

I parked at the curb in front of his apartment building and was surprised to see him sitting on the stairs. He was bare chested, wearing only a pair of basketball shorts and sneakers. I gritted my teeth together to distract myself from noticing. If there were ever a pointless thing for me to notice, Chris Martinez's bare chest would be it.

He saw me coming and opened the door, pushing with the same half scrunch to one side, as if it still hurt. It probably did. That was the side that had met the impact of the Monte Carlo dead on. It had been pretty demolished. He would likely feel phantom pains there for a long time, if not forever.

"Where's the fire?" he asked, and at first I stopped short, thinking he was trying—and failing horribly—to be funny. But the look on his face reminded me that he hadn't seen the letters. He knew nothing about what had happened over the past two hours of my life.

"I found letters," I said. "Bad letters." I shocked myself at how easily and quickly the truth came out of me.

"Let's go for a walk," he said. "I'm kind of stiff from all that time in the car. I need some exercise." Indeed, a trace of his limp had come back.

I had to force myself not to churn up the sidewalk, to slow down and wait for him. I was angry, not in a race.

"So you found letters," he said. He stopped, stooped to pick up a fallen twig, and kept walking, rolling it between his fingers. "I have no idea what that means. What kind of letters?"

"They were letters to my mom from Brandi Carter. And a letter to my dad from Bill Hollis. My dad started the fire that burned down the set at Angry Elephant, Chris. And he refused to pay."

His eyes widened slightly, but he still kept them firmly planted on the twig as we walked. We rounded a corner, headed toward a church.

"Okay?" he said. "And?"

I planted myself in the center of the sidewalk. He nearly plowed into me. "And? Are you serious? My mother is dead, Chris. What is it you don't understand about that? She is *dead*. She's never coming back. Nobody cares about it but me. Nobody ever has."

"I care."

"You do not." I started walking again. He was a few steps behind me.

"I do care, Nikki. But I have other things to think about, too. Your mom is dead, yes. But someone tried to kill me a few months ago. Today's bad guy takes precedence over the bad guy from ten years ago."

I whirled around and started to walk backward. "Oh, well, because an old rival gang member was trying to kill you for taking the drugs away from his dealers, that should totally take precedence over the fact that I think I'm currently living with a potential killer. Nice."

He laughed incredulously. "Okay, well, because you think your dad might have had something to do with your mom's death—which you have absolutely no proof of, by the way—and despite the fact that he's never so much as raised his voice to you, that should totally take precedence over the very real car that hit me. Nice." He matched my glare.

I growled and turned back. Now I was churning up the sidewalk, and not caring if he was able to keep up with me.

"You know, life isn't always about you all the time, Nikki. We were partners once."

I raised my eyebrows, surprised. He nodded.

"Yeah, I remember. We were partners when it was all about looking for your bad guy. But when it comes to mine, we're not partners. It's still all about you. It's always all about you."

"Oh, really?" I said. "So when I was sitting at the community center all damn day looking for Heriberto, that was about me? Or when I was getting plate numbers and Googling Heriberto and busting my brain to try to remember anything that might help you, that was about me?"

"You help me when it's convenient for you. But you don't even consider what might be convenient for me. Maybe I don't have time to deal with your drama."

"Drama?" I said, noticing my voice ratcheting up several notches. "So almost being killed repeatedly is drama now?"

"You're not the only one defending your life," he spat.

We'd turned another corner and found ourselves skirting the church's playground. I tromped through the pea gravel and sat on a swing. It made a rusty creaking noise. Chris stood on the perimeter. I threw up my arms. "So what do you want me to do? Help you find the drugs you stashed? Why would I do that?"

"I don't know, maybe because it would help solve my case?"

"And what about mine?"

He pointed at me. "See, there you go again. *Your* case. My case. Yours. Mine. Not ours. So what are we doing here if we're not helping each other out?"

I had no answer for that. Irritation pulsed through me. I'd been hoping to get some support here, not accusations that I was somehow responsible for ruining our so-called partnership that he, up until this point, couldn't even remember existed.

"I don't know," I said softly. There was a long pause between us, during which the swing I was sitting on continued to screech.

"I know why I was stashing the drugs," he said. "I was trying to flush Heriberto out. He doesn't like when someone messes with his power. Or his money. He has to be the big dog. And someone was buying up all his inventory—a bigger dog. I guess I flushed him out."

"Yeah, I guess you did."

There was more silence between us. I began to swing a little harder so that my feet went to tiptoes every time the swing went back. Chris never left his station at the edge of the playground, though he did move so he was leaning against a scratched bench with a balled-up dirty diaper and a Styrofoam fast-food cup beneath it.

Every time I let my mind wander, it went back to Bill Hollis's letter to my dad. He'd been so cocky, so sure of himself. *I do not lose. I will get my money. Jobs she performed for me long before you came along.* It was all so very Hollis. They had nothing if they didn't have the upper hand on somebody. Even on each other. Luna, pretending to be Peyton.

Dru, trying to buy off Rigo. Bill, spouting off taunts until his very last breath. It was like nothing in the world was more important to a Hollis than power. Power over Peyton. Power over me. Power over Jones. Power over my mom. And as soon as they began to lose that power, they made people disappear. I dug my toes into the gravel to stop myself.

"Wait. What did you say?" I asked.

"What?"

"What did you say? About Heriberto." I pulled myself off the swing and began pacing.

He shrugged. "I don't know, I was just talking. . . ."

"You said he doesn't like it when someone messes with his power or his money. And that he has to be the top dog, always. Right?"

"Yeah, I guess. And?"

"Oh my God," I said. I kicked at the pebbles, hard, sending a spray of them into the air. They clicked as they rolled down the plastic slide. I pushed my hands up through my hair and held on to it at the temples. "Oh my God."

"What?" He had come onto the gravel now, which made him walk even more off-kilter. "Nikki. What?" He reached up and pulled on my wrists to get my attention.

Silver confetti. My whole brain was silver confetti. I couldn't believe I hadn't seen it before.

"It wasn't him," I said.

"Maybe not Heriberto directly, but like I said—"

I shook my head and pulled my wrists free. "No. Not that. My dad. It wasn't my dad." Nobody liked power and money more than a Hollis. My mom was a threat to both. She was also a great way to punish my dad for torching their dream movie. So they took care of Mom the best way they knew how. The same way they made their little Peyton problem go away. The same way they wanted to deal with me. They got rid of the threat by killing her.

He shook his head disbelievingly. "Of course. We're talking about you. I'm going back." He started to walk away, but I grabbed his elbow.

"Don't leave. I need your help."

"You always need my help. This is nothing new."

"Chris. It was the Hollises. That's who killed my mom. If I could just find Luna—"

He got to the sidewalk and faced me, throwing up his arms. "You know, ever since I met you, you've been saying the same thing. *If I could just find Luna. If I could just find Luna.* And every time you find her, shit gets worse. Maybe you should just let her go. Let her disappear and move on with your life, Nikki. Try finding Nikki." He started away, but turned back. "And call me if you ever want to help me for a change."

I watched him as he walked away, keeping my eyes on him until he rounded the corner and disappeared from sight.

He wasn't wrong. The deeper I got into things with Luna

and clan, the worse things got. How many times would I cheat death before she won?

"At least one more," I said aloud. I walked back to my car more motivated than ever. Chris and I might be broken, but Luna would not break me.

I would not let her get away.

23

I THOUGHT SHELBY would never leave her house. I'd been parked across the street for what seemed like forever, waiting. A quick check of the clock told me it had only been about two hours, but being alone made it feel much longer. I tried not to think about Chris while I was waiting, and twice had to force myself to put down the phone while on the verge of texting him.

He didn't want to hear from me.

I felt a little guilty for the way things had gone down between us. Which was exactly why things *needed* to go down that way between us. Guilt was just another reason why I thought relationships were bullshit. I had nothing to feel guilty about. I didn't owe him a damn thing.

Did I?

I probably did. Which told me I'd gotten way too close to him. I knew I had—sitting by his bedside after the accident. Confiding in him. Kissing him. Pressing up against him at igNight. It felt good. Comfortable. I'd ignored and pushed away and beaten back the magenta that tried to fill the room whenever I was with him, but I knew it was there. It was always there, the same as it was when Jones came around me. How did I let things get to that point?

I couldn't tell if he was the one who'd changed or if I was. Was he right? Had I started relying on him to do everything for me? It was impossible to tell.

And I hated that I was having to think about it in the first place.

It was so much easier to think about Shelby and how she could lead me to Luna. Which was saying something.

Shelby finally emerged, shoving through her front door with her hip, a cell phone to her ear. She was talking animatedly to whoever was on the other end—Luna, maybe?—and was wearing a nearly nonexistent black swimsuit covered with silver studs. The bottom half disappeared into a pair of white jeans, artfully ripped along the thighs and rolled up at the bottoms. She stumbled along in strappy crystal-embellished heels that winked in the streetlamps. Even her eyebrows twinkled in the lamplight. Clearly Shelby had shed her punk look for the wealthy glam baby that she was born to be. I curled my hands around the steering wheel. There was something about just looking at her that made me fill with murk. I could have hopped out of my car and plowed her face into the street.

Instead, I sank down in my seat, even though I was pretty sure Shelby Gray was way too into herself to notice someone watching her, and waited as she got into her car, pulled out, and left. I let her turn the corner before I followed.

Shelby drove the same way she did everything in life: like she was entitled to the road and everyone else needed to get out of her way. I could see her silhouette holding up her phone several times, as if she was texting. Or taking selfies. Knowing Shelby, she was doing both—texting selfies. She wove in and out of traffic carelessly, cutting off drivers and forcing them to swerve into other lanes and off the road. I hung back several car lengths—not because I was worried about her seeing me, but because I was worried she would kill me if I got too close.

We drove into the city, Shelby's driving improving zero percent along the way, and when we pulled onto Sunset, I knew immediately where she was headed.

Blue Yonder. Where the fab went to party when they wanted to show off barely there, studded swimsuits and rhinestoned makeup.

She pulled into the parking lot and I slowed, trying to

decide whether I would wait for her to come back out, or just go home. A car honked at me to keep moving, so I followed her, cursing out the jackass whose balls were on fire so bad that he couldn't slow down for ten seconds.

Shelby whipped into a parking spot and took a solid minute to mess with her hair in the rearview mirror. She slathered lipstick on her mouth and finally got out. I decided I would wait for her to walk by, and then would leave. I had no interest in watching Shelby Gray be the center of fabulous for a whole night.

She went straight to the giant wooden doors, clicking along on her ridiculous heels, and I was just about to pull out when I saw someone join her. From my position, all I could see was the back of a small, frail-looking girl. Circle skirt and bikini top. Strappy heels just as ridiculous as Shelby's. And long hair.

Long, blond, celebrity-luxurious hair.

I froze, my hands rooted in place on the steering wheel. My fingers had gone cold and tingly. The interior of my car lit up in gold fireworks. I slammed my car into park and picked up my phone. My thumb was poised over the keyboard, ready to text Chris, when I remembered that he didn't want to be in my drama anymore. He wasn't interested in whether or not I'd found Luna.

Even if I finally had.

* * *

AFTER SOME INTERNAL debating, I decided to go home before following Shelby up to the rooftop of the hotel that claimed Blue Yonder as one of its amenities. I definitely wasn't going to blend in wearing the jeans and tee that I was wearing. But going home to change was going to cost me about an hour. I was counting on Shelby and Luna needing to be seen for at least longer than that.

I was pretty sure I could count on it.

I went home and raced up to my room. Dad called after me from his office, but I yelled back that I was only stopping in and would be home later. He said something in return, but I shut my door. I didn't have time yet to deal with him. I may have been convinced that the Hollises were behind my mom's murder, but that didn't mean I was 100 percent convinced that he wasn't also behind it. It seemed unlikely, given that Hollis obviously hated him. But maybe he was willing to do it to get back in Hollis's good graces. Or to protect himself from the man who'd vowed revenge on him.

Regardless, he'd had so many chances to own up to his relationship with them—I'd questioned him directly, more than once. The fact that he was still hiding it gave me an inky feeling in my gut. Even if I could prove that Bill Hollis killed Mom and acted alone while doing so, would that erase the feeling of betrayal I had every time I thought of my dad now? Would it reverse my lack of trust in him?

I honestly didn't know.

I didn't have time to dwell on it now, anyway. Shelby and Luna were partying and the clock was ticking.

I didn't exactly have a ritzy wardrobe to choose from, but I did have some things that would do. I crammed myself back into that awful pink bikini and covered up with a wrap that my grandparents had brought me back from their trip to Bali a few years ago. It was yellow and black and scarf-like, covered with giant orange and purple and red butterflies. It was silky and beautiful and in no way had I ever planned to wear it. I'd shoved it in the back of my closet and forgotten about it.

But now, it was just what I needed. It took me a few minutes—and an online video—to figure out how to tie it, but by the time I was done draping and twisting and knotting, it actually looked a little elegant. It was sheer and light, and it definitely clung to my form, and you could see the ghost of a bikini beneath. I scraped through my jewelry drawer until I found some gaudy shit I'd collected over the years as Christmas gifts, and draped it over myself. I didn't have any rhinestones or glinty, strappy shoes, so I settled for a pair of leather flip-flops and rushed to the bathroom, where I wound and sprayed finger waves into my hair and painted bright red lips on myself—a leftover from my surveillance trip inside a recording studio a while back. I doubled down on mascara and blush and spritzed a cloud of coconut-scented body spray onto myself.

When I stepped back to study the mirror, I barely recognized the girl in my reflection. I looked . . . like everyone else. It was disgusting.

And also perfect.

TRAFFIC HAD LIGHTENED up as evening drew down, and I got back to the hotel in record time. There were a lot more cars in the parking lot, and I had to drive around a while before I found a spot.

I wished I'd seen which car the blonde had gotten out of, but I'd been too busy watching Shelby and getting impatient. That was the price I paid for not paying attention. *Eye on the prize, Nikki.* And Shelby was only one prize. The small prize. She was the goldfish in a plastic bag when there was a giant teddy bear to be won.

The rooftop was even swankier than I'd imagined. Sofas and cushions and candles everywhere. Music, the clink of glasses hitting glasses, and laughter—fake, forced, kind-of-bored laughter—a cloud hovering above all of us. The entrance was manned by a distractible guy whose eyes were the glossy bloodshot of someone completely high. I craned my neck, pretending to look over his shoulder, an aggravated expression on my face.

"You need something?" he asked.

"My friend is carrying my ID," I said. I ran my hands

down my hips. "No pockets. I was parking and she was supposed to wait for me. She must have forgot."

He scanned the room. "Who's your friend?"

I let my shoulders slump. "I think I saw her go into the
bathroom." I made a frustrated noise. "I don't even have my
phone. You mind if I go find her?"

"Not supposed to let you in without an ID," he said, but
already I could tell his attention was waning as a line formed
behind me.

"I'll come right back as soon as I have it," I said, knowing I could get lost in the crowd and he would totally forget
about me two minutes after I walked away.

He looked skeptical but nodded anyway. "Yeah, go
ahead."

Sometimes it was just too easy.

I lingered along the edge of the room, pausing to gaze
out the windows at the breathtaking view of Los Angeles. I
felt like I could see forever.

"Gorgeous, huh?" I heard, startlingly close to me. I
jumped, turned. A man who looked old enough to be my
dad stood there, grinning at me over a glass of wine. He held
a second glass toward me. "Pinot noir?"

I wanted nothing to do with this toad, but I needed to
assimilate into the crowd. I needed to fit in. I took the glass,
smiled, and clinked it against his lightly. The liquid turned
yellowy brown, but I ignored it. I took too big of a sip. He

watched me over the top of his glass as he drank, too.

He wasn't the worst-looking guy in the world.

"That's a beautiful dress," he said. He reached out and rubbed the fabric between his fingers. My elbow pulled back slightly, ready to jack him in the throat if he even considered touching me further than that. "Almost looks like a scarf."

"It kind of is," I said. I took another sip. "It's from Bali."

His eyes lit up and he dropped the fabric. "Oh! You've been! I hope you had time to visit Karangasem and Besakih Temple. I would venture to say the most sublime spot on the face of the earth. Agree?"

I let out a self-conscious chuckle. "I haven't actually been," I said. "Someone brought me this as a souvenir."

"You should go," he said, his eyes never leaving me as he took a drink.

No, you should go, I thought. *Go away.*

"It's a nice look regardless," he said, gesturing the length of my body with his glass. "A lot simpler than most of the girls here. They try too hard. And you have the curves for it." Fortunately, we both turned to survey the rooftop, taking some of the attention off me, and allowing me to look for Shelby and Luna. They appeared to be stretched out on a couple of lounges, their backs to us. "You going to swim?" the man asked.

"Hmm?" I'd been watching them so intently, I'd pretty

much forgotten I was standing with him. Maybe it was purposeful forgetting.

He pushed aside the edge of my wrap, exposing bare flesh and the top of my bikini bottom. "Looks like you're planning to swim." He arched his eyebrows and tilted his head approvingly as he stared. Puffs of ruby, lime sherbet, rust. *Pop, pop, pop.* A July Fourth finale in my mind. I hated being touched without permission.

Lightning quick, I reached down and grabbed his hand, squeezing and grinding his knuckles together, and twisting his wrist so his thumb was pointing downward. He let out a gasp; wine splashed over the rim of his glass, landing on his shoe.

"Touch me again and you're going to need someone else to hold your wineglass for you."

He tugged against my grip, and I held tight for just a second longer, then let go. I smiled, drained my wine, and handed my glass to him, pressing it against his stomach until he took it. "Nice meeting you," I said, and sauntered away, my entire body vibrating with anger.

He murmured; I couldn't tell what he was saying, but I was guessing it wasn't too nice. I felt good about that. Chris would have loved . . . right. Never mind what Chris would have loved.

I wandered through the crowd, trying to look like I had a purpose so the leches would leave me alone, but also trying to blend in so Shelby and Luna wouldn't notice me. Two guys had joined them, and they were all draped over the lounges together, drinks sweating on the ground at their feet. Shelby kept laughing, throwing her head back, and I clenched my jaw. I hated seeing her having a great time as if everything were normal and the girl sitting right next to her hadn't tried to kill me twice. I was overtaken with a wave of dread, realizing that even if I somehow managed to get rid of Luna once and for all, Shelby would still exist. What kind of person hung out with a sociopath like Luna as if doing so was totally okay? Another sociopath. Just what the world needed. Just what my life needed. With Luna gone, would Shelby simply step up and take her place?

"You need something?" A waitress had appeared next to me, holding an empty tray down by her side. She was looking at me skeptically.

"Um . . . just the restroom," I said.

She pointed in the direction I'd come from. "That way."

I glanced but tried not to let my gaze linger, since the guy whose fingers I'd mashed was still over there. "Thanks."

She started to move on, then stopped again. "You sure you don't need anything? You seem, like, nervous or something. Someone giving you trouble? We don't tolerate that here."

Shit. I chuckled and willed myself to press my nerves

down. "No, I'm just . . . the guy I'm into is here and I'm totally geeking out about it. I'm such a dork."

I had inadvertently nodded my head toward the guys who were messing with Shelby and Luna, and the waitress followed the gesture. "Those guys?" She leaned in, touched my arm. "Trust me, sweetie. You don't want them. They're here all the time. Different night, different girl. They aren't exactly what you would call marriage material, if you know what I mean."

I grinned. "Neither am I." Truth.

She shrugged. "Well, have at it, then. Maybe those two girls won't put out, and you'll have the road paved for you."

She moved on, stopping to pick up empty glasses and bottles along the way. I drifted away, pausing in as many unobtrusive places as I could find. I could feel eyes on me. I hated being in crowds for this very reason. The constant assessing, the feeling of being on show. The pool rippled green and bumpy, what I thought of as "pickle green"—the color I saw when I felt self-conscious.

Finally, the guys got up and pulled off their shirts, wandered over to the pool, and jumped in. The girls egged them on while holding up their drinks, toast-style.

If there was a time, it was now.

I briskly headed toward them.

"Does your parole officer know you're partying?" I asked,

coming around the corner, fast, at Luna. I whipped out my phone, ready to dial the police; I wanted Luna to see me doing it.

She jumped. "What the hell?"

Only it wasn't Luna sitting next to Shelby Gray. It was a different blond girl. The third in Luna's trio: Eve Keller.

Shelby flopped back against the lounge and rolled her eyes. "You've got to be kidding me. Nikki Kill. For the Will Never Go Away files."

I realized I hadn't moved. I was still holding up my phone threateningly. My shoulders sagged. "Are you serious? Eve."

"What the hell?" Eve repeated, this time looking over at Shelby helplessly.

"I told you about her," Shelby said, resigned. "She is obsessed with me for some reason. Won't leave me alone. I heard you were stalking VF at the café the other day, Nikki. Pretty pathetic, don't you think?"

"I wasn't stalking," I said. "I was on a shoot with my dad and when I saw Vee, I went over to say hi and ask a couple questions. I'm trying to—"

"Let me guess," she said, interrupting me. "Find Luna. You're trying to find Luna." She turned to Eve again. "She's like a broken record about it. Completely obsessed. It's totally unhealthy. I've told you before, Nikki, and you seem to be too dense to get it. So I'll say it slowly. I . . . don't . . . know . . . where . . . Luna . . . is."

"You thought I was Luna?" Eve asked, and I could tell by the look on her face that she was secretly thrilled about the mistake. She touched her hair lightly.

"Do you know where Luna is, Eve?" Shelby asked. Eve shook her head. "No. So you can move on now. Luna is not here, and we don't know where she is."

"Has she contacted you at all?" I asked, finally getting my bearings. "I mean, since taking off?"

"If you took off," Shelby said, "would you go calling people to see if they noticed? No. You would hide. I'm guessing that's what Luna's doing. Hiding. Far, far away from here."

"No doubt," Eve said. "Luna's not dumb."

Unlike you two, I wanted to snap, but held myself back. You never knew when you might need someone's cooperation in the future, and Eve seemed to be the one semi-not-horrible friend in the trio. And insulting Shelby just didn't really seem worth my time.

The two boys had gotten out of the pool and were loping toward us, their feet making wet smacks against the concrete, their chests and bellies streaked with mini chlorinated rivers.

"Would you please go now?" Shelby asked, waving me off. "We're sort of in the middle of something, and you're in the way."

"Fine," I said. "But if you hear from her—"

"Yeah, yeah, I'll call you. I know the drill by now. But I

can assure you I'm not going to hear from her. Can we both move on now? And by move on, I mean literally." She waved me off again, a little grander this time.

"Whatever," I mumbled, turning away.

"Have you tried her dad's house?" Eve asked, before I could get out of her sight.

"No."

"You should try there. Last I talked to Luna, she was living with him. I mean, if she's missing, how come there's not some big, like, police search or Amber Alert or something going on? Someone must know where she is."

She had a point. One I hadn't thought of before.

Why hadn't I thought of that before?

"Would you please go now?" Shelby asked impatiently.

The guys had arrived and were busy scrubbing their hair with towels. I could feel their eyes on my dress, could almost feel their eyes under my dress. The waitress had been so right about them.

"God, go already. I swear you are like a fly. Annoying, and impossible to get rid of. I don't like you, Nikki Kill. I don't want you around. Don't make me swat you." She and Eve shared a chuckle as the two guys went *daaaamn* in the background.

"Always good to see you, Shelby," I said in a droll voice.

"I wish I could say the same," she said. And then to my back, "Oh, wait. No I don't. It's always good to see you leaving." She giggled loudly.

Past Nikki wanted to rush her, put her in a headlock, make her cry. But Current Nikki didn't have time for that. Current Nikki had an errand to plan.

Eve was right: it was time to pay Peter Fairchild a visit.

24

I HAD A hard time sleeping. I was too busy planning what I would say to Luna's dad. Would he be hostile, like his daughter? Or would he welcome the help finding her? Maybe he wanted her to go back to juvie, too, so she could get the help she needed. He was Vanessa's *ex*, so obviously he had seen the light at some point. It was possible that he was totally normal, if he couldn't handle being with that nasty mess. In fact, it was better than possible. Given that Luna had run away from him, it was probable. Luna did not do normal. It wasn't in her DNA.

I spent most of the night staring at the ceiling, wondering what kind of relationship Luna had with her dad. How could it be tight, when she'd left him to follow Hollis fame and fortune? Although he had at some point apparently found Vanessa attractive, so maybe he got it.

I found myself wishing I could call Chris and ask him to go with me. And then I was pissed that I somehow felt like I needed to have a man come save me in case things went bad. I didn't need any man. I could protect myself. I'd done it before; I could do it again. Not like Chris wanted to help me. He'd made that perfectly clear.

I felt like I had barely closed my eyes when my alarm went off in the morning. Still, I bolted upright, ready to go. I took a quick shower, dressed, and grabbed an apple on my way out the door. Dad was either not up yet or had gotten up and gone already. Either way, I didn't care. I couldn't care. Not until I had answers.

Answers were at the Fairchild house; I could feel it.

Thanks to the internet, it wasn't hard at all to find where Luna's dad lived. I'd looked it up before, back when I was first researching the Hollises while Peyton clung to life in the hospital. The address stuck in my head: pink, white, melon, copper. 257 Noble.

The weather was beautiful, and I drove with my windows open, sunglasses on, the smell of beach faint in the air. I turned up the radio and sang along, feeling halfway normal for a change. It was the kind of weather that made you want to do fun things—go to a festival or see a movie or hang out at the *dojang* with the doors open and the fans on.

Or capture the girl who's been trying to kill you, and who might be the last link to avenging your mother.

I turned down the radio as I got closer to Luna's house, for some reason feeling like announcing myself with noise was not such a great idea. But when I pulled up to the curb, I realized my fear was for nothing.

I checked the address, and even double-checked on my phone to make sure I wasn't remembering it wrong. Yep, 257 Noble. That was Luna's address. The house she grew up in. Plain and small and boring.

And currently for sale.

Not to mention deserted. There weren't even curtains left on the windows.

I parked at the curb and stared in disbelief. I supposed it wasn't such a stretch to imagine not wanting to live in a tight neighborhood like this one when your daughter was a known murderer, but for some reason being unable to just walk up to the door and talk to Peter Fairchild felt like a blow. Or should I say *another* blow.

I leaned my forehead on the steering wheel and groaned. Option after option after option. Dead end after dead end after dead end. Chris was done helping me search. Shelby was clueless. Even Vee had seemed to give up. Blue had nothing for me. Pear Magic. Angry Elephant. igNight. Blue Yonder. I had literally been everywhere I could possibly think of to find Luna. And she was not in a single one of those places. She was a ghost. A shadow. A memory that nobody wanted to hold on to. Now what?

I turned so my temple was resting on the wheel and opened my eyes.

I could so see why this house wasn't enough for a person like Luna. It was charming. It was unassuming. Black and white with tidy—if not dreadfully plain—little trees and bushes. The only thing colorful anywhere around it was the *For Sale* sign.

I sat up.

Of course. The *For Sale* sign. Caroline Mackey, agent. I got out of the car and took a flyer out of the box attached to the sign. White, white, white, bronze, pink, brown, pink.

Without giving it another thought, I pulled out my phone and dialed.

"Caroline here," a voice sang into the receiver after the first ring.

"Um, hi. I'm wondering if you can show me a house?" I felt squeaky, so I cleared my throat, tried to make my voice sound deeper, more mature.

"Of course. Which house were you wanting to see?"

"Two-fifty-seven Noble," I said. I scanned the paper in my hand. "Three bedroom, two bath? Great starter house?"

"Oh, of course! Yes, it is a perfect starter house. And your name is?"

"Carrie," I blurted. I'd never used my mother's name

before, and the move took me by surprise. I fumbled for a last name, then said the first thing that came to mind. "Carrie Martinez." Surprise number two. I was full of them today. "We, um, I'm a newlywed, and we're, um, looking." I squeezed my eyes tight. I sounded like such a liar, even to myself.

"Wonderful!" she exclaimed. If I sounded like a liar, she was ignoring it. "Can you be at the address in an hour?"

I stuffed the paper back in its box. "Sure."

I HAD AN hour to convince Chris to join me.

I drove until I found a nearby coffee shop and sat at a table by the window, which overlooked a busy boulevard.

Hey, I texted.

No response. I sipped my coffee while I waited. After several minutes, I texted again.

I don't suppose you want to pretend to be my husband for an hour?

I knew he was mad at me, but surely that would get him talking. Surely it would at least make him curious. But the minutes ticked by and there was nothing. I tried again.

You can't stay mad at me forever.

Nothing, nothing, nothing, and then, just when I was about to text again, this:

I'm not mad. I'm busy. You will have to find someone else to play actor with you.

I could feel the bite in his words, even through the phone. He may have been saying he wasn't mad, but he was 100 percent lying.

Come on. You know you're my favorite actor.

Nothing. So much nothing I started to actually get irritated. I was out of coffee and out of patience and it was going to be a hell of a lot harder to pretend I had a good reason to be looking at this house if I was alone. I dialed his number and got voice mail.

"Look," I said, talking through my teeth to keep my voice low. "I know you're mad, and I'm sorry, okay? I will help you track down Leon or Heriberto or whoever you want, but I need you right now. I'm going to be looking at Peter Fairchild's house in, like, fifteen minutes. It's two-fifty-seven Noble. Just meet me there." I unclenched my teeth, knowing that I sounded angrier than I felt. Magenta tears popped into my eyes and I blinked to keep them inside. "Chris, this is dumb. We're a team because you basically forced it. I didn't want to work with you, but you wore me down. I got used to you. Bailing on me now would be . . ." I had to blink again. Damn it. I hated this. I took a deep breath and reclenched my teeth. "It would be a real dick move. I'll see you there."

I was halfway out the door when my phone beeped. A text message.

Don't worry, I'm not forcing you anymore. You're free.

THE HOUSE WAS empty. Bare walls, bare floors, bare shelves. It had a closed-up feeling, but not like it had been closed up for long. Our footsteps echoed on the hardwood in the living room, on the tile in the kitchen; our voices bounced back at us in every room.

Caroline yammered on what seemed like endlessly about the features of the house, and I had to pretend that I cared, which was immeasurably more difficult after the conversation—or not conversation—between Chris and me. I was a mixture of so many colors—disappointment, shame, anger, despair—it was hard to tell what the resulting shade or texture even was. I could only liken it to something rotting. I started thinking of it as rottenshade. *Congratulations, Martinez, you created a new hue.*

There was nothing to see here. Not a scrap of paper or a computer screen or even so much as a footprint to help guide me to where Peter—and perhaps Luna—had gone. But I couldn't just cry defeat. I had come too far. I had to at least try to get information out of good old Caroline.

We had toured the whole house, ending back in the kitchen, where she'd lain her keys, phone, and a stack of flyers for various other houses she was selling just in case this one wasn't the right fit. I stood awkwardly in the middle of the room while she leaned against the counter.

"So why did the previous owner move out?" I asked,

hoping I sounded like the average home buyer. Crossed my arms over my chest. Uncrossed them. Scratched my forearm and crossed again. How did average home buyers hold their arms?

"Major life change," she said, smiling. Caroline seemed to never stop smiling. Her teeth were glossy and intensely white. "He bought a houseboat. Wanted to live on the water."

"A houseboat?"

"Well, I went there to go over paperwork. It was more like a yacht, in my opinion. Between you and me, I don't know where he got all that money. He's still paying a mortgage on this until it sells. Can't be free to tie up at Del Rey every day. I think he just likes being able to say he lives in Tahiti." She winked.

I had an idea where he'd gotten all that money. Luna. She was all that was left of her family. She must have figured out how to get her hands on the Hollis family fortune. Knowing them, they had an illegal stash hidden somewhere, and she knew exactly where it was.

"Just him?" I asked. I bent low to look at the underside of the counter so I would look disinterested in her answer.

"Not sure, actually." I stood; she was still aiming that dorky smile at me. "So what do you think?"

I sighed, trying to look torn. "I wish my husband could be here. I would feel so much better if we could talk to the owner, you know? Get his take on the pros and cons of this place. I don't suppose you could hook us up?"

For the first time, her smile fell. She looked floored that I would even ask such thing. Apparently, asking to speak to the owner was not something people usually did. I tried to save it. "You make him sound like such a personable guy. I figured he probably wouldn't mind."

"I can't—" Her phone rang, one of those loud, old-fashioned rings that all old people have on their phones. She checked the screen. "Speak of the devil!" My heart skipped a beat. I had to resist wrestling it out of her hand and answering it myself. "He must be wondering how the showing went." She looked at me pointedly, then pressed a button to silence the ring. The phone went dark. Damn it. "Hopefully I'll have good news to call him back with. I'll just let him know I'm still with you." Back with the smile. She keyed in her passcode and sent a text, then returned her phone to the counter. "So what do you say?"

I say that the very guy I'm looking for just called you and I can do nothing about it. I say that this has been how my entire life has been going lately—so close, yet so far. I say that a killer could be out on that houseboat and she could just decide to set sail any day now and never come back. And I will be living the rest of my life looking over my shoulder and wondering what happened to my mother. I will spend the rest of my life wondering if my dad was in on her murder. I will never be at peace. Not for a single day. That's what I say.

I say that if you would just give me five minutes alone with your phone, I would . . .

"Can we look at the backyard again?" I asked. I held up my own phone. "I want to take some pictures for my husband."

"Sure," she said, practically leaping out of her pumps to get to the back door. I followed her out, stopping to pretend to tie my shoe, setting my phone on the counter as I did so. I left it there as I stepped through the door behind her. "So, like I said before, you have a really big backyard here. Some shade in the south corner, which is good. The shed can stay or go, depending on what you want. Great neighbors on both sides. Feel free to take whatever photos you'd like."

I reached into my pocket and let a surprised look fall over my face. I checked my other pockets, patting them briefly, and then chuckled and rolled my eyes. "I must have left my phone inside. I can't believe I'm so absentminded. I'm just so excited about this. One second?"

She nodded and went over to a flowerpot, poking around at a half-dead stem inside.

I darted inside and went straight to her phone, praying the colors I'd seen when she keyed in her passcode were right. It was at an angle, and I wasn't paying the closest attention in the world. But that was one of the great things about synesthesia—sometimes it did the paying attention for you.

Cornflower blue. Sea green. Silver. Brown.

I was in.

I was fucking in!

Now all I had to do was memorize his phone number and I would be good to go. I pressed her contacts icon. I didn't need Chris after all. I was perfectly capable of getting shit done all on my—

I nearly dropped the phone.

Peter Fairchild. White, white, white. Bronze, melon, bronze, brown.

Easy number to memorize. It wasn't the number that made my skin crawl, my throat dry, my breath catch.

It was the photo icon next to the number.

White-blond hair, blue eyes, super-tan skin.

Peter Fairchild was the white-blond-haired man.

25

I KNEW IT wasn't going to go well when I showed up at Chris's office early that evening, but I had to take my chances. Part of me—the part that knew him—told me he did care about finding Luna and helping me solve my mother's case. I was going to have to trust that part of me when he was most likely going to be yelling at me to leave and take my drama with me.

Turned out, I was lucky to even catch him there at all. When he came out into the lobby to see me standing there, I could see his shoulders tense. I almost felt bad. Like maybe if I cared for him at all, I would just leave him alone.

But caring for people wasn't in my repertoire. And neither was leaving people alone when I wanted something.

"Don't get that look," I said, brushing past him toward his office. "I'm here for a good reason."

"I was just heading out," he said to my back.

"I can ride along."

"No, Nikki, you can't." He edged around me and stopped in his doorway, blocking me. "This is about a case that has nothing to do with you. Or me. Other than it's my job to solve it."

"Oh, come on. Are you ever going to forgive me? I've said I was sorry."

"If you were really sorry, you would stop doing what you're doing."

"What am I doing?" My voice had taken on a high, squeaky quality that I hated.

"We've been through this and through this and through this. I think you're wasting your time. You aren't going to find Luna. You aren't going to find your mother's murderer. You need to let go already and start to live your life. Stop living in the past. You can't fix it. You can only learn from it."

I cocked my hip to one side, pressing my fist into it. "Says the guy whose secret obsession with his own past almost got him killed. Maybe you should let it go and live your life."

"And you really think Heriberto is going to let that happen?" he asked, voice low.

"And you really think Luna is?" I countered.

"Yes. Actually, I do. I think Luna is long gone. I think she probably hitched the first plane to Dubai, just like her parents would have done. I think she wants to forget that you ever existed. I think she wants everything that's happened to just go away."

"And I think I'm not okay with that. Peyton didn't just go away. Dru didn't just go away. They were killed. And as long as she is out there, I think I have to keep looking. For my sister. For my mom. And everything you just said tells me that you definitely aren't remembering everything that happened." I pressed my lips together, waiting, but he said nothing. I tried switching gears. "Besides, if I ride along with you, maybe I would decide I want to be a cop after all." He rolled his eyes, the seriousness slowly sliding off him. All the opening I needed. I grabbed his arm. "You could change a life, Detective Martinez. Inspire a future officer of the law." I saluted, grinning.

He held out for another long moment, and then let his arms drop. "Fine. Come with me. But you stay in the car unless I tell you to get out. You got that?"

"Aye, aye, Captain Control Freak." I saluted again, but he'd already turned his back.

"SO WHO ARE we busting?" I asked as soon as we got into the car.

"First of all, I'm not busting anyone. I need to question someone about a murder that happened under an overpass two nights ago. Routine stuff. Secondly, *we* aren't doing any-thing. *I* am asking questions; *you'll* be in the car. Got it?"

"Sure, sure."

We drove along for a few minutes. I watched out the window as we drove deeper into the rough side of the city. I wondered what it would be like to call these streets work. My job. A squad car my office. For the first time ever, I didn't get a sick feeling at the idea of putting on a blue uniform. For the first time ever, it seemed like it could be a possibility. If I could pass the written exams, of course. Could it really be that hard?

I was probably still riding the high of figuring out who the white-blond man was.

"So to what do I owe the pleasure of having you on this ride-along?" he finally said, breaking the silence. Sarcastic. Still a little bitter.

"Don't say it like that," I said.

"So your presence in my office doesn't have anything to do with what you found at the house you tried to get me to look at with you this morning?"

"You know, I think I liked it better when I was telling you to get off my ass all the time," I said sourly. "You were way nicer then. Of course, that was before you got scrambled brains." I knew, even as the words were leaving my mouth, that they were the wrong ones.

"Nice, Nikki. Really nice."

"Sorry," I said, sitting in a fern-colored awkwardness.

He let the heaviness hover for a minute while he turned into an even shadier area—one of those abandoned-looking streets that immediately took me back to the day we went to the Dom Distribution warehouse. My palms started sweating with the memory. "So what did you find?" he finally asked, quiet, contrite.

"The house is completely gutted. Nothing and no one to be found."

"So you got nothing?"

"I did, actually. I hacked into the Realtor's phone and got this." I held up the palm of my hand, on which I had scribbled Peter Fairchild's number the moment I'd gotten back in my car.

"You hacked . . . never mind. Whose is it?"

"Peter Fairchild. Luna's dad. Also, it turns out, her getaway driver. The thing is, I've seen him before. I know who he is, where he works, everything." Well, not quite everything. I still didn't know what exactly he had to do with my parents. Why he was hanging around in the background of their photos.

Chris raised his eyebrows. "And?"

"And he's the director of that movie over at Pear Magic."

"Interesting."

I nodded. "It gets even better. He was the guy who pretended to be an agent. I'm convinced Jella was Luna in disguise. He's trying to hide her. He sold his house to buy a yacht."

Chris turned into a parking lot and came to a stop. An empty, rusted grocery cart was overturned at the nose of our car. "A yacht," he repeated once he'd turned off the car.

"A houseboat," I said, emphasizing the word *house*. "Right after Luna mysteriously disappeared. Coincidence?"

"You think Luna is living on the yacht."

"Can you think of a more Luna place to hide?"

I had only just then noticed a knot of people nearby, tucked up high under an overpass, clustered on a single filthy blanket. They were watching us carefully. Chris caught me looking.

"Is this who you're questioning?" I asked.

He nodded. "Here's the thing. When a homeless person goes missing, nobody even realizes it, right? They're invisible to the rest of the world."

"Sad thought."

"True thought. But the thing is, they actually are missed. Their circle of friends misses them. And those friends also might know more than they even realize they know. They just don't bother to come to us with the information. They figure it's pointless."

"Because they're invisible," I said.

"Yep," he said to the window. "Our job is to see them

anyway. To remember that no invisible person is really invisible."

Made total sense to me, but I wondered how many cops would look at it that way. How many would think to talk to the other homeless about their murdered friend? Maybe all of them, I didn't know. But for some reason I guessed not. For some reason, I guessed that was one of the things that made Chris special.

The sun was starting to make me sweat along the hairline.

"It's also my job to convince them that I'm not going to bust them. That I'm going to leave them just invisible enough to get away with whatever drugs and stolen shit they've got going on over there."

"So it's better for me to stay in the car," I said. "I get it."

"Exactly. That was why I didn't think you should come in the first place. This isn't a spectator sport, as much as TV would like us to think it is."

"Fine, whatever, I'll wait." I snapped down the visor. "But you know how fast I get restless—" I stopped. When I'd pulled down the visor, something had fallen into my lap with a clink. I picked it up.

A key.

A single key on a ring, a number etched onto a tab that also hung from the ring.

Brown, silver, bronze.

"One forty-nine," I said. I held the key up questioningly, expecting Chris to yank it away from me, too, and chastise me for not minding my own business.

But his face was frozen. He looked almost pasty. His eyes bored into the metal of the ring; his mouth hung open just slightly.

"What?" I asked. I glanced at the key and back at him again. "What's one forty-nine? An address?"

"A locker," he said. His voice was rough, as if it came from somewhere far away. "I'm almost positive I remember a locker."

I squinted at him, confused. "Like, a gym locker?"

He finally moved, his hand closing around the key and tugging it from me. "A storage locker," he said. "Holy shit, Nikki, I know where Heriberto's drugs are."

THE STORE4CHEAP LOCKERS were just off the highway, surrounded by a tall chain-link fence and a gate
that locked by code. We pulled up, and Chris punched in a
few different number sequences. None of them worked. He
cussed after each try. I could feel the frustration fuming off
him. To remember things bit by bit had to be maddening.

Eventually, he gave up and went inside, flashed his
badge, and the attendant let us in. If only the attendant had
known what we were hoping was inside that locker.

A ton of drugs meant to be peddled by children and
instead confiscated by a cop on a secret mission.

I was pretty sure we would all be in deep shit if anyone
had figured this out.

Chris unlocked the door and rolled it open. Inside were two giant moving boxes. We stepped inside, turned on a battery-operated lantern, and shut the door behind us. The air felt close and stale and smelled dirty and somehow a little oily, like exhaust. I wanted out. Everything looked gunmetal gray, and I knew that meant it wouldn't be long before that gray bubbled up into black bumps and panic would set in and I would have some sort of embarrassing meltdown. I tried to concentrate on the smell of Chris to keep me grounded. But I could feel the slate nerves crackling off him like static. His yellow was intense in here. Almost too intense.

He stood over one box, hands on hips.

"Well?" I asked. "You going to open it?"

"I know what's inside," he said. "I remember. I know what's inside both of them."

Still, he didn't move, and if something didn't happen soon, I was going to go crazy and start clawing at the door, so I bent and opened the flaps of a moving box. Inside, bags upon bags filled with powder and crystals and pills. Heriberto and his boys could have given the Hollises a run for their money when it came to pushing.

I reached in and scooped up a handful of bags, then let them drop.

"Holy crap," I breathed. "You've been at this for a while."

He nodded. "Sam."

"Huh?"

He scratched the back of his neck, and then one eyebrow, wincing at the memory. "Ever since I realized it was Sam. It was one thing for Heriberto to be dealing. That goes with the territory. Using someone like Sam to do his dirty work, though . . ." He shook his head. "These aren't just any kids, Nikki. These are kids who will eventually end up in the gang. If they're not already. These kids have no future. And I couldn't let that happen with Sam. Not after everything Rebecca did to get me out."

I picked up and dropped another handful of bags. I couldn't even imagine how much money was in that box.

"How did you afford all this?" I asked.

He pointed to the other box. Slowly, curiously, I walked over and opened its flaps. And was nearly blown away by the greens and reds and yellows of twenties and fifties and hundreds. Stacks and stacks of them. I gasped.

"Are you kidding me?" I dropped to my knees next to the box. I glanced at him, but he was looking down at his feet, his face set in grim concentration. "What did you do, rob a bank?"

"Close," he said. "I robbed Heriberto."

I sank back so I was resting on my heels, the hard concrete floor digging into my knees. "You're kidding, right? You? I don't believe it."

When he leveled his eyes at me, they were so angry they were nearly black. Slowly, he shook his head.

"How?"

"I found out where they were keeping it. My brother Javi knew. I visited him up at State and he told me where to look. I watched and I waited and the first chance I got, I robbed the bastard. And I bought his drugs with his own money. And stashed them here. It was like he didn't even exist."

It was a brilliant plan, really. The gang probably thought it was another gang who'd stolen from them—not a cop. The kids kept selling, so they didn't get busted up by Heriberto and friends. Heriberto thought he was making money, but he wasn't. And the drugs went nowhere.

"So what went wrong?" I asked, standing up and brushing off my hands. Suddenly they felt filthy. Probably simply because I knew what the money had been used for. I knew where it had been.

"Rebecca," he said. "It wasn't enough anymore. I was starting to see a change in Sam. He was getting tougher or . . . or something. More like cold. So I went to her. I told her I was going to get her out just like she did for me. I had the money and I was going to somehow get it to her and help her leave L.A."

"And someone saw you there."

He nodded. "I was an old rival in their neighborhood. And a cop on top of it. Of course someone noticed me. Heriberto put out a hit. That's all there was to it. I was so close to getting her out. So close to   " He trailed off, lost in thought.

"Chris?" He didn't answer. I bent low and waved in his face. "What? So close to what?"

He didn't answer, but quickly closed the flaps on the boxes and in just another motion, whipped up the garage door.

"Close to what?" I asked again, following him out, so confused I only barely registered how cool and fresh the air felt against my skin after being inside the locker. He slammed the door shut behind us and locked the padlock. "Hello, close to what?" I repeated.

He raced around to the driver's side of his car and pushed a button to pop the trunk. He practically launched himself inside, brushing aside jumper cables and other pieces of equipment, and lifted up the carpet. Beneath, inside the well where the spare tire sat, was an envelope. He pulled it out, closed the trunk, and upturned the envelope so the items inside fell out. Photos.

"Close to busting them," he said.

I riffled through the stack. Surveillance photos. Photos of Heriberto handing drugs off to kids. Photos through a window of Heriberto sitting at a kitchen table, counting money, a cigarette dangling from his mouth. Photos of Heriberto cleaning a gun. Close-ups, albeit grainy, of the gun in his hands.

"That gun will match the bullets taken from a couple guys who were killed outside a convenience store last year," he said. He slid the pictures around until he found one of Heriberto sitting on a porch rail. "Those shoes," he said, "will match shoe prints taken at the scene. And we have an empty cigarette wrapper from the scene too. Same cigarettes." He moved his finger to a close-up of Heriberto's hand holding the cigarette. "The shoe prints and cigarette wrapper were okay evidence, but we needed more. I got more. I got a picture of him holding the gun. And I got Rebecca. She was going to testify."

"No wonder they wanted you dead," I whispered. The thought flashed through my mind that it could have been so much worse, what happened to him. Heriberto could have succeeded in killing him—getting rid of the cop who could take them down. I also became convinced of something else. Chris was right. There was no way they were going to leave him alone now. He had no choice; he had to finish what he'd started.

We heard the rattle of the gate opening. Nighttime had fallen on us while we were inside the locker, so technically Store4Cheap was closed. We both froze, then locked eyes, then worked together to stuff the photos back into their envelope.

"We should go," Chris said.

I took the envelope and we hurried into his car, rolling

out of the aisle just as the car that had come in started down our aisle at the other end. All I could see in the side mirror were headlights. But they were headlights that weren't slowing.

Chris noticed it too and began driving faster, going over the speed bumps so hard I came up out of my seat. The headlights continued behind us, slow but picking up speed.

"Come on," I whispered, as the gate, which had just closed, trundled open at a maddeningly slow pace. I glanced in the mirror again. The headlights were still coming. "Come on," I repeated.

Finally, the gate was open enough for us to get out. We cut off a minivan in our haste. It swerved and honked, but Chris ignored them. I turned in my seat. The car behind us had gotten through the gate just in time. It nearly sideswiped the minivan, which honked again and slowed to a stop on the shoulder.

"Hold on," Chris said. Calm. Rational. Deadly.

I wrapped my hand around the door handle and tensed my legs for leverage. Chris punched it and we took off like lightning.

The car behind us sped up too, but it wasn't as fast as Chris's car. Plus, Chris was a better driver. He darted in and out and around cars by what seemed like feel alone. There were honks and shouts and cars plunking off onto the shoulders, but Chris never stopped. Never touched another car with his. Just kept his eyes on the road, his foot planted all the way to the floor and his mouth pressed into a scowl.

I looked. The car was still there. It was back a little bit more now, but it was still there.

"Keep going," I said, even though I knew it was useless for me to even speak. He would have kept going whether I had been in the car or not.

We hit a stretch of open boulevard and Chris zoomed ahead, the speed starting to make me feel woozy.

"He's still there," I reported.

"Hold on," he said for a second time, as matter-of-factly as if he were telling me to hold his drink while he went to the bathroom.

I squeezed the handhold tighter, and he took a corner so fast we fishtailed. But he hardly slowed down as he took another corner and then a third. There was a bowling alley straight ahead and we bounced over the curb into its parking lot, my teeth clacking together from the jarring bump. I bit my tongue; I tasted blood. Chris immediately turned off his headlights and whipped the car into a parking space, blending us in with the other fifty cars that were in the lot.

"Duck," he said. I didn't move at first, so he put his hand on my head and pushed until I moved down in my seat. He moved down in his, too. It was only then, in the sudden silence, that I noticed he was breathing heavily. "Stay down."

But I couldn't help myself. I sat up just an inch or two

so I could see through the back window. There were head-lights coming down the street we'd just come from. I held my breath, ready to tell Chris to gun it again.

But instead of turning into the lot as we had, the car turned the other way and drove slowly away from us.

I watched as it passed under a streetlamp.

It was black, with the words *Monte Carlo* coming out at me in silver.

27

I T WAS ALMOST impossible to sleep after our little high-speed tour of the city. Chris had taken me back to my car and had followed me all the way home. I suspected that he even sat outside my house for an hour or so, just watching.

I puttered. I ate. I watched TV. I texted Dad, who was apparently on location in San Francisco. He responded: I would have told you I was leaving if you were ever home. It's like living with a stranger. Anger. *Well, back at you, Dad.* I took a shower to calm myself and played around on social media for distraction, and petted Hue for at least half an hour, and next thing I knew it was late—like, super late—and I was turning pages in the journal I'd stolen from Pear Magic, because I had nothing else to do, and now that I knew the author was Peter Fairchild, I had a better idea of what I was looking for.

8:10 A.M. AWAKE

8:22 A.M. SHOWER, DOOR CLOSED

9:10 A.M. BREAKFAST, CEREAL, DRY, COFFEE, CREAM, SUGAR, DIDN'T FINISH

9:30 A.M. STUDYING, OPEN TEXTBOOK, GEOGRAPHY

9:56 A.M. CIGARETTE BREAK 1, COMPLETE TO FILTER, NO BRAND CHANGE, DISCARDED BUTT SAVED, RETRIEVED, AND LOGGED

There was something about the journal that had bugged me. I couldn't quite put my finger on it. I flipped through some more pages.

3:15 P.M. BRIEF TRIP OUTSIDE, RETRIEVES SOMETHING FROM CAR, GOES BACK INSIDE.

4:00 P.M. WATCHES TV, REALITY SHOW

4:30 P.M. ASLEEP ON COUCH

This didn't make sense. Why would Peter Fairchild's journal talk about studying for geography and watching reality TV?

I flipped through more pages:

3:04 P.M. PICKS UP GRADUATION CAP AND GOWN. TALKS TO PRINCIPAL.

3:20 P.M. IMPATIENT AS DAD TAKES PHOTO IN FRONT OF
SCHOOL; ARGUMENT

4:50 P.M. COOKING: POTATOES, ONIONS, GROUND BEEF

I let the journal drop in my lap. I felt teleported backward through time. The day I picked up my cap and gown, I had been surly as hell. The last thing I wanted to do was step foot on that campus again, where I was Convo of the Century. I had asked—begged, pleaded—for Dad to just pick it up for me, but he'd refused. He'd wanted to take pictures of me in front of the school.

Ultimately, I lost the battle. Dad followed me to the school and jumped out as soon as I emerged with cap and gown. He attacked me like paparazzi and it pissed me off. We argued. Loudly. Right there in front of the school at dismissal time. I'd said a lot of things that I ended up regretting about five minutes later. I wasn't sure at that time what I could trust with my dad and what I couldn't. But the look on his face when I'd said those things told me he was disappointed. I'd gone home and cooled down, and then gone downstairs to cook us both a nice dinner.

And there it was, logged in the journal I stole from Peter Fairchild.

It was a journal about me.

But there was something else about it as well. Something familiar. I realized what it was—a thin magenta glow around every letter. I went to my desk and pulled open a few drawers until I found it—last year's yearbook. Clumsily, frantically, I flipped through the opening pages, scanning. Finding nothing, I opened the back.

There it was.

I can't wait to see what this summer brings. LOVE! Jones

Each and every letter ringed with a magenta glow. I took the yearbook to the bed and compared it to the writing in the journal. It matched perfectly. I slammed the journal shut and saw on the back cover a notation from an L.A. County juvenile detention center that it had been inspected and approved.

Son of a bitch.

Jones had been watching me. He'd been writing it all down. And he'd been feeding it to Luna.

My gut lurched up into my throat. I jumped up and crossed the room, pulling my curtains shut angrily. I went through every room in my house doing the same. I felt violated, and even though Jones was dead, Peter and Luna weren't, and I still felt vulnerable. Who were they using to report my every move now?

Restless, I turned on some music and cranked the volume. I turned out the lights and sat on my bed, letting the music envelop me. Letting it hatch a plan inside me. In the darkness, I fumbled through my nightstand for my leftover pack of cigarettes and an old lighter. The flame flicked open the darkness for just a moment, and then there was the red glow of the end of my cigarette.

I needed to calm down. I needed to get some sleep. To center myself.

I had a boat to crash the next day.

28

"N ICE OF YOU to stop by."

I jumped, nearly dropping the yogurt I'd taken out of the refrigerator on the fly. I hadn't even noticed Dad sitting at the kitchen table, his bathrobe open to expose a white V-neck, boxer shorts, and tube socks. What I used to call his Dad Uniform, back when I felt comfortable enough with him to tease him. He had his laptop open and was browsing the news.

"You scared me," I said. "I was just leaving."

"Broken record," he said to the screen. "I almost forgot you lived here."

"Don't be dramatic." I pulled the foil off the top of

the yogurt and licked it clean, grabbing a spoon out of the drawer at the same time.

His eyes flicked up to me. "It's dramatic to miss your daughter?"

"It's normal for someone my age to be gone all the time. If I was like everyone else, I would be off at college right now."

"But you're not like everyone else."

I paused with a spoonful of yogurt halfway to my mouth. "Thanks for that."

He shut the laptop and took off his glasses, then laid them on the table and rubbed his eyes with his thumb and forefinger. "Well, it's the truth, right? You're gone all the time. You're with some mysterious man I've never met. You're not going to school. You're not working. Where in the world are you all day?"

"I'm busy being eighteen," I said defensively.

"You're busy hiding things from me."

That was it. A pop of ragemonster red on the ceiling and a splash of indigo in my yogurt, fern and ink seeping across the floor and under my feet. I was done.

"Really?" I asked, setting my half-eaten yogurt on the counter. "You're going to talk to me about hiding things?"

"Nikki, let's not turn this into a big deal," he said wearily. "I just got out of bed. I've been working and I'm tired and I'm not awake enough for theatrics."

"Oh, sure, you're right. This isn't a big deal." My Chucks were on the floor next to the garage door, and I went to them. "What *you're* hiding, though, is a big deal." Once it was out of my mouth, I could hardly believe I'd said it aloud. But it was too late to go back now, and I wasn't even sure if I would have.

"What are you talking about?"

"Mom!" I practically shouted. I had one shoe on and was working the second one, but my hands were shaking now. "You're hiding what happened with Mom. You knew, Dad. You knew about Hollywood Dreams. You knew about Peyton. You knew about Bill Hollis. You burned his studio down and you knew he wanted revenge. I think you even knew he wanted her dead." I finally got my other shoe on, and I found my finger angrily jabbing the air in his direction. "You knew everything. You kept evidence in that box under your desk. I don't know if you physically killed her yourself, but you might as well have. Because you let the killer in, didn't you? You left her alone on your supposed date night, knowing how powerful Bill Hollis was."

Dad's face had remained a stunned oval. It had gone ghostly white and then filled in high up on the cheeks with pink splotches. "Nikki," he said, his voice raspy.

"You lied to me," I said, my throat constricting with angry rusty starbursts. I almost felt like they were going to choke me. "You said the police couldn't solve her murder, but all these years you never said their only suspect was you and that they just didn't have anything concrete on you. You lied to me, Dad, for my entire life. So don't get all high and mighty on me about hiding things. I could never hide anything as well as you."

"Nikki," he repeated. He sounded small, defeated. "You don't understand."

I pulled my keys out of my pocket. "Spare me, okay? I don't need any more of your lies." I opened the garage door, then turned back while the big garage door rumbled and creaked open. "Oh, and what I'm hiding from you is this. I'm going after Luna. And her dad, Peter. Because somehow Mom's murder is tied to the Hollises and to him, and Luna's the last one standing. And because she's tried to kill me twice, and I won't ever be able to live normally as long as I know she's out there. Not that I would really know what normal is anyway. But, honestly, I have been looking for her because I want her dead. And if I have to kill her myself, then so be it. Like father, like daughter, right? There. How's that for honesty?"

I stomped down the wooden step into the garage, slamming the door behind me. My colors were going crazy—rage and sadness and giddiness and relief—and I let them float me all the way to the car. I didn't know what was going to happen when I came back home—*if* I came back home— but I knew everything between Dad and me had changed, all in the course of one conversation.

And that wasn't necessarily a bad thing.

I backed out of the driveway and pointed my car toward the beach. As I rolled past my house, I could see Dad standing in a front window—the one in the spare bedroom—watching me leave, his bathrobe cinched around his waist and a serious look on his face.

I T WOULD TAKE me twenty minutes, give or take, to get
to the marina. I hopped onto the 405 and turned on my
Bluetooth.

"Call Martinez," I said.

The robotic voice answered, "Calling Martinez."

The phone rang and rang then eventually went to voice
mail. It wasn't really all that early. He actually should have
been at work for a couple of hours now. Maybe he was in a
meeting. I left a message:

"Hey, it's me. I know you've got your own stuff going
on today, but I thought I'd let you know that I'm headed to
the marina to check out a houseboat. I'd love it if you'd join

me. That badge of yours would probably make it a lot easier to find the right boat, if you know what I mean. I'll pay you back. I'll ride along while you take care of your storage problem. I know you love that idea. Call me."

I hung up. Chris may have thought that I couldn't do anything without his help—and my phone call wasn't going to dispel that at all—but I wasn't worried. After my confrontation with Dad, I was feeling pretty fearless. What could Peter Fairchild really do to me now?

I was probably better off not thinking about it. The top of my foot, which I'd once broken on the back of Luna's head, throbbed at that thought.

It was a beautiful day, and the marina was hopping. I always loved the way the boats looked, all lined up and bobbing in the waves. Their names, printed proudly on their sides, beckoned me in colors and textures that dazzled my brain. I loved the smell of the sea and the cry of birds and the hum of engines as boats came and went, their ocean adventures calling to them. It was a place where my synesthesia wasn't a burden. A place where I could let go and enjoy the show.

But today it was a place where I had to pay attention. There were about five thousand boat slips, and after just a few minutes, they all started to look the same. Fortunately, good old Caroline the Realtor had spilled the beans when she said she thought Peter Fairchild just liked saying he lived in Tahiti. *Tahiti*, a foamy tangerine word. Also the name of one of the basins.

Still a lot of boats to comb through, but definitely less than five thousand. I started walking, barely glancing at the smaller boats, the sailboats, the fishing boats, the pontoons. I craned my neck as I passed every houseboat, trying to get a look inside, or at least on deck. Trying to find their names. Hoping for a *Luna* or *Peter* or SS *Fairchild*.

BuxtonTudor III

Norfolk

Alligator One

Loyalist

Claudette

Celeste

I stopped. *Celeste*. Midnight with star pops of light. Not celestial, but close. The *Celeste*. I was suddenly uneasy but unsure why. There were probably a million Celestes in this world. Just because Celeste Day worked for Peter Fairchild didn't mean a boat in his marina named *Celeste* had anything to do with her. Right?

Slowly, I went back to scouring the marina.

Saga

Gallion 10

Experiment

Bob's Babes

No Peter. No Luna. No Fairchild. Not even a *Hollywood Dreams.*

I got to the end of the marina and started back, rereading all the names, even though I knew I hadn't misread or missed any of them. I even read the names on the sides of sailboats just to be sure that Caroline hadn't gotten it wrong, or just had a very different definition of *yacht* than I did.

Actually. I stopped and turned slowly, trying to ignore the minutiae for a moment. Trying to see the boats as a whole. Very few would actually be big enough to be considered a yacht. I focused on those as I walked back.

Prime

Second Time Around

Sea Gypsy

Celeste

Again, I stopped. But this time not for the midnight with pops of light. This time for what was painted on the bow. I'd missed it on my first pass. How could I have missed it? Big swirly letters adorned the boat's nose.

Candy cane. Mustard.

VP.

There was no doubt in my mind. *Celeste* was Peter Fairchild's boat.

PETER FAIRCHILD CLEARLY intended to call this home. He had built a sturdy flight of boarding steps. The door at the top was closed, but I hadn't come all the way out here to stare at a closed door and go home. Since when did a closed door stop me from going inside a place?

Quickly, I glanced around the marina. I was pretty much alone for the time being. I pulled out my phone.

Again, the other end rang and rang. No answer. I pulled the phone away from my ear and checked the time. Even if he'd slept in, he'd be awake now. Maybe he was still in a meeting. Or he'd busted someone and had been busy writing reports.

Still. He would have called me back.

"Hey," I said to his voice mail. "Just letting you know I found the boat. I was hoping we could go in together, but you would appear to be . . ." I glanced up at the yacht, which looked a lot bigger once I had decided aloud that I was going to be boarding it. "So anyway, call me if you get this. Or just . . . come here. The boat is called *Celeste*." I pulled the phone away to hang up, but thought better of it and brought it back up. "Hey, and call me either way, okay? I'm just . . . you haven't given me shit all day and it feels weird."

You're worried, Nikki. You can say it. You are hard-core magenta-and-gray-spotted worried. It doesn't have to mean anything, other than that you're human.

"Yeah, but when did I turn into that?" I asked aloud as I hung up the phone.

I pushed thoughts about what could be happening with

Chris out of my head and walked up the stairs, my heart pounding harder with each step. If I was right, and Luna was on this boat, what then? I could hear Chris now: *Once again, Nikki, you're barging into a situation based on one of your hunches and without a plan.* I hesitated halfway up, and then kept going. Apparently barging into situations without a plan was working well for me.

Or at least I was surviving.

I tried the door. Of course it was locked. I knew it would be. Who would leave a luxury yacht unlocked and available for anyone who wandered by to steal out of? Still, I was disappointed. It was never fucking easy.

I went back down the stairs and walked back to my car to see if there was anything inside that I could use to break in. Last I had seen my penknife, Blake Willis had it in a plastic evidence bag. I had never gotten it back. I had nothing. Not even a credit card to slide down the doorjamb. Not to mention, this was hardly going to be some flimsy lock, and who even knew if there might be an alarm system if I got in?

I felt my way through the seat cushions, hoping to find a bobby pin or fingernail file, all the while knowing it was hopeless because I wasn't exactly the kind of girl who used bobby pins or filed her fingernails. I was more the quick brush and ponytail kind of girl, and I had noticed myself gnawing on my nails more than once since trying to quit smoking.

I popped the trunk. Maybe the tire iron would be helpful. If I were able to pry the door open, it would leave a statement, that was for sure. But sometimes statements had to be made. Especially statements like, *I found you, Luna, you crazy bitch, and now you're going to pay.*

I had to slide out of the way as a catering truck backed past me, all the way to the dock, beeping obnoxiously—a sound that pealed through the serene air like a knife through fabric.

"Jeez, watch where you're going!" I shouted at their closed windows. The two guys inside didn't even notice that I existed. Satisfied with their entry, they parked the truck and both hopped out, throwing open the back doors and pulling out a ramp.

I pawed through my trunk, looking for the tire iron. Once I found it, I knew it wouldn't work. Not unless I wanted to just bust my way through the door, *The Shining*–style. Maybe not the subtlest entry, even for me.

"Shit, shit, shit." I slammed the trunk and leaned against the back of my car. I'd found one thing in the backseat that was useful. I pulled out a cigarette and the lighter that had been tucked into the cigarette packet and lit up, idly watching the Ambrosia Catering guys do their work.

If Chris arrived and I was smoking, he would have a hissy fit. But I would actually kind of welcome a hissy fit if it ended with an idea of how I was going to get into that yacht.

The caterers were continuing to come and go, each dipping into the back of the truck and emerging with an armload of boxes. They dutifully carried them down the dock, all the way to . . .

I bolted upright, dropping my cigarette. I barely glanced at it as it fell.

They were going into the yacht. *The* yacht. A woman in an old-timey apron—housekeeper?—was holding the door for them, stepping out of the way to let them pass. They disappeared, the housekeeper shouting instructions behind them.

This was almost too easy. It was a gift.

Without thinking, I darted up the ramp and into the truck. There were a few tubs left. I grabbed the first one I could get my hands on and hauled it down the ramp, grunting the whole way. I could hear clinking inside that sounded like wine or beer bottles. They were stocking up. For what? Were they leaving town? Had they figured out that I had found them and planned to skip out before I could do anything about it?

I could hear the voices of the two men approaching. Panicked, I opened my car door and jammed the box inside, then dove in behind it. I waited, listening for their thunking metal footsteps on the truck floor and their voices getting farther away again. When I was pretty sure they were gone, I crawled over the seat. They were at the top of the steps again. I started my car and moved it to a spot on the other side of the marina. I could still see the yacht, and the delivery truck. I watched as they emerged from the yacht with a clipboard, stared bewilderedly into the back of the truck, one of them gabbing into a cell phone, and then got back in the truck and drove away—undoubtedly to retrieve the box of booze they'd "forgotten" to bring.

As soon as the truck was out of sight, I raced back to my spot and got out. It was going to be a long walk heaving this box, and my knees already felt weak from nerves. But I would make it. Or I would die trying.

Bad choice of words, Nikki.

I was sweating and breathing hard by the time I got to the top of the stairs. I knocked on the door, bringing up one knee and balancing the box atop it. I heard a faint voice from inside and then the woman opened the door. She looked surprised, first taking in me and then the box and then me again.

"Are the guys gone?" I asked. "Sorry, I'm from Ambrosia Catering?" I lifted the box a little higher to show it to her. "Our delivery guys forgot a box. I think it's alcohol. Can't forget that." I let out a breathy, conspiratorial laugh.

"Oh, yes," she said, standing on her tiptoes to look over my shoulder. "They left to find it. You must have just missed them."

"Darn it," I said, following her eyes over my shoulder, as if I were looking for them, too. "I was hoping to catch them. Is it okay if I just bring it in myself? I'll give them a call."

"Of course." She stepped out of the way.

And I was in.

G RANTED, I HAD never exactly been inside a yacht before, so I didn't have anything to compare it to, but I had to physically force myself not to gasp when I walked inside.

It was huge. Way bigger than it looked from the outside. I was standing in a foyer, complete with chandelier, a luxurious living room to my right, a dance floor to my left. A grand staircase wound its way to an upper deck.

Someone—the housekeeper, I suspected—had sprinkled confetti across black, glass-topped tables. Balloons skittered aimlessly around the dance floor.

"A party," I said, mostly to myself, but the housekeeper heard me.

"I'm sorry?" She looked at me quizzically. *Duh, Nikki, why wouldn't the caterer know there was going to be a party?*

I gave a stupid-me eye roll. "I mean, I know there's a party. I meant to ask, what are they celebrating?"

"The movie is finished!" she said excitedly, as if their success was hers. "Miss Celeste is exhausted and sick, but she demanded a party to celebrate. She is proud of Mr. Fairchild's success. Come, the kitchen is downstairs."

I followed her through a set of doors into what looked like a captain's quarters, everything white linen and sleek lines. Near the captain's chair was a staircase. Another spiral, this one disappearing into the bowels of the boat.

"You'll forgive me for asking," I said as I tried not to tumble under the weight of the box. "But is this ship Celeste Day's ship?" She gave me another perplexed look. "I've never met an actual celebrity before," I said sheepishly. Not adding, of course, that until I started looking for Luna and her dad, I'd never heard of Celeste Day at all. "It belongs to Mr. Fairchild," she said. Her voice had taken on an icy tone. Clearly I had overstepped my bounds. "He is quite fond of Miss Celeste. I'm certain that's why he named the ship after her."

"Ah." That was weird, though, wasn't it? Was he sleeping with his teen star? "Does he always name his ships after his leading ladies?" I attempted a laugh, but it sounded forced even to me.

"This is his first big film," she said, bustling to a door. It opened into a walk-in refrigerator, which was stuffed with booze, including three more Ambrosia Catering boxes. She invited me to place my box inside with a sweep of her arm. "And his first ship. It's quite the perfect marriage, don't you think?" I was still holding my box. "You can set that in here for now," she said, prompting me. "We'll let the bartender decide what to bring up to the bar later."

"Oh." I had to keep her talking. I had to look around. I had to answer the most important question: Was Luna on this ship, too? "Can I go ahead and unpack while I wait for the guys to come back? I don't want us to get behind schedule."

She gave a curt nod but didn't move from her position, holding the refrigerator door open with her butt.

"I've kind of followed Mr. Fairchild's career," I said, opening the box and taking out two wine bottles. "I'm curious—does his daughter live here with him?"

This time the woman frowned. "Mr. Fairchild's daughter is . . . away," she said.

"Vacation, huh?" I plowed on, acting clueless, even though my heart had dropped with disappointment. Luna wasn't on this ship. Maybe Chris was right. She was in Dubai, living the life with her parents' money. She was nice enough to set up her doting daddy before she left, so he could keep house with a hot young starlet. How kind of her.

The housekeeper mashed her lips together, then leaned in. She whispered, "She's getting some rehabilitation." She said the last word with great gravity.

"Drugs?" I whispered, playing along.

The housekeeper shrugged. "She's had some difficulties in her past," she said. "Could be drugs, I suppose. My impression is it was much worse."

"I heard she was in jail," I ventured, my spine tingling. If she figured out who I was—that I was the *much worse* she herself was referencing—I was toast.

The housekeeper twisted her hands in her old-timey apron. "I can't say," she finally said. "Mr. Fairchild has been very good to me. His family problems are none of my concern. I only know that he does not believe he will see her again."

"Ever?" I asked.

"That's how I understand it. He said it would be best for everyone if we just forget she exists. Can you imagine a father saying that about his own daughter?"

Shit. That proved it. Luna was gone. She'd run away and was never coming back. That should have made me happy. So why was I so enraged I wanted to start throwing these wine bottles against the walls of his posh little boat?

"No, I can't," I said absently.

There was a faraway knock. The housekeeper peered up the spiral stairs anxiously. "It's probably the caterers coming back," she said.

I smiled sweetly. "I'll just finish up here, and if they don't need me, I'll let myself out."

She looked unsure—as if she'd been given directions to never let anyone out of her sight while on the *Celeste*. But she also looked like she trusted me. Our conversation about Luna seemed to have relaxed her a little bit. "Okay," she said. "I do have more dusting to do. You wouldn't think a boat would get so dusty. It's a mystery to me."

She said the last as she trotted up the stairs. I waited for her to disappear and for the sound of the door opening, and then I bolted, letting the walk-in slam shut on the half-emptied box. I had to get out of there before the Ambrosia guys came in and realized they'd been gifted a coworker who didn't actually exist.

The housekeeper's voice floated down toward me, intermixed with the voices of the two men. I stood at the base of the stairs and gazed up. No way could I go back up this way. I would be intercepted for sure. Instead, I hurried through the kitchen and out a side door, which took me to some sort of Jet Ski garage. Two Jet Skis were parked in front of a rolling door, life jackets lining the walls. Seriously cool and swank, but not really a great place to hide. I kept moving, finding myself in a fitness room, and then a recreation room. There was a bar down here, along with some card tables, a pool table, and three really huge flat-screen TVs. The lower deck of this ship probably cost more than my house.

God only knew what the upper levels held.

I was about to find out.

I ducked through a door on the other side of the recreation room, spilling into a spa room, with mirrored makeup stations and three massage tables. The air smelled like oils and lotions, and if I wasn't desperately trying to find a place to hide, it might have been tempting to just lie back and enjoy the aromatherapy.

I kept going. On the other side of the massage room was what looked like a big storage area. I turned in circles, assessing whether I could hide here. It mostly seemed to be filled with tubs and boxes, and a tall, partially disassembled Christmas tree in one corner. In order to hide in here, I would have to empty a box.

I could barely hear the voices anymore, which made me relax a little. If they were excited, I might hear some yelling or at the very least calling out.

Still, I pressed forward, and found myself in an engine room. Also no place to hide. But there was a set of stairs at the end, presumably leading to the main deck and beyond.

I stood at the bottom of the steps and bit my lip. If the housekeeper decided to come down these stairs, there would be no hiding. There would also be no explaining why on earth I was on the opposite end of the ship that I was supposed to be on. Not to mention, why hadn't my supposed coworkers ever heard of me?

I was in too deep to go back now. I could make up a story about needing to use a restroom and getting lost. I could play up the whole golly-gee-willikers-this-is-a-mighty-big-boat thing. Maybe she would believe me. Maybe she would at least believe me long enough for me to get away before she called the police.

But I didn't want to get away. And I did want the police to come. Or at least one particular officer.

I pulled out my phone and fired off a quick text, hoping it would go through from the depths of a ship.

Party at Luna's tonight. Be there or be square. I'll be—I paused, thinking. Where would I be? **around,** I finished.

I sent the text, chewed my nail, and wrote another.

Actually, don't be square. Just be there. Or here. Or not. Whatever.

Half a second after sending that one, I winced, wishing I hadn't done so. I sounded like a confused dork even to myself. I opened my text box one last time.

I'll find you.

There. That would be enough. Hopefully. I wasn't exactly sure he would still be willing to do something like this for me. I wasn't exactly sure I would blame him if he wasn't.

The texts sent, I pushed my phone back into my pocket

and started climbing stairs, hurrying, but trying to keep my footsteps as quiet as possible. I passed the main deck, figuring that would be the most likely place for the housekeeper to be hanging out, and pressed on to the upper deck.

I came out in a little hallway. On my left I could see a dining room, so filled with shining silver and crystal it hurt my eyes. On my right, I could see . . . the ocean. The entire room was made of windows. Just as there had been couches and tables and candles at Blue Yonder, so were there here. Probably a hundred people could sit in the lounge area and stare out at the water or step onto the small deck outside for a dip in the glass-walled pool, and probably tonight there would be.

Up here, I couldn't hear the water lapping against the sides of the ship or the hum of the refrigerator or the soft rumble of the kitchen appliances or the birds outside. I definitely couldn't hear the men talking anymore. All I could hear was my own breathing, and the soft shush of my shoes on the carpet as I walked warily down the hall. Cabin after cabin opened up on either side of me—six of them in total, their beds identically made in melon and turquoise linens. Guest beds.

I ducked into a stateroom and opened a closet. Other than a life vest, it was empty. Which meant lots of room to hang out, but nothing to hide behind. I assumed every cabin would be identical in that way, so when I came across another stairway at the ship's stern, I headed up.

The top deck was obviously just for the sun goddesses. Luna probably avoided this deck like the plague, given the fair skin that she was so proud of. Deck chairs were lined up like soldiers. I felt high above the water, the breeze whipping salt into my hair. Just me and the sun.

I sat on a lounge and closed my eyes, taking the tiniest moment to soak it in.

This was Luna's life. This was what it was like to grow up part of the Hollis clan. This had been Peyton's normal. This had been what Dru was accustomed to. Could it ever feel ordinary to me? Probably not. Ordinary had nothing to do with this life. Come to think of it, ordinary had nothing to do with my life, either.

I was so not a Hollis it wasn't even funny.

Maybe that had been the message Dad had been trying to send me this whole time. Maybe he hid things from me to protect me. Even if he'd had something to do with Mom's murder. Even if she was dead because of him. Maybe he was trying to spare me the same fate.

Or maybe he was persona non grata to Bill Hollis, and you just didn't get to be Hollywood elite if someone like Bill Hollis wanted you locked out.

I had to stay on this yacht until the party. I had to confront Peter Fairchild. I had to find Luna.

I got up and jogged one deck down, passing all the

staterooms swiftly, my focus sharpening on possible hiding places. Closets—not the best. Beneath the dining room table—surely the housekeeper would be up there at some point, polishing silver or whatever she did to prepare for parties. Behind the upper-deck bar—that would be opening at some point this evening, I was sure of it.

Then I saw it. A tiny door flush with the wood under the grand staircase that went from lower deck to top deck. A perfect place to hide.

The door was locked, a tiny key lock visible in the wood. I bent to inspect it, then went all the way back to the lower deck and rooted through the spa room until I found a handful of bobby pins and a paper clip. I worked quietly, hearing the hum of the men's voices again. I tiptoed to the door and listened to their conversation. They were talking about onions. Nothing at all to do with the strange disappearing employee who had somehow ended up delivering their wine. Thank God.

Tools in hand, I went back upstairs, pausing only long enough to see what the housekeeper might be doing on the main deck. She was running a rag in tight circles along the brass bar rail, humming softly to herself.

If she'd realized anything was amiss, she definitely had a strange way of showing it.

I started to duck back into the stairwell when something on the flat screen over the bar caught my eye. The TV was turned on—a special news report. The sound was off and I could barely make out the words at the bottom of the screen, but my stomach twisted in knots just the same. *Local Drug Bust Turns Deadly.* The screen showed a live shot of a street surrounded by cop cars, lights whipping in circles, doors thrown open. They were surrounding two cars, one blocking the other in a driveway. The film was being recorded from a helicopter, and when it panned out wide, there was a body on the ground right next to one of the cars, a sheet tossed over it. It was almost impossible to make out through the fireworks going off in my head. Almost.

Even through the rust popping in my vision, I knew what I was looking at: bubble gum, pearl, blue. Bronze, silver, foamy sea green. JSB946. Rebecca Moreno's license plate. Her car being blocked by a car I recognized. One ringed so yellow I could taste butter when I looked at it too long.

I couldn't breathe. My hands shook around the bobby pins, and I even dropped one. It plinked against the floor and my heart hammered. Surely the housekeeper was going to hear that and turn around. Would it matter, though? Would I really care if she caught me? Would I still care about Luna if Chris was . . .

I shook my head. I couldn't go there.

He hasn't been answering your calls, Nikki.

I had to believe he was safe. It was the only way I could finish this.

He hasn't texted you even once.

He was a good cop. He knew what he was doing.

He remembered why they wanted him dead in the first place. And they found his storage locker, Nikki.

I sipped in breaths, trying to get my feelings under control. Damn it! This was why I didn't do feelings. He was fine. And if he wasn't, it was his own fucking fault for trying to White Knight the entire world.

The housekeeper turned in my direction and I only managed to just barely pull my head back into the stairwell in time. My synesthesia had lied to me before. The TV was far away and there was no sound. The colors could have totally tricked me into seeing something that wasn't there. One of those license plate letters could be wrong. And who knew how many people drove cars just like Chris's?

He was alive. He was fine. He would be calling any minute. And I needed to be in a place where I could talk to him when he did.

I climbed to the upper deck and went back to the staircase door. I dropped to my knees, straightened the bobby pins, and stuck them in the lock, wiggling and twisting until it opened.

Damn, I was getting good at this.

I pulled open the door and peered inside. It was dark and dusty and God only knew what kind of bugs might be lurking, but save for a few empty boxes, there didn't appear to be much in there. A perfect place to hide.

I crawled in, feeling grit under my palms, and pulled the door shut. I fumbled in the dark until I found the lock and swiveled it so that it was shut again, then slithered behind the boxes. I couldn't sit up straight, so I curled up on my side and closed my eyes, hoping that when I opened them again, they would be adjusted to the dark. I slowed my breathing, and my heartbeat followed. I rested my head on my arm, pulling my hair over my shoulder so it wasn't lying in the dust.

My stomach growled. I ignored it. I had no choice. I had to stay here and wait.

My chest felt tight, filled bumpy gray and black with fear. I ignored it. I had no choice.

I checked my phone. Nothing from Chris. I ignored that, too.

I had a party to go to tonight.

I had a date to wait for.

Two, really, if you counted Luna.

And why wouldn't I count Luna?

31

I WAS AWAKENED by a deep rumble and the sense of movement. I opened my eyes, confused and frantic. It was pitch dark, and my entire body was cramped from being in the fetal position, and at first the movement and the dark and the discomfort tricked me into thinking I was back in Jones's van, racing to Tesori Antico. But I could smell boxes and dust and ocean water. It was the last that jogged my brain back into place.

I pulled myself to sitting, pressing my palms flat against the floor. We were definitely moving. I crawled back to the door, which I could make out by a tiny sliver of light shining through the edge. I pressed my ear against the wood, but the engine hum only got louder, drowning out any noise from the room.

I sat back and licked my lips. I was thirsty, and still hungry, and hot, and my shoulder ached. And I hadn't thought about how I was going to get out of here.

There you go, Nikki, barging into places without a plan again.

Chris.

I shimmied to one side so I could get to my phone. Chris hadn't texted me back. Hadn't called me, either. If I'd been able to see anything, I was certain everything would be gray and black. I dialed his number. It rang and rang and eventually went to voice mail. I tried not to think about the body lying on the ground outside Rebecca Moreno's house.

"Hey," I whispered. "Just letting you know that I've set sail. I have no idea where we're going or how long we've been moving. I'm safe." I started to hang up, then thought better of it. "I hope you are too."

I felt the movement slow, the engine noise lowering an octave and getting quieter. Now I thought I could hear a thump of bass. Music was being played somewhere. I also thought I could hear distant laughter. I pressed my face against the stripe of light and tried to see out. I could only see shifting shapes, which was really all I needed to see to know I was completely fucked. There was no way I was going to be able to come out from under the staircase without being noticed.

I eased back, resting against the wall. I could feel the thump of feet at the back of my head, as expensive shoes clomped up and down the stairs. I weighed my options, which seemed few and far between. Come out with figurative guns blazing, try to slip out stealthily, or just stay inside. My leg cramped, giving me the answer for the last option. I was clearly not very good at the second option. Which left just one.

I checked my phone again. Still nothing from Chris. I closed my eyes and bounced my head softly against the wall behind me.

"Think, Nikki, think."

I turned on my phone flashlight and looked around. Like I'd thought, there was nothing but me, empty boxes, and the pipes and wires on the walls.

Wait. The pipes and wires on the walls.

I ran my fingers down one of the wires. It was thick, white, and I had no idea what it powered. I also had no idea what would happen if someone were to rip a live wire out of a wall. Especially while sitting on water. Probably nothing good. But maybe not anything really that bad. Maybe just enough to cause a disturbance.

And causing disturbances was something I excelled at.

I turned off my flashlight and waited for my eyes to adjust again. They did, and I grabbed a handful of wires. I braced my feet against the wall and said a quick prayer.

"Please, God, don't let me die in here. But if you do, make it quick."

Without giving it another thought, I pushed against the wall with my feet and yanked on the wires as hard as I could. Nothing happened. The wires had pulled away from the wall a little, and that was it. I let out my breath and panted, my arms slack at my sides.

Well. At least I wasn't electrocuted.

But I was still stuck in this place.

Building up courage was a little harder the second time, because I was afraid I'd somehow damaged the wires and just touching them would light me up like a sparkler. But after a few readying breaths, I planted my feet on the wall again, wrapped my hands around the wires, and pulled.

Something loosened, and then a wire pulled free completely. There was a muffled cry of surprise. I opened my eyes to see the strip of light had gone out.

It worked. Holy shit! It worked! *Score another one for no plans, Martinez.*

I released the wires as if they were on fire and thrust myself forward, feeling for the lock. I found it, swiveled it upward, and pushed the door open just a fraction. There were about twenty people in the room, most of them standing at the bar, and the ones that weren't were so wrapped up in the drama of a power outage, there was no way they would see me. Not if I moved fast.

So I moved fast. I didn't even bother to shut the door behind me. I spilled out onto the carpet, got to my feet, and booked it to the stairwell.

THE REST OF the ship still had power, and word hadn't yet reached other decks about the outage upstairs. The main deck was wall-to-wall people, some of whom I recognized from Pear Magic, all dressed in fancy gowns and expensive-looking suits. All drinking and talking over one another. It wouldn't be long before someone would start investigating what was wrong on the upper deck, and then they would find the open storage door and the loose wires inside. I had only a minute or two to make sure the rest of the ship was in the dark.

I raced downstairs, no longer worrying about the sounds of my footsteps. Nobody was on these stairs—they weren't fabulous enough. It would be impossible to Make an Entrance on a back staircase. I plunged into the engine room of the lower deck and looked around. Nobody here, either. The circuit breaker box was there, though. It was time to take care of that.

I scurried into the storage room next door and looked around until I found a toolbox. Inside were the usual— screwdrivers, wrenches, nails, a hammer. I picked up the hammer and wont back into the engine room.

My skin buzzed in silver squiggles. Bubbling and burbling

yellows and oranges burst up into rusty splats. Beneath it all was a field of bumpy gray and black. I had to take a few deep breaths to stop the kaleidoscope from spinning.

As soon as I felt stable, I threw open the circuit box and smashed it with the hammer. The first hit sent a jolt of neon green up my arms, but I didn't let that stop me. I swung again and again, even after I was bathed in darkness, pieces of plastic flying around me and skittering across the floor.

Satisfied, I dropped the hammer and walked out.

I HAD GONE to school with overdramatic rich girls long enough to know what kind of mayhem was going to ensue. People would scream in fear—dainty little squeals that they would later pretend to be embarrassed about. They would cluster together, all talking over one another. They would suppose this and suppose that, and nobody would have the first clue what to do, because there was always someone else hired to know how to take care of these kinds of things. I remembered thinking during one of our many fire-alarm pranks that I would be the only person to survive if there was actually an emergency at our school. The rest of them would die, in the most lovely, photogenic poses they could think of.

It wasn't much different on a dark ship full of actors in the middle of the ocean.

For the first time, I was able to waltz right through the main deck without turning a single head. I wound my way through, listening to the ridiculous theories and complaints and the occasional couple who didn't seem to really even notice anything was going on. I paused every time I came across anyone who even remotely resembled Luna, the boiling oranges and yellows licked ragemonster and drained into a sea of ink, until I realized it wasn't her. Also, no Peter Fairchild, who would make a very satisfactory runner-up in the Who Becomes Nikki's Punching Bag First contest.

I scoured the entire dance floor, the packed living room area, the bar. I pushed my way outside, where the people seemed much more chill about the power outage. I heard rumors of someone named Tony checking out the breaker to see what had happened. The lights should be on soon, the consensus outside seemed to be. The party would go back to full swing.

I sank onto a lounge chair in a shadowy corner and studied each face, each voice on the deck. No Luna. No Peter.

Frustrated, I pulled out my phone and checked for word from Chris. Still nothing. I shouldn't have checked—now my nerves were out of control, the slate sliding over me, dampening the fire colors.

I got up and went back inside, taking everything more slowly this time, staying on the fringe of the crowd but paying close attention to each person. I continued to search in a second living room next door, where people were quivering on couches like this was the *Titanic* and the whole damn thing was going down. Beyond that, I passed through a less formal bar area—nearly empty, save for an entwined couple making full use of the dark—and into a quiet hallway.

More cabins. I hadn't had the chance to explore these earlier because of the housekeeper. A quick look in the first one told me it belonged to Peter Fairchild. Men's shoes lined the floor at the end of the bed. A jacket hung from the closet door. Colognes and aftershaves were scattered atop the dressing table. I took a quick tour of the room, looking for anything that might help me bust him, but of course I found nothing.

I peeked in another room; it was empty.

But there was a third room at the end of the hallway, and I heard voices coming from it. I edged along the wall and positioned myself just outside the door, near a hallway bathroom, so I could see inside.

A man and a girl. The girl crying, the man bent over her, gently murmuring, consoling her. Even from the back, I could tell it was Peter Fairchild, his white-blond hair nearly glowing in the dark. My skin crawled and I felt a tingle go up my spine. Finally, I had found him.

He shifted position, and I could see the brown wavy hair of Celeste Day peeking out from the side. But there was something off about her. She was shorter than she'd originally appeared at Pear Magic. And there was something about her cry. Something familiar. I inched closer so I could hear them.

"This was supposed to be my big night," she whimpered. She blotted her eyelashes—carefully, carefully, just the lashes—with a tissue.

"And it still will be," Peter assured her.

"The tabloids are here," she said. "They're supposed to be here to cover me. To make me officially part of the scene." Her cry had gone angrier, and the familiarity deepened.

"And they still will."

"How can they?" she seethed. "There are no lights on this piece-of-shit boat. How is anyone supposed to see me? How is anyone supposed to appreciate me and all that I've done?"

He put his hand on her arm, a calming, almost sweet gesture. "They will. The lights will come on and everyone will see you, Luna. I promise."

"Don't call me that," she growled.

"I'm sorry," he said. "It's a habit, I've told you. I will always see my little girl under that face, even if you get a million surgeries." He ran a thumb down her cheek. "Even if you change your hair a hundred times or buy a hundred colors of contacts. You're beautiful, just like your mother. Much prettier than that silly little starlet was, Luna."

She slapped his hand away "I am not Luna. I am

Celeste. Why can't you get it through your thick skull that I am Celeste? Not a silly little starlet. I am a star. Luna was a nobody. Luna is dead. I am not a nobody. I will not let you make me a nobody again."

Realization washed over me like a tidal wave, and I swam in a gray and black sea. Of course. That was why her cry was familiar, why her voice was familiar. She wasn't disguising it because she thought they were alone. But now I could see it. In her movements. In her posture. In her pitiless crocodile eyes. I sagged against the wall.

"You were never a nobody," Peter was saying, but I couldn't pay attention to his words, my mind was racing so hard.

I heard footsteps coming up the stairs and pressed myself into the shadows of the restroom.

"Sir?" a voice said. I peeked out to see a short man in a sharp uniform standing in the doorway.

"What is it, Tony? Why don't you have the lights back on yet?" Peter snapped, irritation lining his face as he advanced on poor Tony.

Tony held up the hammer that had been hanging slack at his side. "Someone destroyed the breaker box, sir. Smashed it to bits."

Peter took the hammer from Tony. My stomach lurched.

"Destroyed it?" he said, almost to the hammer itself, as if he expected it to be able to answer him.

"Yes, sir. It is not fixable tonight. We will need to replace the whole thing. There are also wires loose in the upstairs storage room. Door was unlocked and open."

Peter's face twisted. "Wires loose?"

"Yes, sir. Someone wanted the lights out tonight."

Peter gazed at the hammer again, turning so he could gaze between both Luna and Tony. When he moved, Luna was fully exposed. She looked up, but her stare went past Peter and past Tony, directly across the hall and into the shadows of the bathroom.

I felt my face light up when our eyes connected. Ice filled my entire body. Gray and black ice.

"Who in the world would want to sabotage the *Celeste*?" Peter asked, still dismayed.

Luna's reptile eyes glowed as they stayed locked on mine. Her chin was tucked into her chest, her shoulders taut.

"Nikki Kill," she answered. Then to me, "Boo."

32

THE FIRST THOUGHT in my mind was that I was trapped. The second thought that Chris would have said he told me so. Both thoughts were blasted away by the third thought, though, and that was, *Run*.

We all seemed to take off at the same time, Peter knocking Tony to the ground in his haste to get to me. I had to jump over Tony's chest, my toe nicking his shoulder and pitching me forward. I caught myself just as my fingertips brushed the floor and I churned my feet harder, plunging back into the confused crowd on the dance floor.

Now there were real screams, blossoming from annoyed shouts, as first I shoved through, and then Peter, and then Luna. I bumped into another man in a uniform who was carrying a long Maglite. I grabbed it out of his hands and chucked it backward, watching only long enough to see it glance off Peter's face. He stumbled, paused, touched his bleeding forehead, and raced forward, the hammer tight in his grip now, his teeth bared in a snarl.

The crowd closed Luna in as we took off even faster.

No plan, Nikki. You have no goddamned plan, I admonished myself as I headed for the grand stairwell. I tipped a vase off a table at the bottom of the steps. It shattered, sending water and flowers and shards of glass across the floor. Anything to slow Peter down. Anything to give me time.

My lungs felt like they were on fire, and I wished I hadn't had that cigarette earlier that day. Mostly, I wished Chris was here to help me out. It was one thing to think you could beat Peter Fairchild at his own game; it was another to be faced with him, especially when he was brandishing a hammer at you.

I got off on the floor where I'd hidden under the stairs and ran directly into a woman who had been standing at the top of the stairs, peering down curiously. We landed in a tangle on the floor, and I rolled wildly to get off her. I could hear Peter's feet nearing as I raced down the hall toward the utility stairs that had been my safe space all day. I heard someone yell, "That way!" and cursed under my breath. Nobody on this ship knew who the real bad guy was.

I paused only for the briefest moment, my shoes skidding

on the floor. I didn't have time for decision making. I had to just choose: up or down. I chose up.

When I reached the top deck, I slammed the stairwell door shut. Three women in bikinis startled and then hurried toward the grand staircase when they saw me coming. I was breathing so hard my throat felt hot, and I was desperately looking around for a way to protect myself.

"No," I said between breaths, reaching out to the women. Ragged, scary. "Help me."

But the women left anyway. I was alone with the wind and the ocean and nowhere to go to get away from Peter Fairchild.

I T WAS JUST moments before Peter wrenched the door open. I raced behind a lounge chair and picked up a heavy deck umbrella. It wasn't much of a weapon, but at least it was something. I clutched it in front of me so hard my arm muscles ached.

Peter came toward me, still holding the hammer. His face was an evil snarl. He walked with an unsteady gait, as if his legs had been weakened by the run. He was breathing just as hard as I was, but his breath wasn't coming out like asphalt. It was belching out of him in outraged feathery fern and ink. The wind blew my hair across my face, and I tossed my head to get it out of my line of sight.

I swung the umbrella at him with everything I had. I

missed by miles, of course, but it slowed him down. I walked backward, knowing that before too long I would be up against the ship's rail and would be out of options. I would have to fight back or die.

"I should have known," he said, his hand tightening around the hammer so that I could hear his skin creak against the wood. "I should have known it would be you. You just couldn't leave well enough alone, Nikki. You couldn't leave Luna alone."

I swung the umbrella at him again. "Everyone thinks Luna's long gone."

"She could have been," he spat. "After that shitty studio in Vegas turned her down, we found the perfect actress. Such a resemblance, and easy to get rid of. We spent thousands on cheekbones and a nose job. The transformation was perfection, and finally she had what she always wanted. A chance in Hollywood. That was all she wanted—a chance. And first her bitch stepsister took that from her. And then you. You took that from her. She was starting over. And you're back. You won't be satisfied until we kill you, too." He swung the hammer and missed.

"I wasn't following Luna," I said. A small lie. I wasn't sure where I was going with it. I was only sure that it was buying me time. "I was following you."

He paused but only a little. "Why?"

I swung the umbrella, twice. "You know who killed my

mother," I said. "You were there. I wanted to know if it was my father."

He stopped for real this time, lowered the hammer, and laughed. "Milo?" He laughed again. "Milo couldn't put a match out with a fire hose. No, he didn't kill her."

"Bill Hollis, then," I said. My arms were killing me.

His face drew itself into a hateful line. "No. Believe it or not, Bill Hollis did not run the entire world. Even if he thought he did."

I shook my head, uncomprehendingly. "Then who?" I asked.

"She was mine," he bellowed.

"My mother?"

"No, you stupid girl. I didn't want your used-up mother. *Vanessa* was mine. I would have done anything for her. And I did." He pounded the air with the hammer as he talked. "I supported her. I ruined careers for her. I hurt people for her. Anything she asked for. We were Vanessa and Peter. We were VP."

Candy cane and mustard lit up in my mind. He wasn't the vice president of anything. He was still holding a torch for Vanessa Hollis.

"And then she left me. Met that bastard, Bill Hollis, and left me. Hired that moron Basile and he started doing my job. I was out, stuck with a snot-nosed kid who looked exactly like the woman I wanted. The one I rightfully deserved."

He pointed to his chest with the hammer. The movement startled me, and I thrust the umbrella forward again.

"I don't understand," I said. Wind pushed my hair across my face; it stuck to my bottom lip. "What does this have to do with my mother?"

"She should've stayed gone. Your mother should have stayed gone. But she came back. Your father burned down the set and Bill Hollis made her come back as his personal whore. And God knew what that man wanted he always got." He pounded the air with the hammer again, spittle flying from the corners of his mouth. "Trust me, I was happy that Carrie came back, but Vanessa was jealous. She cried on my shoulder." He pointed the hammer at himself again. "Mine. Not Bill Hollis's. Mine. I had her back. And then Carrie went away again—well, we all know why now, don't we? We all know about Peyton. But at the time, nobody knew. She just disappeared. And the minute she left, Vanessa forgot that I existed. Went right back to Bill, as if he gave even an ounce of shit about her. Not like I did."

"My mom didn't steal him," I said. "She was blackmailed by him."

"I wish she would have!" he yelled. He began advancing on me again. I tensed the umbrella again. "If she would have stolen him, maybe Vanessa would have given up on him. Instead, when your mother came back again, Vanessa came to me. She wanted me to make her go away for good."

"You? You're the one who killed her?"

He pressed the hammer against his lips as his eyes smoldered through the memory. "I did everything Vanessa ever wanted."

I felt a tear run down my cheek. My poor mother had been trapped by Bill Hollis. She had no way out, just like I had no way out here. Would we both die by the same man? Trapped by Hollis lies? "You didn't have to kill her."

"I wasn't going to. I was going to scare her, make her and Milo leave town. I didn't want to kill her," he said. "Until I looked into her face and saw . . . I saw Vanessa. I saw someone who was willing to do anything—even betray the man who would die for her—for Bill Hollis. She betrayed Milo the same way Vanessa betrayed me, all for that man. Next thing I knew I was bashing her head in with a tire iron. She was gone, and Vanessa was happy. And for the rest of her life, I kept Vanessa happy. I was there for her to run to when things were going wrong."

"She wasn't worth it," I said. I swung the umbrella again, but my swings were getting worse. My hands were getting numb. My arms were getting weak. "The world is better off without her."

He growled and came at me, swinging.

"No, Nikki," I heard. "The world would be better off without you." Luna had come up the stairs. She stretched her arms out to her sides and posed. "What do you think?

Am I the most amazing actress or what?" Her features softened as she rested her hand over her heart. "Thank you all for coming to my premiere. Those of you who know me know what a long road it's been from Albany to here. But I believed." She burst out laughing. "You should see your face. It's like you're seeing a ghost. Boo." She fake-lunged at me, and I jumped, bringing the umbrella up. Now I was trying to keep an eye on both Peter and Luna. "You kind of are seeing one, actually. The ghost of that big loser Celeste Day. If she weren't glugging around at the bottom of the ocean as of a few days ago when my last surgery was healed, she would be thanking me for putting her on the map. Right, Daddy?"

I thought about the girl in the makeup chair back at Pear Magic. Was Luna saying what I thought she was saying? Was Celeste Day gone? Had Luna killed her? "You won't get away with it," I said.

"Already have. Daddy's plan was brilliant. Find a nobody actress who has no ties back home and give her a role." She made a scissors motion with her fingers by her face. "A little injection here and there, a centimeter or so off the nose, some contacts, great stylist, and the nobody actress can disappear without anyone knowing the difference." Again, she posed. It was uncanny, hearing Luna's voice, seeing Luna's eyes behind this strange face. She'd always been so good at imitating other people—especially Peyton—but this was creepy. "I hate being a brunette, but I'll be a famous brunette. Finally. Fuck Hollis and his plans. He was too slow. He never appreciated my potential. And neither did you." This time she lunged at me for real.

I jumped back and dropped the umbrella, stumbling too close to Peter.

Peter swung the hammer, grunting. I blocked high, feeling the pain all the way through my teeth when the wood struck my forearm. I heard a crunch and felt instant nausea. I cried out, even as Luna laughed in my ear. He swung again, wild and weak this time, and I blocked low with the same arm. Again my world lit up with pain, but I gritted my teeth. I couldn't let myself feel it. But I knew I couldn't keep blocking forever. Eventually the pain would get to be too much.

Evade, Nikki, I heard Gunner say in my head. *Let him swing at the air.*

I straightened again, keeping my eye on the hammer as Peter brought it back over his head. This time, when he swung, he put all his effort behind it. At the last minute, I ducked and swiveled to the side in one smooth motion.

The hammer landed with a sickening *clop.* Luna's eyes went surprised for half a second—looking almost like normal eyes—and then fluttered closed. The force of the blow whipped her head to the side, blood spouting in all directions; I felt it on my face like ocean spray. There was a hole in her temple where the hammer had met it. Her body had gone limp. I jumped away, extricating myself from between them and falling backward onto my butt, and watched as Luna's body slumped to the ground, her eyes open and vacant.

Peter dropped the hammer and screamed, something unintelligible, as he went to her. I crawled on my hands and knees to grab the hammer, which had bounced within reach. The handle had Luna's blood on it, and a hunk of brown curly hair stuck to the ball of it, and my arm was aching and shaking so hard I could barely hold it, but I didn't care. I scooted away from Peter.

He turned from the rail, his face a gash of rage, and started to come after me.

"Don't even think about it," I heard.

Chris was standing at the top of the grand staircase, his gun trained on Peter Fairchild. Peter stopped, his hands up, and I collapsed forward, hanging my head between my knees while Chris arrested him.

It was finally over.

34

THEY HAD JUST finished setting my arm and were busy getting my discharge paperwork in order when Dad arrived at the hospital. He pushed through the curtain, a panicked expression on his face.

I tried a smirk that failed, my chin going all stupid wobbly. "Fancy meeting you here."

"Oh, Nikki." He came to my bedside but seemed afraid to touch me. "How bad is it?"

I shrugged. "I'll live."

"Why did you keep this from me?"

"I think I can probably ask you the same thing," I said.

We locked eyes for a long moment. And for the first time in maybe forever, I felt a real connection there. There was nothing to be hidden between us. He pulled a chair close enough to the bed that he could hold my good hand. He stared at his shoes, seeming to be weighing where he should begin, so I helped him out.

"You knew about Mom and Hollywood Dreams," I said. "And you knew about Peyton, right?"

He nodded and then shook his head. "I knew about the job, yes, but I didn't know about the baby until after she came back."

"And you didn't, like, demand a paternity test? What if Peyton was actually yours?"

"Your mother said the baby wasn't mine, and I trusted her."

My chin dropped. "You *trusted* her? She was sleeping with other men for money. How could you trust her? I'll never trust anything I knew about her."

"That's why I hid it from you, Nikki. Because she was an amazing person and a wonderful mother, and the thought of you not trusting her memory kills me," he said. "It was hard to accept, but eventually I did. Hollis was going to come after me for the fire. I was prepared for it, but he ended up going after her instead. She agreed to go back to Hollywood Dreams, and back to him, to keep him from hurting me. I didn't know until after all was said and done. I'd been waiting for him. I'd been keeping those letters as some sort of evidence in case something happened to me. And while I was waiting, he was using your mother."

"But even after you knew about Peyton, you let her go back."

"I tried to stop her. She told me she didn't have a choice. She said if she didn't go back to him, he would do everything he could to ruin us. It was supposed to be temporary. We were going to figure out a way to get her out. I confronted Hollis, and he threatened to have us all killed. Even you. We were trapped by him."

I pulled my hand out of his grasp and ran it through my hair, which felt tangled and greasy from the ocean wind, the dusty closet, the fear. "God, Dad, and you didn't think maybe to just call the police? Mom would have gotten a slap on the wrist for her part."

His eyes were fiery with hatred. "And Bill Hollis would have gotten even less." He stood, paced to the other side of the room. His back was to me. "The man had so many police officers and politicians in his pocket, he could never be touched for anything. I found that out the hard way after she died." He spun so he was facing me again. I could see how tired he was. Not just like he'd gotten a bad night's sleep, but like he'd gotten a bad life's sleep. "I was the only suspect. Why? Because Hollis knew his wife was behind your mother's murder, and he told the police to convict me or no one. They didn't have anything on me. We were going to have a date night that night. I left to buy flowers, and when

I came back . . ." He turned up his palms helplessly.

That explained why Dad had never trusted the police. Why he never pursued solving Mom's murder. Why he didn't want me to become a cop. The police he'd dealt with were bought and paid for.

"So you didn't say anything to anyone about the baby, because you were afraid of what he might do."

"Yes. She was afraid that if Bill Hollis found out, he would do something to the baby. Or to her friend. Or both. I never put it together that the kid he was always with in the papers was that kid. I assumed all three of those kids were Vanessa's. I think your mother assumed the same. Her friend stopped writing after a while. She told your mother it was too dangerous. What we didn't know was that Hollis had taken the kids and threatened to kill her if she talked."

I thought about poor Brandi, who'd only ever wanted to help. If Hollis had been telling the truth about her, she'd been burned up in a fire. Dad was right—Bill Hollis was ruthless and powerful. Nobody could stand up to that.

"And after she was gone, I couldn't bear to go public with the letters. I couldn't bear the world knowing about her being a part of that world. It wasn't who she was." He came back to me, sank back into the chair, rubbed the back of my good arm. "I don't know how you found out, Nikki. Your mother and I never wanted you to be involved."

"How could I not be?" I asked, my voice a whisper. "I was

involved the day Peyton was born. And I was really involved the day Peter Fairchild killed Mom."

There was surprise on Dad's face. "Peter . . . ? You found out who did it? Are you sure?"

I held up my arm. "How do you think I got this?"

Dad let out an incredulous huff of air, shaking his head. "It wasn't even Hollis himself."

"It wasn't Bill Hollis at all," I corrected him. "Vanessa was the one who wanted her gone."

"All this time . . . ," he whispered.

There was silence in the room, and in that silence I was struck with the strange loyalty of it all. Mom went back to Hollywood Dreams to protect Dad from Bill Hollis's wrath. Dad kept Mom's secret to protect her from Bill Hollis's wrath. In the end, their story was one of true love—even when true love was excruciatingly painful. Even when it was deadly.

But there was more to it than that. Brandi took Peyton to protect her from Bill Hollis's wrath. Dru paid off Rigo to protect him from Bill Hollis's wrath. Everyone worked so hard to protect themselves from Bill Hollis. And in the end, it had all been Vanessa. The one with the real power.

That was what it had all been about, really. Power. Bill's power over my parents. Vanessa's power over Peter. Luna's power over Peyton. Even Peyton was playing a power game with her family when she died. And ultimately, it was lack of power that destroyed my family. Not just our lack of power, but Peter Fairchild's as well. My mother lost her life because he had lost his beloved Vanessa.

But where everyone was wrong was in thinking Bill Hollis would always win. In the end, he didn't. His control, his money-hunger, was his undoing. It was the undoing of all of them. Vanessa finally had her man and lost him to two kids who belonged to my mother and Brandi. Luna finally had her stardom and was in a morgue. Bill Hollis finally had his chance to take me down, and he failed.

Was I acting out of power, too? Was that what all this was—this dogged pursuit of answers?

No. No way. I was dragged into this mess. I was made to care about Peyton. I was grieving Dru. I was avenging my mother. But never was I looking for power.

I was looking for closure.

Hell, if I was being completely honest, I was looking for love. Sloppy, annoying, terrifying, magenta love. Because no matter how many times I told myself I didn't need it, I did. Everyone did.

"I never meant to lie to you, Nikki," Dad said. I could see tears in his eyes, behind his glasses. "I was trying to protect you. And to protect your mother's memory. I wanted you to remember only the good things about her."

"That is all I can remember," I said. "Constructing this new version of her has been awful. Because the mom in my memories was kind and gentle and loving and so beautiful."

"And that was exactly who she was. Just like you."

I let out a snort. "Okay."

"No, I'm serious. You look just like her. It's like living with a ghost sometimes."

I stared at him. How many times had I had the same exact thought about living with him?

The curtain fluttered as someone rooted around for the split. Then it parted, and Chris Martinez stuck his head through.

"Oh. Sorry. I'll come back," he said, ducking back out.

"No," I called. "You can come in."

There was a pause, and then his whole body appeared through the curtain. Wary. Awkward.

"I want you two to meet," I said. I turned to Dad. "No more secrets." I took a breath. This felt so weird. "Dad, this is Detective Chris Martinez. Chris, this is my dad, Milo Kill."

Chris stuck out his hand. My dad looked at it, and then at me. "Detective?"

"The one who killed Bill Hollis, actually." I took another breath, then let it out. "The one who inspired me to go into the academy."

This time they both raised their eyebrows at me. I stared them down, daring them to say something. Neither did. Smart men.

Dad shook Chris's hand. "I take it you're who she's been spending so much time with?"

Chris nodded.

"Well, I guess I should thank you for keeping an eye on her. Nikki's always needed a little extra . . . supervision."

Chris barked out a laugh. "You're telling me!"

"Shut up," I said, putting venom behind it, but not really feeling it. I sounded more pouty than intimidating.

"I'll go get the car," Dad said, and before anyone could argue, he was through the curtain, his chuckle following him down the corridor. Chris and I were alone.

"I thought you died," I said angrily. He didn't respond. "On TV? Drug bust turns deadly? What the hell happened?"

"Heriberto's dead," he said flatly.

"Jesus," I said. "You okay?"

"It wasn't me," he said. "I showed up to arrest them, brought a couple officers with me, but as soon as we got there, you left that message about finding the yacht."

I gawped at him. "So you just left?"

"I just left."

"But your car . . ."

"I was blocked in, and I was in a hurry, so I grabbed a car from another detective. After I left, Heriberto apparently came out of his house and started shooting. It was over pretty quick."

"You just left."

He gave an impatient nod. "Yes."

"Why?"

He took a few steps, so that he was standing just in front of me as I sat on the edge of the bed, my knees dangerously close to his hips. "Because it was you."

The air between us had gone into a buzzing violet. I felt it pressing on my chest. "I thought you were done saving me."

"Actually," he said, "there was a bullet hole in the front seat of my car when I got back. If I'd been sitting there, it would have hit me. So I guess you could say that you saved me."

I laughed. "It's getting so old saving your ass, Detective." I rolled my eyes dramatically.

"I've told you a thousand times," he said, mocking what I'd repeatedly said to him months before, when we barely knew each other. "Call me Chris."

He reached out and touched my cast with his finger; the violet almost took on a physical presence, it was so strong.

"You remember me telling you to call me Miss Kill a thousand times, huh?"

"I remember more every day," he said.

I raised my eyebrows. "And you still want to be around me?"

He bit his lower lip and nodded, slowly, seriously. "More than ever."

Violet coursed between us, brighter and brighter, until I could hardly breathe. I'd seen violet before—with Dru, with Jones—but I'd never actually felt it taking hold of my body. Chris must have felt it too, because his hand snaked up from my cast, up the length of my arm and into my hair. He cupped the back of my neck and pulled me toward him.

I had seen colors my whole life. I had lived in color, as Peyton had. I had swum in a soup of confusion and sadness and happiness and fear and love and mystery for as long as I could remember.

But when Chris's lips touched mine, a rainbow sprouted between us, brighter than the Vegas Strip and deeper than rivers of paint and richer than any Hollis ever thought of being. I let myself slide along the colors, even though they scared me and took my breath away. They also felt right. I reached up and placed my hand on his chest. I could feel his heartbeat speeding under my fingers.

He pulled away just slightly, pressing his forehead to mine. "Am I still yellow?" he asked.

"Actually," I said, barely able to get words out, "you're totally magenta."

"Is that a good thing?"

"It didn't used to be," I said. I was breathing his breath, the tip of my nose brushing his. "But, yeah, with you, I think it's probably a good thing."

He swept both arms around me and I allowed myself to fall into him.

A really good thing.

EPILOGUE

B LUE WAS STILL unpacking when I got home with the cake. The girl had a million little statues and gems and runes and bowls that I joked were her virgin sacrifice bowls.

"You are definitely a witch," I said, sliding the cake onto the counter and taking the ice cream to the freezer.

She laughed and reached into the box, pulling out a couple of metal rods. "Am not."

"What the hell are those?"

"Divining rods," she said, as if I were clueless. Which I kind of was.

I unpacked the cheese and crackers I had bought and laid them out on the counter. "All I know is you better not ever try to use those on me."

She laughed again. "You don't use divining rods on people, Nik. You use them to find ghosts."

"Oh, good, that's so much more sane," I said. "You find glasses today?"

"Yep, in the cabinet." I opened a cabinet and she had washed, dried, and neatly stored a dozen drinking glasses. "And all the plates and silverware are party ready."

I opened the drawers, checking out all the things she'd put away while I was at work answering phone calls at the station. "Not a party," I said. "Just my dad and Ruby and Vee."

"And Chris," she said.

I felt myself blush. When would the blushing wear off, for cripes' sake?

"And Chris."

"Speaking of . . ." She rolled her eyes upward toward Chris's apartment, a floor above us.

"No, he doesn't know yet."

"Nikki!"

"I'm about to tell him. Jeez. Leave me alone, Mom." I was forever calling Blue *Mom*. She was tiny and young, but definitely a caretaker. She'd been there while my arm healed, through my post-yacht nightmares, and through all my major freak-outs as I sat for my exams. She even went to the library and checked out books to help me learn how to ignore my colors so studying went easier. I wasn't sure if they always worked, but it felt good to have someone care enough to try.

"He wants to know."

"I know."

"He will be disappointed to find out from someone other than you."

"I know."

I started down the hallway to my tiny bedroom.

"You should tell him now, Nikki!"

"I know!" I shut the door and changed clothes, peeling off my "secretary clothes," as Chris liked to call them, and pulling on leggings and a sweatshirt. I tossed my low heels into the back of my closet—God, I hated heels—and dug out my comfy Chucks. These shoes had been through so much. They'd walked the tile of Peyton's hospital room. They'd been carelessly discarded by Dru's bed. They'd stood on his blood. They'd been lost at the beach. They'd been to a swanky dinner in Vegas. They'd strolled with Jones and kicked Luna and chased Peter Fairchild. They'd walked into my new apartment to start a new life, away from the place where my mom died and my dad hid so many secrets.

Some days I thought it was time to get rid of the shoes. Most days, I thought I never would.

I stuffed my feet into a pair of socks and the Chucks and gathered my hair up into a ponytail. I checked the time on my phone, then texted Chris.

Workout?

Already there.

Nervous?

What would I have to be nervous about?

I'll show you in a minute.

"He deserves to know, after everything. . . ."

"Oh my God, are you still talking?" I said. I grabbed my key to the new downstairs fitness room—really, just a treadmill, a heavy bag, and a sparring mat—that we'd talked the landlord into when we moved into Chris's building, and walked past Blue, making *yak-yak* motions with my hands.

"I'm excited, okay?"

I looked at her with exaggerated wide eyes. "You don't say."

"Just go. Tell."

"Okay, okay."

CHRIS WAS ALREADY sweaty when I got there.

"Hey, neighbor," I said. "Warming up? I don't blame you. You need all the advantages you can get."

"Or I need to wear myself out a little first, so I don't accidentally hurt you."

I cocked my head to one side. "Hurt me?" I craned my neck, looking past him. "Did you bring an army I don't see?"

"Army of two," he said, flexing both biceps.

I pretended to yawn. "Pretty puny army."

"Oh, really?" He rushed me, grabbed me around the waist, and pulled me to the ground, flipping so he was on top of me, holding my hands down on the mat on each side of my head. "Hmm. I like this hold." He leaned down and kissed my neck. My world lit up purple.

I tamped down the color and dug my chin into his shoulder, pressing hard so that he let up. I bucked to the side and tossed him off me, then pulled up onto my knees, facing him, my hands at the ready.

"Oh, so it's like that, huh?" he asked, a devilish smile on his face.

"It's always like that."

"Trust me, I know."

He started to advance on me and I tensed my stance in anticipation. "I passed," I blurted.

He stopped. "You did? When did you find out?"

"This morning. Flying colors . . ." I thought about it. "So to speak."

His arms went slack as joy lit up his face. "I told you. I knew you could do it."

"Just the entrance exam," I said. But we had both known that was going to be the hardest part for me. "I still have a lot of training to go through."

He knee-walked to me and wrapped me in a hug. "Congratulations. I'm so proud of you, Nikki."

I launched all my weight forward, knocking him

backward, then jumped up, placed my knee on his chest, and threw a strike, stopping centimeters away from his throat, letting out an intimidating *ki-yah* as I did so.

He raised his hands, a symbol of surrender. I leaned close, brushing my cheek against his and hovering my lips just above his ear. "That's Officer Kill to you."

ACKNOWLEDGMENTS

Seeing Nikki all the way through her journey has been an amazing and intense process that required the dedication of a lot of people. I feel honored to have so many passionate professionals believe in my abilities and help me bring you the best stories I possibly can. I would like to thank them here.

First up, always, is my agent, Cori Deyoe, who is probably Nikki Kill's biggest fan (besides my dad. Thanks, Dad!). I would be nowhere without Cori's support, encouragement, strong shoulder, and gentle editing.

What an awesome team I got to work with at Katherine Tegen Books! It was such a pleasure brainstorming with, writing with, and revising with this phenomenal team: Melissa Miller, Claudia Gabel, Kelsey Horton, Stephanie Guerdan, Valerie Shea, Kathryn Silsand, and of course, Katherine Tegen. I know there are many more who lent a hand in getting Nikki's story in shape, out the door, and onto bookshelves—even if I didn't directly work with you, please know your efforts are much appreciated.

Joel Tippie slam-dunked the book cover designs for the

entire series. He really "got" Nikki and found a way to perfectly express her emotional journey in art. Thank you, Joel, for so masterfully capturing the color of Nikki's world!

As always, I want to thank my support system. Family, friends, community—you know who you are. You're the ones who tell me I can do it, who share my books with your friends, who express pride and patience, and who are just general badasses. I love you all.

Finally, I want to thank you, Readers, for not only reading my stories, but just for being readers. You book lovers support the writing community, and we literally couldn't do this without you.